A Season of Change

D.C. Elmore

Explore
www.dcelmore.com

Global Book Publisher

Copyright © 2006 by Dreama C. Elmore

Editor: Beth Krippner
Cover Design by Jaime Flores

ISBN: 1-4196-5365-2
LCCN: 2006910473
Publisher: BookSurge, LLC
North Charleston, South Carolina

Printed in the United States of America

Dedicated to R.T. Sojitra

● ● ●

You changed my entire world with
your love and I couldn't survive
a day without it.

Acknowledgments:

R. Lovan
B. Krippner
J. Flores

A Season of Change

CHAPTER ONE

Sierra Stanton clamped her eyes shut and gripped the gray plastic armrests of seat 10F. The tanned skin on her knuckles turned white as the Boeing 737 battled another round of turbulence. The sudden rise and fall of the airplane mimicked that of her chest as she fought to keep from hyperventilating. In desperation, she thought about what she had read online and repeated it over and over again: *There is only a one in eleven million chance of being involved in an aircraft accident.*

Typically, Sierra met her challenges head on, but the entire year up to this point had proven to be insurmountable even for her. Her career was suffering and her personal life was nonexistent, hence her publicist's insistence on taking some time off. To make matters worse, she had an extreme fear of flying. There was no amount of alcohol that could keep her from cursing underneath her breath at the distance at which she had been coerced to travel for a little peace and relaxation.

To her credit, Sierra had tried to be prudent in the handling of the present situation. Right before takeoff, she had lowered the oval window shade and attempted to convince herself that there was no difference between an airplane and a large bus except the view. She had brought a variety of reading material to distract her. She had also filled her iPod with all her favorite eighties songs to keep her mind from entertaining other horrific thoughts. Unfortunately, the side of her that refused to play along with her ingenious plan had plagued her mind throughout the flight with visions of the plane plummeting to the ground and everyone onboard being vaporized on impact. Now that same culprit begged to know how close the plane was to the snow-covered mountaintops as it made its steady descent from 30,000 feet.

Sierra took a deep breath and forced her eyes open. She peeled the fingers of her left hand off the armrest. Swallowing hard, she grabbed the plastic edge of the window shade and shoved it upward. The untainted night sky reached in and swallowed up her green, wide-eyed curiosity. The snow-covered mountains with their jagged peaks loomed ominously beneath the thin metal hull of the plane. Sierra couldn't help but nibble nervously at her bottom lip.

"From the look on your face, this must be your first time flying," an obnoxiously loud voice in close proximity said.

Sierra turned almost mechanically toward the young man sitting next to her. He was no more than twenty-five. His dark brown hair was longer in the front and it shaded his brown eyes. The two of them had not spoken to each other since takeoff, when a brief greeting seemed to suffice. Further communication on Sierra's part would have fallen on deaf ears as the young man had completely made a mockery out of what being a gentleman was all about in his attempt to acquire a flight attendant's cell phone number. She had politely, but firmly, turned him down.

"It's my second," Sierra said, keeping her voice amicable. "I was about ten years old the first time."

The young man straightened in his seat and took hold of Sierra's right hand. "There's absolutely nothing to fear," he said, squeezing it gently. "I fly all the time, but it does help to engage in friendly conversation."

His bogus chivalry made Sierra's skin crawl, but she wasn't the type to drop to someone else's level. "That sounds like a fine idea," she replied. "Do you travel a lot for work?"

"Hell, no," the young man said. "It's strictly for fun. What about you?"

"It's fifty-fifty," Sierra replied. "I usually drive."

The young man moved his eyes down Sierra's body. "Do you usually travel alone?"

Sierra smiled politely and pulled her hand away to scratch her right ear, though it didn't really itch. "No, do you?"

The young man's eyes flickered with amusement. "Not usually, but this trip was last-minute."

"Is that so?" Sierra said with feigned interest.

"Some of my buddies wanted to go snowboarding," the young man replied. He stretched out his legs into the aisle and moaned. "This is exactly why I prefer to sit in first class and not back here where the other half travel. I can easily afford it and there's just more room."

Sierra nodded. "And I'm sure there's a lot more privacy."

The young man didn't reply.

"So you were saying," Sierra said, feeling a twinge of guilt for her blatant honesty.

"I'm a top-notch snowboarder," he said, puffing out his chest. "Who better to have along?"

"I guess no one," Sierra replied.

"The fact is, I'm one of the best in the country," the young man said, glancing over at Sierra. "I'm surprised you don't recognize me. I've been on the cover of a couple of magazines."

"I'm sorry," Sierra said, striving to conjure up any recollection. "The last article I scanned about snowboarding talked about the guy from Carlsbad, California. You know, the kid with red hair."

The young man shifted uncomfortably in his seat. "Yeah, I know who he is."

Sierra sensed the young man's envy for an accolade that was beyond his reach. "I'm sure you're just as good."

"That's what they say," the young man said quickly. "I'll probably be on the front of a cereal box after the next Olympics."

"That's great," Sierra said with a little more emphasis than was warranted. "I'll have to look for it." She watched as the young man's hand traveled to his back pocket. She didn't need the services of Sherlock Holmes to figure out what his next move would be. She'd already witnessed his pickup method with the flight attendant.

The young man handed Sierra a business card from his wallet. "The name's Mark. My cell number is in the bottom right-hand corner."

I might not have figured that one out on my own, Sierra thought sarcastically, taking the card. "Thank you, but I'm not looking to learn how to snowboard."

Mark arched his right eyebrow and grinned devilishly. "I was thinking of a different sport actually. I mean you're in town alone and I'm in town alone, so maybe we could throw back a few cold ones once we land and spend the rest of this evening getting to know one another a little better. What do you think?"

The plane banked to the left. Sierra slapped her hands back down onto the armrests, but refused to disengage from the conversation. "I think you're making a big assumption that I'd be interested in that."

"You're not?" Mark said, obviously perturbed that his usual tactic of wowing women with his snowboard spiel had failed miserably.

Sierra held Mark's gaze. "Look, you seem like an interesting guy, but I've had what you're offering and I'm just not into that."

Mark leaned back and rubbed his chin between his thumb and forefinger. When his eyes widened, Sierra thought for sure he had come to the right conclusion that she was a lesbian. "I've got it," he said proudly, as though he'd just figured out some ancient riddle. "You're still hung up on the last guy who broke your heart."

"That's not it," Sierra said, shaking her head.

"It's okay," Mark said. "I completely understand."

"I'm pretty sure that you don't," Sierra replied.

Mark looked around to make sure no one was paying too much attention to their conversation, and then leaned forward. "I do understand and I can tell you the best way to get on with your life."

"This I have to hear," Sierra said, entertaining his ego.

"It's simple," Mark replied, leaning back into his seat. "You have to sleep with another guy."

"What if you're trying to get over a woman?" Sierra said.

Mark shrugged. "Same rules apply. It's exactly what I did to get over the last girl I was seeing. That's how I know it works."

Handsome package but only one head thinking and it isn't the one between his shoulders, Sierra thought. *Obviously his last girlfriend figured that one out as well.* "I'll keep that in mind."

"Flight attendants please take your seats," the co-pilot announced over the intercom.

The landing gear lowered into place as the aircraft made its final approach. Sierra tugged at her seatbelt one more time but kept her attention on Mark. No matter how absurd their conversation was, it was keeping her mind occupied.

"So?" Mark said. "Are you sure you don't want to have that drink with me? I'll buy."

"I appreciate the offer, Mark, but I have to pass," Sierra said.

"Your loss," Mark replied flatly. "If you change your mind, you have my number. This time of year can be quite brutal to spend alone, especially in a new place so far from home. Every year on the news I hear about the ones who can't deal with their loneliness or depression any more and choose an immediate end to their suffering."

Sierra restrained from reaching up and slapping the living daylights out of Mark.

She was quite aware of how the holidays drove some people to kill themselves and her heart went out to those lost souls. What she couldn't handle was the desperate asshole sitting next to her using it to try to get into her pants. "I'll keep that in mind if I become grievously desperate," she said, enjoying the well-deserved insult she directed at Mark.

His mouth twitched as though he ached to spit some unsavory comment to refute her assessment of him, but kept in check. "You do that," he said.

Sierra tucked Mark's business card into the front pocket of her jeans. It was truly absurd how many men, not just Mark, hit on her. Whether she was grocery shopping or running on the boardwalk that zigzagged between the palm trees in front of her house, there was always some guy trying to give his phone number or get hers. Of course, to be fair, there were just as many women asking for it as well. In the lesbian community, it seemed that an all points bulletin was broadcast whenever a couple broke up and it included a full disclosure of fact and gossip for the receiver of such news to pick and choose from.

Refusing to dwell on the past, Sierra shifted her focus to the daunting task that had been the sole reason for this last minute vacation: writer's block. Before she could contemplate what the first step should be in resolving that issue, a child in the row behind her screamed out that he could see the ground. His follow-up question, though, hurled Sierra's thoughts into an abyss of despair.

"Mom, I don't see the runway," the boy said. "Where is it?"

"It's there, honey. Don't worry," his mother calmly replied.

"I don't see it!" the boy said even louder.

Sierra pressed her forehead against the thick, plastic shield that protected the actual window. It felt cool against her sweating brow as she peered into the darkness. She couldn't see the runway lights or any other telltale signs that the Denver International Airport was anywhere in proximity either. She only knew that the ground was getting closer and closer as they young boy had claimed.

Throwing her head back against the seat, Sierra closed her eyes and braced herself for the impending explosion. The plane's landing gear contacted the runway, creating an ear-piercing squeal from the brakes. The roar of the reverse thrusters silenced the passenger cabin momentarily and catapulted Sierra's imagination into the flaming ball of death she was sure to find herself in if she were able to peel her eyes open for a brief moment.

The sudden crackle of the intercom startled Sierra and she held her breath, waiting to hear the pilots screaming in agony for someone to save them.

"Ladies and gentlemen, thank you for flying with us," the pilot announced cheerfully. "Please keep your seatbelts fastened until we arrive at the gate. An airline representative will be happy to help you locate your connecting flight after you have disembarked. If Denver is your final destination, bundle up before stepping outside. It is only a whopping twenty-nine degrees."

It wasn't until Sierra felt Mark's hand back on top of hers that she opened one eye, then the other. She exhaled slowly and deliberately. "Thank goodness."

"It gets easier," Mark said, patting her hand. "Do you want to go for that drink now? It really will help you unwind and forget all about the stress of the flight."

Sierra pulled her hand away yet again. "No thanks," she said firmly. "I'll be just fine."

Mark shrugged. "Whatever."

The moment the seatbelt sign was no longer illuminated, Mark unlatched his seatbelt from the silver clasp and got to his feet. He stepped into the aisle and attempted to brush the wrinkles out of his beige slacks, but it was a fruitless attempt. Frustrated, he grabbed his jacket from the overhead compartment and looked back at Sierra to give her a quick wink. "Call me if you change your mind."

Sierra mustered a halfhearted smile. *Don't hold your breath*, she thought. "Take care and happy holidays, Mark."

With the plane safely on the ground, Sierra turned back to the oval window and embraced the beautiful snowcapped mountains, uncompromised by the veil of darkness surrounding them. Though her mind didn't conjure up any images for a best-selling novel, she felt a wave of relief at being so far away from the place that she no longer considered home. Deep down, she knew it had never really felt like home, but it had come pretty darn close.

The flagrant, non-holiday attitude being vocalized by some of the travelers within the narrow aisle that ran between the rows of seats caught Sierra's attention. She'd tried to ignore the human traffic jam buzzing with disdain, but she couldn't keep from people-watching. Most of the passengers had permanent frowns on their faces as they shoved their carry-on items into the legs of the people standing in front of them, as if that would speed up the disembarking process. Others shouted into their cell phones so that whomever was on the other end would be sure to hear their instruction to meet them at the baggage claim. Of course, there were one or two passengers who projected their annoyance at having to wait, either by sighing obnoxiously loudly or by refusing to budge and let someone gain access to an overhead compartment.

Silently amused, Sierra was in no rush to join these unhappy souls as they pushed and shoved themselves down the aisle, nor was she in any condition to. Her legs were still weak. The small instances of strength in her muscles were fleeting, evaporating like the bubbles blown by a child through a small plastic circle. It had been an exceptionally long day, preceded by an extremely long year.

Sierra continued to take deep, calming breaths while trying to harness the remaining energy left in her body. When the last of the passengers had gathered their belongings, she forced herself to stand and stepped into the aisle. Her legs didn't tingle, though they felt asleep. They were slow to react and her walk was more like a shuffle. She grabbed her laptop bag and leather jacket from the overhead compartment and headed toward the two flight attendants who were wishing the departing passengers happy holidays.

Sierra offered a kind smile as she passed the flight attendants, but wasted no time on pleasantries. She hurried down the Jetway, imagining the bright lights of the terminal disappearing and as a result, a giant black void swallowing her whole. Once on solid ground, it took all the pride she had left to keep from dropping to her knees and kissing the worn carpeting. Instead, she followed the signs to the shuttle that would take her to the baggage claim and to the main exit of the airport.

• • •

Sierra pulled both of her suitcases behind her and walked toward the doors that led to the awaiting taxis, shuttles and buses. She paused to slip on her jacket and readjust the laptop bag's strap over her shoulder. As she stepped outside, her cheeks instantly stung from the harsh wind that seemed to be laced with tiny, unforgiving icicles. Fleeting clouds of gray escaped from her mouth with every exhalation and her eyes burned terribly as though abraded by invisible sandpaper.

The designated shuttle service that her literary agent had arranged was easily identifiable; it was painted a bright blue. Sierra had to wait only a few seconds for the driver to open the back of the van and take her suitcases. She handed him the laptop bag as she tried to keep her face somewhat warm by tucking the lower half of it into the collar of her jacket. When he was finished securing her belongings, she stepped aside and climbed quickly into the van, being careful not to slip on the ice-covered running board. The driver continued loading suitcases and gear from the other shuttle van passengers who darted from the sanctity of the airport into the bitter cold for their reserved passage into the heart of Colorado's winter wonderland.

Sierra took a seat at the end of the middle row next to the window. It was going to be a one-hundred-twenty-mile trip to the lodge in Vail and she wasn't about to be smashed between two strangers for the entire trip. *This was a great idea,* she thought, vigorously rubbing her upper arms with her hands to create some warmth. *Who needs sunshine anyway?*

• • •

Shortly past midnight, the shuttle van pulled up in front of the lodge where Sierra was staying. The trip from the airport had taken a total of three-and-half hours due to a horrific accident involving three cars, an SUV and a semi-truck on the I-70W freeway. It had temporarily shut down both sides of the road. Fortunately, the shuttle van had been the third vehicle allowed through on the only lane the state troopers decided to open.

Sierra had watched while the rescue workers struggled to free the victims from their mangled vehicles. Her eyes had pooled with tears as one driver was eventually covered with a blanket after all of the resuscitation efforts had failed. She knew that one family would be receiving a call that everyone prays they never get. The only person that appeared to be uninjured was the semi-truck driver. He sat motionless in the back of one of the ambulances and stared at the wreckage strewn all over the highway. Intermittently, he would shift his attention to the sheriff's deputy questioning him before hanging his head again.

The shuttle driver made his way around to the passenger side of the vehicle. When he slid open the side door, he did so just wide enough to allow Sierra the room to climb out and avoid subjecting the rest of the passengers to too much of the cold.

Sierra scooted past the other passengers in her row and carefully stepped down onto the running board. "Let me help you," the driver said, extending his hand up to her.

Sierra took his hand and stepped down onto the road. "Thank you."

The driver closed the door. "Go ahead and get inside," he said. "I'll bring your suitcases in so you don't catch a cold."

"You're so very kind, Sierra said. "Please don't forget the laptop bag."

The driver tipped his hat. "Of course not, madam."

Sierra trudged up the lightly dusted, snow-covered steps leading to the lodge's front entrance. Her footprints vanished almost instantly as the relentless wind filled the depressions her shoes had made. She hurried across the large wooden porch, grabbed the wrought iron handle, and pulled open the heavy wooden door. She, the porch, and a portion of the stairs were flooded in bright, white light. The radiating warmth that rolled out like a welcoming mat enveloped her and beckoned her to enter. Taking a small step past the threshold, she wiped her feet on a large mat that was surprisingly not soggy from the other guests she presumed had come and gone throughout the day.

The shuttle driver hurried past her and set both suitcases and the laptop bag down beside the registration counter. Sierra reached into her pocket and pulled out a twenty-dollar bill as the driver walked back toward the door. "Thanks for the ride," she said, holding out the cash.

"Thank you, madam," he said, taking the money and tucking it into his jacket pocket. "Please keep us in mind for any additional transportation needs that you may have during your stay."

"I will," Sierra replied. "Have a great night."

"You, too," he said, before closing the door.

Sierra looked around at the impressive craftsmanship of the lobby with its high-beamed ceiling and carved-stone entryway. To the immediate right, there were a couple of benches she figured were used to take off ski boots so as not to scuff up the hardwood floors. Off to the left was a small burning fireplace, a couple of pine rocking chairs, and a small square table covered with a variety of skiing magazines. She walked to the deserted registration area and looked over the counter to see if anyone might be rummaging behind it and didn't hear her come in. Alone, she tapped the palm of her hand on the tiny bell as directed by the red sign with bold white lettering. "Hello?"

A rush of cold air caught the back of Sierra's hair and blew it forward. She turned around as four very athletic men in their early twenties filed in one by one through the doorway. One of them offered her a friendly wave, closed the door and followed the other three over to an exquisite wooden staircase. Sierra waited for them to ascend the stairs before ringing the bell again.

The soft crackle of another fireplace caught her attention and she left her belongings next to the counter to take a closer look. She walked past a large entryway that opened opposite the staircase. Game tables, big, cozy couches, overstuffed chairs, and end tables ornate with holiday-themed accents greeted her as she stepped into the room. A modest-sized Christmas tree stood in the far corner. It was beautifully decorated with white twinkling lights, large, colorful bulbs, and an exquisite blown-glass star nestled on top. Beneath it were a few brightly wrapped packages with miniature candy canes taped on each one.

"May I help you?" an elderly woman's voice called out from behind Sierra.

Startled, Sierra pivoted and caught her foot on a thick, rectangular brown rug that blended in with the dark wood flooring. Unable to maintain her balance, she found herself sprawled out on her hands and knees on the floor.

"Goodness gracious!" the woman said, rushing toward her.

Sierra smiled reassuringly at the woman who was old enough to be her own grandmother. She accepted the feeble outstretched hand and got to her feet. "It's been one of those days."

"I do apologize," the woman replied. "I didn't mean to frighten you."

Sierra brushed her hands off on her jeans. "That's okay. It wasn't your fault, ma'am."

The woman took Sierra's hand and patted it gently. "The name's Delores, but everyone just calls me Dee. Do you have a reservation, honey?"

Sierra nodded. "Yes, I do ma'am. I mean, Dee."

"Quick learner," Dee replied, letting go of Sierra's hand. "I like that quality in a person, Ms. Stanton."

"How did you know my name?" Sierra said, pleasantly surprised. "Have we met somewhere before?"

Dee walked toward the registration counter. "My dear, you're the only one left on today's check-in list that hadn't arrived. I simply used deductive reasoning."

Sierra grinned. "I guess that means it's a full house."

"It always is this time of year," Dee replied sweetly, stepping behind the counter. She pushed her silver hair back from her face and slipped on a pair of reading glasses that magnified her pale blue eyes. "Now, let's get you checked in. You look exhausted."

Sierra leaned against the counter. "I am."

Dee punched some information into the computer before handing Sierra a keycard to get into her room. "All right, you're all set. Let me give you a rundown of the accommodations so you won't be completely out of your element when you wake up in the morning."

"That sounds great," Sierra replied, fighting off a yawn. "You have no idea how out of my element I am."

Dee smiled. "Hogwash! You have a fighting spirit behind those tired eyes."

Sierra blushed. "I guess."

"Well, I know," Dee said.

Sierra dropped her eyes. "So tell me about those accommodations."

Dee shuffled a stack of papers into a neat, organized pile. "You're staying in a one-bedroom suite. It contains a full kitchen, a small dining area situated next to the balcony, a cozy living room, and a private bath with massaging jets."

"Wow," Sierra said. "I would have been happy with just a bed and bathroom. It sounds terrific."

"Well, my dear, it doesn't stop there," Dee said. "We have all the little extras as well. Each suite is equipped with hairdryers, ironing boards and irons, DVD players, cable TV with surround sound, and Internet access. We understand that a lot of our guests have business they must attend to, even on vacation."

"I'm very impressed," Sierra said. "Anything else I should know?"

Dee held Sierra's gaze. "Everyone comes here searching for something. Sometimes its rest and relaxation and other times it's to get their life in order. I've seen people try to escape their pasts up here while others start their lives together. Whatever brought you here, Ms. Stanton, I hope you find what you're looking for."

"Me, too," Sierra said, inadvertently glancing down at the faded white circle on her ring finger.

"You're on the third floor," Dee said. "I can have someone carry up your luggage if you so wish. Or if you'd rather do it yourself, I suggest taking the elevator."

Sierra looked over at the massive staircase. "I'll take the elevator."

"You're in room 311," Dee said. "Please let us know if you need anything to make your stay more comfortable."

Sierra placed the laptop bag's strap around her shoulder and grasped each suitcase handle. "I will. Thanks, Dee."

• • •

Sierra switched on the light before closing the door behind her. The suite was exactly as Dee had described. She rolled the suitcases over to the king-size bed and dropped her laptop bag onto the mattress. Taking off her jacket, she tossed it onto the recliner that was to the right of the headboard and sat down on the edge of the bed. She ran her fingers through her hair. Her entire body ached from exhaustion and sleep deprivation forced her eyelids to close every few seconds until she willed them to open again.

Stubbornly, Sierra stood back up and dragged one of the suitcases onto the bed. She unzipped it and rummaged through the contents until she found a small travel bag filled with all her beauty essentials. Slipping off her shoes, she scooped up the bag, went into the bathroom, and fumbled for the light switch, inadvertently turning on the heating lamp. It was a welcome addition to the coolness of the room and she set the timer at its maximum limit of thirty minutes.

Sierra stripped off her clothes and turned on the shower. She removed the shampoo, conditioner, soap and razor out of the travel bag. When steam began fogging up the mirrors, she placed the shampoo and conditioner in one corner of the bathtub and the soap and razor in the adjacent corner. She stepped underneath the warm spray and bent her head forward so the water splashed onto the back of her head and cascaded down between her shoulder blades. Trying to relax the tension that had grown into a bustling metropolis beneath the muscles in her back was pointless. The never-ending flow of memories powered the stream of electricity keeping the little bustling city from ever sleeping.

With an irritated sigh, Sierra shrugged off the little bit of hope that she had to relax and picked up the shampoo to wash her hair. About ten minutes later, she had scrubbed every inch of her five-foot-nine frame, including a couple of detours to shave her legs and underarms. After one final rinse, she turned off the water and stepped onto a small hand towel to dry off. She slipped into a T-shirt and boxers before grabbing her comb to tackle the few tangles left in her dark blond hair that the conditioner had not conquered. A few seconds later the warming light switched off.

Leaving the vanity lights on, Sierra pulled the bathroom door closed so only a small sliver of light escaped through the crack. She walked over to the bed, zipped up the suitcase, and placed it back on the floor along with the laptop bag. Folding the comforter and sheets back away from the pillows, she walked over to the light switch that controlled the floor lamp next to the recliner and turned it off.

With the thin ray of light seeping through the bathroom door to guide her, Sierra made her way back over to the bed and collapsed as the strength in her limbs dissipated. She grabbed the other king-size pillow from its lonely position on the empty side of the bed and hugged it against her chest. The backs of her eyelids were instantly transformed into dual movie screens. The simultaneous feature playing on both was a repeat of a horrific year that would end in less than thirty days with her raising a single glass of champagne with no reason to celebrate once again.

Desperate for peace of mind, Sierra tried to fight off the tears that pooled in her eyes. *Just go to sleep*, she thought. *Please, God, I just need one night of good sleep.*

CHAPTER TWO

Turning over onto her side, Sierra looked at the digital clock on the nightstand. Its neon green numbers illuminated the nine o'clock hour. For the three-hundred-eighty-seventh day since losing three of the most beloved people in her life, she had suffered from anxiety attacks. This night had been no different. She had awakened almost every hour trembling and teary-eyed. She had hoped the morning would be kinder to her battered soul and offer a little more tranquility, but it had only prolonged her suffering. Now exasperated, she tossed the covers off to the side and sat up to stretch her arms above her head. There was no sense fighting what she was still not strong enough to confront: the complete obliteration of her faith in love.

Sierra hopped out of bed and instantly shot up onto the balls of her feet. The wood floor was unbearably cold and she tiptoed across the room to the balcony. Thick, beige curtains were drawn closed over the French doors. She drew one side of the curtains back and squinted against the blinding light that filtered into the room. The treetops, the rooftops the ground itself were all hidden by the accumulation of fluffy, white snow.

Sierra tried to push open one of the French doors to see how deep the snow was on the balcony, but it wouldn't budge. Peering through the panes in the door, she took in all that she could from the place she would call home for at least the next thirty days. The towering mountains surrounded the 1.2 million acres of the White River National Forest and the thirteen-square-mile town in which the lodge was located, creating the effect that Vail was another world entirely.

Sierra walked back toward the bed and wiped away a tear that came dangerously close to spilling onto her cheek. *What an amazing place to share with someone*, she thought.

Sitting down next to her suitcases, Sierra unzipped each one. She searched for anything that might offer a little warmth until she bought something more suitable to wear. A few hideous color combinations later, she settled on a navy blue jogging suit and a long-sleeved white T-shirt. It wasn't ideal, but at least it matched.

After taking some time to put away the rest of her clothes in an oak dresser, Sierra placed the suitcases into the closet along with her laptop bag. She slid the door closed and for a moment held onto the handle, wishing her mind would be suddenly flooded with ideas for her next best-seller. She could just imagine ripping the closet door open, pulling out the laptop, and pecking away at the keys as her story came to life in Microsoft Word. Sighing, she

released the door handle and walked into the
bathroom to get dressed.

• • •

Sierra leaned over the banister to observe
the flurry of activity taking place below as
she waited for the elevator. It appeared
that everyone staying at the lodge was
presently crammed into the confines of the
lobby. Apologies flew as skis and poles
collided and winter enthusiasts rushed
around to get to the ski lifts as early as
possible. Children wearing hats and gloves
in every color huddled close to their
parents to keep from being trampled. Some of
them bounced around with sleds, urging their
parents to hurry up because the snow would
be gone by the time they got out there.

When the elevator arrived on the third
floor, Sierra decided that taking the stairs
wasn't such a bad idea after all. There was
something unnerving about stepping into the
confines of a metal box that resembled a tin
of sardines. She hurried down the stairs and
let go of the railing as she skipped the
last two steps. Darting across the lobby
into the sanctity of the room she had
visited the night before, she made her way
toward the Christmas tree that was partially
blocked by the corner edge of one of the two
tables that were set up on that side of the
room.

The first table contained four large
stainless steel thermoses with easy-to-
dispense black nozzles at each base. A large
stack of Styrofoam cups was placed in one
corner along with a variety of sugar packets
and a bowl of tiny sealed cups of half-and-
half. The second table had a three-tiered
fruit plate, a basket full of muffins

ranging from banana nut to chocolate, and a large tray with small boxes of dry cereal lined up one right after another. Off to the side of the tray was a pitcher of milk sitting in a tub of ice.

Sierra took a Styrofoam cup off the top of one of the stacks and read each thermos label. Though she was tempted to try the hot chocolate, she really needed coffee, and not the decaffeinated kind. She moved over to the last two thermoses and placed her cup underneath one of the black dispensers. The inviting aroma of high-quality brewed coffee beans wafted upward and she inhaled deeply as the rich liquid filled her cup.

Sipping carefully, Sierra scanned the room as the dark liquid trickled down her throat and warmed her being. Two other guests were enjoying their choice of a hot liquid breakfast as well at a small, round table on the opposite side of the room. The couple was working diligently on a crossword puzzle. By their outward appearance, they were of Hispanic descent and in their late sixties. Their intermittent laughter at figuring out a word on some random clue, however, reminded Sierra of two teenagers in love. She couldn't help but wonder how long they had been together.

Sierra curled up in one corner of a very large couch positioned directly in front of the fireplace. With her back against the armrest she could keep an eye on the couple and enjoy the reddish-orange flames dancing around the logs. She took another sip of coffee and watched as the older man placed his hand tenderly on the woman's. His hands were large and even at such a great distance, Sierra could tell that they were calloused and worn. His hard work had obviously not been in vain. The couple sported very expensive clothing and the rock of a diamond on the woman's ring finger spoke even louder about their wealth.

If only money could buy love, Sierra thought, closing her eyes. *I'd sell everything I own.* She pushed herself up from the couch and walked back across the room, dropping her coffee cup into the medium-sized trash receptacle just outside the entryway. There were a few stragglers still gathering their gear in the lobby, but it was nothing like the maddening chaos it had been a short while before. Sierra zipped up the jacket to her jogging suit and double-checked to make sure she had her wallet. Then she strutted over to the front door and used her shoulder to push it open. The frigid wind instantly penetrated the thin material of the jogging suit as she stepped out onto the porch.

With her unprotected hands shoved deep within her jacket pockets, Sierra stepped down onto the first snow-covered step. The snow crunched beneath her shoes. By the third step, the snow was ankle-deep and the icy wetness had seeped into the interior of her shoes. One more step would result in half the length of her calf being subjected to unnerving cold. This realization caused her to pause and reassess her need to go shopping.

"You'll never survive going out dressed like that," a playful voice said. "You'll freeze your butt off first."

Amused, Sierra turned around and was immediately greeted by an outstretched gloved hand. The woman's eyes were hidden behind a ski mask and a scarf stretched from her chin to her nose. A knitted cap was pulled down over her ears and forehead.

"Asha Amin," the woman said, shaking Sierra's hand.

"Sierra Stanton."

"It's very nice to meet you," Asha replied, releasing Sierra's hand slowly. "Where are you headed?"

"Actually," Sierra chuckled. "I was on my way to buy some warmer clothes."

"Why don't you let me give you a lift then?" Asha said, motioning Sierra to follow as she walked toward one of four snowmobiles parked to the right of the porch.

"That's okay," Sierra said, trying to keep her teeth from chattering. "I'll be fine."

Asha placed her hands on her hips. "Are you really telling me that you'll be okay even though you're already freezing to death?"

Sierra nodded.

"You haven't even made it two feet from the porch yet," Asha said, tapping her foot in the snow. "Even I'm a little chilly and I'm wearing a snowmobile suit."

Sierra pursed her lips. "I'll be fine."

Asha patted the back part of the snowmobile seat. "No offense, but your feet would fall off before you got across the street and I don't think any of the stores sell shoes that would fit after that."

Sierra couldn't resist smiling. "Okay, you win. I can't argue with that."

Asha jumped onto the snowmobile and started the engine. She pulled up alongside the steps and patted the seat again. "Come on."

"Thanks," Sierra said. She straddled the seat and wrapped her arms loosely around Asha's waist.

"You'll need to hold on tighter than that," Asha said.

Sierra tightened her grip as the snowmobile surged forward. She tucked her head down into the back of Asha's jacket to try to keep her face from being exposed to the wind. Wisps of black hair poked out from underneath Asha's knitted cap and Sierra could smell the slightest hint of rosemary mint as it brushed against her face. *Why did she have to smell so good?*

Within a few minutes, Asha eased the snowmobile to a stop. "Here we are," she said, wiping away the snow that had collected on the lenses of her ski mask.

Sierra looked up at the wooden sign dangling from the store's entrance that read "Top of the World Ski Shop." On each side of the entryway were two large windows outlined in an assortment of Christmas lights that caused a kaleidoscope of color to cascade down onto each display. In the window to the left, there were mannequins dressed in the season's latest fashions. In the other window, another mannequin had been posed so that he was carrying skis over his shoulder.

"Thanks for the lift," Sierra said, scooting off the back.

Asha pulled the scarf away from her mouth. "How long do you think you'll be?"

"Uh, I wouldn't think longer than an hour," Sierra said, staring at Asha's full lips and the dark skin that surrounded them. *I wonder if she's Indian.* "I'm not a huge fan when it comes to trying things on."

"Well, ski apparel is something you'll want to try on," Asha said. "Otherwise, you'll either be miserable because you feel like you're in plastic wrap or look like the abominable snowman."

"I'll keep that in mind," Sierra replied, dropping her eyes away from Asha's lips that had separated into a beautiful white smile.

"I have a few errands to run, but I could swing back by and pick you up," Asha said, pulling the scarf back up over the bridge of her nose. "They'll have the roads cleared by mid-afternoon and a snowmobile doesn't do a lot of good without snow."

"That's okay," Sierra said, resisting the familiar twinge of curiosity building up inside her. "I'll be fine."

"All right, then," Asha said. "Don't forget thermal underwear. You'll definitely need some."

"Thanks for the tip," Sierra replied.

"See you around," Asha said. She steered the snowmobile away from the store and continued down the street.

Sierra pulled open the heavy, glass door that was decorated with a large, green Christmas wreath and a bright, red ribbon tied into a bow. She stepped inside and welcomed the warmth. From behind a counter, positioned in the center of the store, a young woman watched her curiously. Sierra waved and the woman politely waved back.

The variety of styles offered under the store's one roof was impressive. Sierra moseyed around for a few minutes, trying to absorb all her options and orchestrate a game plan. Each rack designated for women held sizes ranging from zero to twenty-eight. There were an abundance of colors, thicknesses and materials. It was almost maddening even to the most eager shopper.

What do I know about buying cold-weather gear? Sierra thought sullenly. *I live in one of the southernmost parts of Florida. I spend my money on shorts, tank tops and tropical rain gear. Now here I am pretending to know what I'm doing and guessing at what I need.*

After about twenty-five minutes of going back and forth between racks, Sierra had narrowed her choices down to eleven outfits including a snowmobile suit. She headed into the fitting room and tried the snowmobile suit on first. Staring in the mirror, she turned from one side to the other, shocked by the amount of bulk the suit added to her hips and butt. *It's warm, though*, she thought. *Who knows, maybe I'll get to take another ride on that snowmobile.*

Sierra slumped into a chair nestled in the corner of the dressing room. She peered up at her reflection in the mirror, then back down at her left hand. The thin, pale reminder of once having someone that crossed the top of her ring finger was slowly fading. She looked back up and studied the lines that had formed at the corners of her eyes. *Three more years until I'm forty*, she thought. *And look at me now. I am completely alone.* Shaking her head, she stood back up, unzipped the snowmobile jacket, and tossed it onto the chair. She slipped off the matching overalls and hung both items back onto the hanger.

Sierra's mind wandered back to Asha. *I've got to stop thinking about her. This is crazy. I don't even know what she looks like and even if she is a lesbian, I'm not here to have a fling. I'm here to write!* She tried on the remaining outfits in irritated silence.

After slipping back on her jogging suit, Sierra grabbed the bundle of clothing hanging from the hook and glared at her reflection one more time. This past year had made her cynical. It had slowly chipped away her hope to find true love, and along with it, her ability to write. She closed her eyes. *Please, God, just give me one more chance to find unconditional love.*

Sierra stepped out into the store and replaced three of the eleven outfits back where she had found them before moving to the accessories section. She quickly located a shelving unit with thermal underwear and picked up two sets in her size. Minutes later, she had moved on to shoes. Unable to decide between two different pairs of snow boots, she opted to get both before grabbing a couple pairs of thick wool socks off an end cap. Her arms were stretched to their capacity as she headed toward the cash register to get the damage report.

The young woman behind the counter had a brass-colored name badge pinned to her shirt claiming that she was Devi, employee of the year. She had dark, olive skin and her hair fell softly around her face like fine, black silk. The dark chestnut hue of her eyes matched the warmth of her smile. She took her time ringing up Sierra's items, ensuring that each security tag was removed. "That'll be $1497.54," she said once all the items were bagged up.

Sierra handed Devi her MasterCard and waited patiently for the transaction to be completed. After a few seconds, Devi handed Sierra the receipt to sign just as the door buzzer sounded. Devi looked over and smiled. Sierra couldn't resist turning around to see who had invoked such a reaction. She blushed when she saw Asha standing just inside the doorway.

"How's it going, stranger?" Devi said. "I could have sworn I saw you an hour ago hanging out front and being too snobbish to come in and say hello."

"Just because you're my little sister doesn't mean I'm at your beck and call," Asha replied playfully.

"Yes, it does," Devi said. "It's in our unwritten contract as siblings."

Asha shook her head and shifted her attention to Sierra. "I was on my way back and thought I would check to see if you were still here."

"I'm still here," Sierra replied, suddenly disappointed that Asha hadn't removed anything more than her scarf again.

"Would you like a lift?" Asha asked. "Or do you prefer taking leisurely walks in the freezing snow?"

"Well, since you put it that way." Sierra said, quickly scrawling her name on the bottom of the receipt. "I guess I could handle going for another ride."

Asha's grin spread even wider. "I'm glad to hear that. Do you need help with your bags?"

"No, I'm okay," Sierra said, her heart feeling as though wild horses had suddenly thundered across it. She grabbed the bags off the counter. "I'll be right there."

• • •

Sierra stood just to the left of the lodge's front entrance and waited for Asha. She shifted from one foot to the other, trying to keep the blood she thought for sure was freezing in her veins circulating throughout her body. The brief moments of warmth that escaped each time a guest opened the front door to the lobby made the decision to wait even harder. She didn't want to appear rude after Asha had done so much for her, but her jogging suit felt like the thin piece of paper that was wrapped around a Popsicle, wet and sticky.

Asha steered the snowmobile skillfully back to where it had been parked an hour or so before. A sign affixed to the porch's wraparound railing read "Reserved for Search and Rescue." Switching off the engine, she trudged over to the steps and peered up at Sierra. "You didn't have to wait for me," she said, taking off her gloves and tucking them underneath her arm.

Sierra opened her mouth to reply, but the lobby door sprang open. Asha stopped in her tracks less than two feet away as a flash of frizzled silver hair exploded from inside and stepped in between them.

"Thank goodness you're back," Dee said, throwing her arms around Asha's waist and hugging her tightly.

"Is everything okay?" Asha said, pulling her scarf away from her mouth and peering over Dee's head at Sierra.

Dee stepped back and offered a crooked grin. "Of course it is, dear. Can't I just be happy to see you?"

Asha peered down at her. "All right, what's up?"

Dee poked Asha in the ribcage playfully. "I was wondering if you would mind running up to the house and getting my sweater. It's a tad chilly."

"No problem, Grandma," Asha said. "I'll be happy to get it."

"Thanks dear," Dee said. She turned and smiled politely at Sierra. "It seems like it gets colder every year."

"I'm sure," Sierra said. "I've been here for less than twenty-four hours and I don't think I've ever been this cold."

"I see you've at least expanded your wardrobe," Dee said, eyeing the bags Sierra held in her hands.

Sierra smiled. "I'm trying to."

Dee nodded and looked over at Asha before slipping back into the lodge. Asha pulled the scarf around her nose and mouth and slipped her gloves back on. "Would you like to go snowmobiling after I get back?"

"Sure," Sierra said, surprised by the offer. "I just need to change into something warmer."

"Without a doubt," Asha replied. "What if I ring you from the lobby when I return? I'll only be a few minutes."

"That works," Sierra said, moving toward the door.

"Will you be the one answering the phone?" Asha asked. "Or is someone else staying with you?"

Sierra felt the caterpillars that had been quite dormant for some time in her stomach instantly sprout wings and turn into butterflies. "No, it's just me."

"Good," Asha said, smiling. "I'll see you in a little while."

"Don't you need my room number?" Sierra asked.

Asha leaned forward. "I have a woman on the inside who will trade the number for a sweater, remember?"

Sierra could feel Asha's warm breath on her cheek and though she couldn't see Asha's eyes, she sensed that they were watching her intently. "I remember, but isn't insider trading illegal?"

Asha stepped back and looked around as if searching for spies. "It's only illegal if you get caught," she whispered.

"Well, you'd best not get caught," Sierra said, pulling open the lobby door.

"I won't," Asha replied. "I'll be back in no time."

• • •

Sierra shivered uncontrollably as she wiped her sopping wet tennis shoes on the entryway rug. Her feet were freezing. In fact, every inch of her was cold except for one area in particular. It was warm and wet with desire for a woman whose face was still a mystery. She blushed as if those milling around in the lobby could somehow read her mind. *I must be desperate,* she thought. *How could I possibly be thinking about this woman going down on me when I have no idea what she looks like? I still don't even know if she's a lesbian!*

She shook her head and started for the elevator. The mouthwatering aroma of fried chicken intercepted her senses and her stomach growled with anticipation. She followed her body's insistence for food and allowed her nose to guide her into the large recreation room. A couple of staff members were busy setting up a lunch buffet where the continental breakfast had been earlier.

"It'll be another five minutes or so before everything is ready," the shorter of the two men said, offering Sierra a warm smile.

"It smells terrific," Sierra replied. "Unfortunately, I don't have time to enjoy it today."

The shorter man paused from his task of breaking up the freshly baked rolls into individual servings and studied Sierra. His eyes were a brilliant blue surrounded by long, dark eyelashes. His black hair was parted down the middle and feathered back, leaving just a few strands to fall on either side of his forehead. He had a slender waist but his chest and arms were well defined. "Wait a second," he said, grabbing a couple of rolls along with some squares of foil-wrapped butter. He placed them on a small, round plate and strutted across the room. With an easy smile, he held the plate out to Sierra. "I can't let a sister run around hungry."

Sierra switched her bags from her left hand to her right and accepted the plate. "Thank you," she said, with a grateful smile. "Is that a house rule?"

"Girl, the owner's granddaughter would have my hide otherwise," he said, still smiling. "By the way, the name's Ryan."

"Sierra," she replied. "Thanks for the snack."

Ryan looked down at the four bags Sierra held in her hand. "Do you need help with any of that?"

"No, but thanks anyway," Sierra said. She took a step toward the lobby before something that Ryan had said struck her. "Ryan?"

Ryan looked back at her.

"You were talking about Asha, right?" Sierra said.

"That's correct," Ryan replied. "As strange as it sounds for obvious reasons."

"Their attributes are so strikingly different," Sierra said.

"I'm guessing you and Asha have met?" Ryan replied.

"Kind of," Sierra said. "She gave me a ride earlier."

"Wow, she works fast," Ryan snickered.

Sierra shook her head. "I didn't mean it like that."

"I have no idea what you're talking about," Ryan said, playfully defiant. He sashayed back over to the buffet bar to resume his task of breaking up rolls for easier handling. "Any more questions?"

"Is she for real?" Sierra said.

Ryan brushed his hands off on the apron tied around his waist. "What do you mean?"

Sierra glanced at the clock on the wall. "Never mind, I've got to get going. Thanks again for the rolls."

"No problem," Ryan said, crossing his arms in front of his chest. "And Sierra?"

"Yes," she replied.

Ryan's face was momentarily serious. "What you see is what you get with Asha."

"I'll keep that in mind," Sierra said.

"Just don't hurt her," Ryan said, dropping his arms back down to his sides. "She's been hurt enough." He turned back to the rolls and began breaking more of them up.

Sierra's stunned gaze bored into the back of Ryan's head, but that was the extent of her indignation. There was no reason to verbalize the grievous error in his assumption that Asha would be the one to get hurt. She knew full well that even if Asha turned out to be the woman of her dreams in some third-dimension fantasy world, it would be her getting hurt in the end and not Asha. History had a way of repeating itself and she had never discovered the magical key to unlock a lifetime of happiness and avoid constant disappointment.

Exiting the recreation room without another word, Sierra skillfully balanced the rolls in one hand as she carried the shopping bags in the other. Her mind was preoccupied by the many unknowns about Asha. For one thing, as Ryan had so blatantly alluded to, Dee was as white as Wonder Bread and Asha was definitely not.

What would be the harm in doing a little research? Sierra thought, sidling up to the registration desk and looking around for Dee. She tapped the bell a couple of times and waited.

Within a few seconds, a man with curly, brown hair and a thick mustache emerged from the back. "How can I help you?" he asked.

Sierra found herself tongue-tied. Surely she couldn't ask this guy about Asha's family or if she was involved with anyone. "Um, can you tell me if I have any messages?"

"I sure can," he replied. "The name's Jack. What's your room number, Miss?"

"Stanton," Sierra replied. "It's 311."

Jack looked through a small stack of handwritten messages. "Sorry, Ms. Stanton, I don't see any here. Have you checked the automated message system from the phone in your room?"

"No, not yet," Sierra replied.

"Well, just so you know," Jack said matter-of-factly, "we only take handwritten messages if a non-registered party comes to the front desk and requests to speak to a guest staying at our lodge. We buzz the room, but if there's no answer the person has to leave a message. We respect the privacy of all our guests and try to ensure their safety."

"That's a good rule of thumb to follow," Sierra said. "I won't be having anyone coming to visit, so I guess I won't need to worry about it."

"What?" Jack said, his eyes reflecting disbelief. "There will be no one joining you during your stay?"

"Hey," Sierra said, arching an eyebrow. "Don't rub it in."

Jack leaned forward. "I'm sorry, Ms. Stanton. I meant no offense. I'm just surprised that a beautiful woman like yourself would be spending the holidays alone."

"You and me both," Sierra replied. "I'll see you around."

Jack didn't respond.

The lobby door flew open and Sierra hurried toward the elevator. She didn't want the woman strolling in to see the telltale signs in her eyes that she had been betrayed by someone she had loved. A man might not recognize it, but a woman definitely would.

Sierra was about to set her bags on the floor to press the button for the elevator when she glimpsed the woman out of the corner of her eye. "Let me get that," the woman said, stepping up next to Sierra.

"Thanks," Sierra replied, trying not to be distracted by the beautiful creature that stood at least an inch taller than she.

"My pleasure," the woman said softly. "I hope you're having an enjoyable stay so far."

Sierra could see that the woman had a swimmer's build that probably developed somewhere between high school and college. She had long legs, narrow hips and broad shoulders. Sierra was afraid to gaze too closely at the woman's face although she could tell that her features were exquisite. "I'm having a great time."

"Well, that's what this place is all about," the woman replied.

The elevator doors parted and Sierra stepped toward one side, expecting the woman to be right behind her. Instead, the woman was making her way over to the recreation room with a bundle of clothing tucked underneath one arm. Just as the elevator doors were closing, the woman glanced back toward the elevator. Sierra looked away, blushing as though she had been caught peeping through the woman's bedroom window.

When the elevator doors parted on the third floor, Sierra hurried to her room. She locked the door behind her and tossed the bags onto the bed. Setting the plate of rolls onto the night stand, she collapsed onto the bed next to the bags and stared up at the ceiling. She was exhausted. The restless night of sleep combined with her pathetic eating habits were starting to rear their ugly heads. She kicked off her shoes and peeled off her damp socks to rest for a moment, but the aroma of the freshly baked rolls coaxed her into sitting back up. Taking one of them, she didn't bother with the butter as she sunk her teeth into its soft shell. The taste was heavenly.

After brushing bread crumbs off her chest, Sierra began to rummage through the shopping bags. A few indecisive minutes later, she settled on a gray and pink camouflage pair of ski pants and the white jacket with matching camouflage stripes down each sleeve. She changed quickly and sat down on the edge of the bed to wiggle her feet into one of the new pairs of boots. After lacing them up, she stared down at the phone on the nightstand. "Ring," she said softly. "Come on, ring."

Beads of sweat trickled down the back of Sierra's neck and the moisture building beneath her breasts sizzled. She glanced at the clock and wondered if she would pass out before Asha even called. Then a terrible thought crossed her mind: She might actually get stood up. When the telephone rang, she almost jumped up and down. She took a deep breath instead and scooped up the receiver. "Hello?"

"Hey, it's Asha. Are you about ready?"

"As ready as I'll ever be," Sierra replied. "I'll be down in a second."

"I'll meet you out front," Asha said.

Sierra dropped the phone on the cradle and grabbed another roll as her stomach loudly grumbled to be fed. She took a bite as she tucked her wallet into one of the zipper pockets of her jacket. Stepping into the bathroom, she double-checked her appearance. Her eyes looked tired, but the dark circles beneath them were minimal. *Just give me the strength to get through this day,* she thought. *And keep the memories of this year at bay.*

CHAPTER THREE

The snowmobile sailed over the four-foot-high snowdrift and Sierra cried out with glee. She tightened her arms around Asha's waist and gingerly tucked her hands back into the sleeves of the jacket. Although she had been on the back of the snowmobile for less than twenty minutes, her fingers felt like frozen French fries. There was no one to blame but herself; she had forgotten to purchase gloves in her whirlwind shopping spree at the Top of the World Ski Shop and was paying dearly for her oversight.

Just a little while longer, Sierra thought. *Surely I can make it a little bit more before I have to tell Asha we need to turn back.*

Asha steered the snowmobile deeper into the forest and skillfully maneuvered it in and out of the towering tree line. Sierra closed her eyes and inhaled the light pine scent that clung to the air. Each deep breath seemed to clear away more and more of the cobwebs that had cluttered her mind. Ideas trickled from her imagination, slowly gaining momentum, until plots and characters were capsizing over each other. She felt actual joy in her heart as though the dam of hope had given way and flooded the dry, desolate valley of despair into oblivion, leaving the flowers of inspiration blooming in its aftermath.

The snowmobile's abrupt stop pulled Sierra back into reality. She peered over Asha's right shoulder, half-expecting the machine's tiny engine to be on fire, forcing them to walk back. Instead, she saw Asha pointing in the distance toward a small herd of deer. Their dark brown color stood out in contrast to the snowy clearing that they were grazing in. A few of them had raised their heads and turned their gentle brown eyes to stare at the intruders who had invaded their sanctuary. The rest continued nuzzling the ground in search of food, though their ears flicked back and forth, listening just in case the unwanted guests tried to sneak up for a closer look.

Sierra rested her chin on Asha's shoulder. "My God, they're beautiful."

Asha leaned her head gently against Sierra's. "Yes, they are."

Once again Sierra felt the stir of desire elbowing its way through cynical resistance. "What should we do?" she said. "I don't want to scare them."

Asha straightened back up. "We'll just take it nice and easy." She steered the snowmobile to the left and gradually picked up speed.

Sierra kept her eyes on the deer until they had faded into the picturesque setting, blending back into nature. She tucked her head back behind Asha's jacket and flexed her hands open and closed. Her fingers ached to be wrapped around a warm coffee mug and her body craved the hot, dark-roasted liquid. She knew that it was time to head back but she dreaded saying it.

The snowmobile slowed to a stop again and Asha switched off the engine. Sierra panicked. *Did Asha somehow read my mind?* she thought. *Will she make me walk back? I don't even know where I am!*

"Look," Asha said.

Sierra raised her head and peered over Asha's shoulder once again. Directly in front of them was a small stream, its waters traveling silently beneath a thin layer of ice. The surrounding pine trees stood like silent soldiers, tall and majestic with limbs of white. They protected the area from the unforgiving winds that would disturb the tranquil solitude if given the opportunity.

"What do you think?" Asha said.

"I'm speechless," Sierra replied.

"I thought you might like this place," Asha said. "I come here whenever I need to get away and think."

"So you do live here?" Sierra asked.

"I come here and take care of my grandmother from November to February every year," Asha replied.

Sierra resisted asking about the obvious difference in their ethnicity. "What do you do the rest of the year?"

"I'm guessing you want to know what I do for a living," Asha said.

"If that isn't being too personal," Sierra replied. "If I had to guess I'd say you're either inherently wealthy, your spouse has some high-powered job, or you're lucky enough to be employed where they grant four-month vacations every year."

Asha chuckled and shook her head. "I haven't inherited any money and I'm definitely not married, but I do have a job that allows me to work whenever I want to."

"Oh my God," Sierra gasped in mock horror. "You're a prostitute!"

Asha cracked up laughing. "Not quite, but I'm glad you have a sense of humor."

Sierra unintentionally squeezed Asha's waist. "I'm glad you're glad."

"Me, too," Asha replied.

"It feels so good to laugh," Sierra said, feeling the heat of embarrassment redden her checks. The tug on her heart brought forth images of miniscule monkeys swinging back and forth on the strings of Cupid's harp. "So are you going to tell me what you do or am I going to have to keep guessing? I have a pretty wicked imagination when I'm in the right mood."

"I'm guessing you're in that mood now?" Asha said.

Sierra fought the girlish giggle that seemed to bubble up within her. *Oh, if you only knew what kind of mood I was in,* she thought. *It's been so long since I've been in someone's arms.*

"Sierra?"

"I'm so sorry," Sierra said, leaning into Asha. "I was suddenly a million miles away."

"I completely understand," Asha said. "This place has that effect on people."

"I feel like I'm in a Thomas Kinkade painting," Sierra replied. "It's truly incredible."

"I'm glad you like it," Asha said. "Now are you going to answer my question or keep avoiding it?"

Sierra laughed. "Yes, I'm in that kind of mood. It's dangerous to leave my mind wandering for too long."

Asha grinned and turned around slightly. "I own a circuit board company out on the West Coast. We supply boards for the commercial and medical industry as well as the military. I'd go into more detail, but it's classified and if I told you, I'd have to kill you."

"That's okay. I like my life just fine," Sierra said as an ornery grin pulled at her lips. "Then again, I do like to live on the edge."

"Is that so?" Asha replied, curiosity evident in her tone.

"Yes, that's so," Sierra said. "In fact, I'm going to take a risk and ask you another question."

"Fire away," Asha replied.

Sierra took a moment to formulate the words. She didn't want Asha to know that she had already been asking about her. "How come your grandmother works so many hours at the lodge? Don't you worry about her?"

Asha shrugged. "She owns it and she's stubborn as a mule. The winters are the toughest on her as it gets very cold up here, and it's the holiday season so it also gets very busy. I do what I can to help out, but she misses my grandfather something fierce. This was their dream."

"That's really wonderful to pitch in the way you do," Sierra said.

"I wouldn't have it any other way," Asha said easily.

Sierra crossed her arms in front of her chest. Her body shook uncontrollably and her teeth chattered so violently it caused her head to hurt. "Asha, I hate to cut this short, but would you mind if we headed back? I'm freezing."

"Of course I don't mind," Asha said. "I'm so sorry you're cold."

"It's my own fault," Sierra replied. "I was having too much fun to say anything."

"It makes me happy to hear that," Asha said, switching back on the snowmobile. "Hang on, okay?"

"Okay," Sierra replied as the snowmobile lurched forward. "By the way, are you hungry?"

"Starving," Asha shouted as they picked up speed.

Sierra held on tighter to Asha's waist. "Would you like to have a late lunch with me?"

"I'd love to," Asha replied. "I'll just need about a half an hour to get cleaned up. Will that work?"

"That works," Sierra said. She almost expected the snowmobile to lift off the ground as her spirits soared from the depths to which they had been accustomed for quite some time.

● ● ●

Sierra stripped off her clothes and jumped underneath the warm spray of the shower. The water momentarily stung as it rinsed the cold away from her skin and eased the chill that seemed to have buried deep within her bones. She showered in record time and was running a comb through her hair when the phone rang. Racing for it, she paused, took a deep breath, and picked up the receiver. "Hello?"

"Hey, it's Asha."

"Wow, you're fast," Sierra replied. "I just stepped out of the shower not more than two minutes ago."

"That's okay," Asha said. "I'll just wait for you in the lobby."

"Don't be silly," Sierra said before she thought things through. "You're more than welcome to come up."

"I'll give you a few minutes to get dressed though, okay?" Asha said hesitantly.

Sierra glanced down at the towel that was wrapped around her body. "That'd be great," she replied, slapping herself in the forehead with the palm of her hand. *I'm such an idiot.*

"See you then," Asha said.

Sierra dropped the receiver back onto the cradle and quickly dressed. She had just finished drying her hair when she heard a knock at the door. "Just a sec," she shouted. "I'll be right there." She double-checked her appearance one last time in the mirror and hurried over to the door. Taking another deep breath, she threw her shoulders back and swung open the door. Dee smiled up at her.

"Good afternoon, Ms. Stanton," Dee said.

"The same to you," Sierra replied, forcing the complete obliteration of her excitement from reflecting in her voice. "Is everything okay?"

"I'm afraid not," Dee said. "A couple of skiers decided to crash into one another. We have reports of broken bones and a significant gash on one of the skiers' faces. Asha was called in to assist until other emergency personnel arrive."

"I see," Sierra said, leaning against the door frame for support. "I hope everything turns out okay."

"It will," Dee replied confidently. "Anyway, Asha wanted me to ask you if she could have a rain check on lunch."

"Absolutely," Sierra replied. "I thoroughly enjoyed spending time with her today."

Dee eyed Sierra suspiciously for a moment. "Yes, Asha is a wonderful woman. I'm assuming that the two of you have hit it off?"

"I'm not quite sure what you mean," Sierra said, suddenly feeling as though she was under the microscope and her blood was being examined for lesbian tendencies.

Dee held Sierra's gaze. "I just mean that it would be nice if the two of you became friends."

Sierra bit her bottom lip. "Yes, it would."

"Well, I'm sure I'll see you later," Dee said, turning to go. "Have a pleasant afternoon."

Sierra stepped into the hallway. "You have a nice afternoon, too."

Dee looked back at her. "You should definitely come down and listen to our live music tomorrow night. It's grown to be quite a tradition here on Sunday evenings."

"I'd love to," Sierra said. "When and where?"

"In our restaurant toward the back of the lodge," Dee replied. "I suggest getting there a little before seven o'clock."

"Oh," Sierra said worriedly.

"What's the matter, dear?" Dee asked, walking back over to Sierra.

Sierra shrugged. "I'm not a fan of dining alone."

Dee took Sierra's hand and patted it. "My dear, I've seen couples come in and never speak a word to one another through the entire meal. Now, that's what I consider dining alone. Besides, Asha will be there and I'm sure she'd be more than happy to join you."

Sierra couldn't resist the grin that pulled at the corners of her mouth. "Then I'll see you tomorrow evening, if not before."

"Good," Dee said, letting go of Sierra's hand. "Please don't forget to wear something elegant. The evening's theme is 'A Black Tie Affair'."

Sierra closed the door and fell back against it. *Oh my God, I have nothing to wear!* She rushed over to the nightstand, picked up the phone, and dialed zero.

"Front desk, this is Jack. How can I be of service?"

"Jack, its Sierra Stanton. Do you know where I can get something formal to wear?"

"Yes, ma'am," Jack replied. "There are quite a few shops that sell formal attire. Or, if you prefer, we have a seamstress on hand who can design whatever you need."

"Can she whip something up within twenty-four hours?"

"I'm not sure but I'll see what I can do," Jack offered.

"Please let me know right away," Sierra replied.

"Of course," Jack said. "I'll call you back within two minutes."

• • •

Sierra spent all of Saturday evening jotting down her thoughts and expanding on plot ideas in her trusty notebook. She took a brief recess to order room service and was delighted by its presentation as well as its taste when it arrived. The *filet mignon* was butterflied and the center was perfectly pink. Each bite was tender and juicy, melting almost like warm butter on her tongue. The vegetable medley was made up of crisp baby carrots, perfectly steamed broccoli and garlic-roasted asparagus. Lemon wedges were also included as a convenient way to cleanse the palate between bites.

When eight o'clock rolled around, Sierra dialed room service and asked that her dinner tray be retrieved. The nice man on the phone requested that she set it outside her door so they wouldn't disturb her. She appreciated their consideration for her privacy and did as instructed. Then she jumped in the shower to clean up before her scheduled appointment with the lodge's on-site seamstress, Monique.

At exactly eight-thirty p.m. sharp, Monique arrived, wearing a flowing black pant suit that complemented her small frame. Her actual height was about five-foot-two, but her pumps made her look about five-foot-five. In her hands she carried a collection of different fabrics, a fashion book highlighting the latest styles, and a bag of essentials. She breezed into the room and laid everything out on the bed. "All right, what kind of look are you trying to attain?"

Sierra tapped her index finger against her lips. "Well, it's for tomorrow night's 'A Black Tie Affair'."

"Okay," Monique said, flipping open a sketcher's pad. "I understand that it needs to be elegant, but what kind of reaction are you going for?"

It took only a second for Sierra to respond. "Tastefully distracting?"

"I can do that," Monique replied, with a wicked smile. "Now let's get some measurements."

• • •

Sierra awakened Sunday morning feeling better than she had in quite some time. Her body buzzed with energy and she wasn't about to pass up the opportunity to run. She flipped open the booklet that had been placed on the small two-person dining table that listed all the amenities the lodge had to offer. Searching through its pages, she found that the workout room was on the fifth floor along with a lap pool, Jacuzzi and sauna.

Within minutes, Sierra was dressed and had her hair pulled back in a ponytail. She dug through the suitcases for her running shoes. Initially, when she was deciding on what she would bring on the trip, the running shoes had been a toss-up. Sierra's literary agent, Dana, who had come by to make sure Sierra wouldn't miss her flight, had made the final decision. Dana had tossed them into the suitcase, declaring it was better to be safe than sorry.

Sierra slipped on the running shoes and bounded toward the door. She reached in and grabbed a hand towel from the bathroom before dashing into the hallway. There was plenty of time for her to get a solid workout in, expand on some more of her writing ideas in her notebook, and get cleaned up before tonight's dinner and live entertainment. *Watch out, world,* she thought triumphantly as she stepped onto the elevator. *I'm starting to feel like me again.*

• • •

At five minutes till seven o'clock, Sierra stepped off the elevator and hurried over to the registration counter. Her pantyhose didn't protect her feet from the cold wood flooring so she stood on her tiptoes and leaned on the counter. Dee looked up and smiled. "My goodness, you look terrific, dear."

"Thank you," Sierra said, blushing slightly. "Did my shoes arrive?"

Dee removed a box from underneath the registration desk and set it on the counter. "I believe this is what you're looking for."

Sierra removed the lid and looked at the one-inch black pumps. "They match perfectly! Let's hope they fit."

"Well, there's only one way to find out," Dee said.

Sierra slipped the shoes on and took a step back. "What do you think?"

"You'll turn every head in the room," Dee said. "I can't believe Monique was able to design something that exquisite on such short notice. She really outdid herself this time."

"She sure did," Sierra replied, fidgeting nervously with the small black shoulder straps of the cocktail dress. "I've never owned anything like this before. I'm not so sure the world is prepared to see this much skin."

Dee grinned. "It's flattering, so don't worry. Besides, it complements your curves and I really like that Monique left the back open."

"It's a little hard to get used to," Sierra admitted, running her hands nervously along the neckline of the dress. "I feel a little naked."

"You'll be fine," Dee said. "Now, get going or you'll miss the start of the music."

● ● ●

Sierra hurried around the registration desk and down the hallway toward the restaurant. She stepped up behind two couples who were easily in their forties and were dressed to the nines. The two gentlemen were in black tuxedos with white shirts and black cummerbunds and black bow ties. Their two female companions wore similar white dresses with black pearl necklaces and one carried a black purse.

The maître d' guided the four patrons to their table. He waited for them to take their seats before handing each one a menu. Sierra started to fidget with the thin straps of her dress again when she glimpsed the two women lean in and kiss. She watched, mesmerized by their loving gestures toward one another, and didn't notice that the maître d' had returned. "They come every December to enjoy the holidays with us," he said finally.

Sierra's cheeks reddened. "Do you know how long they've been together?"

The maître d' grabbed another menu. "Well, this makes my fifteenth year here and the four of them started vacationing here about a year after I started."

Sierra glanced back over at the table. "At least it gives me hope that I'll find my special someone someday."

The maître d' smiled. "Well, Christmas is a magical time of year."

"That's what they say," Sierra replied.

"Have faith, Miss...?"

"Stanton," Sierra said.

"Oh, Miss Stanton," the maître d' exclaimed, taking her hand. "We have a table reserved for you." He led Sierra across the room and sat her down at a table directly in front of a black baby grand piano.

"Thank you," Sierra said, allowing him to push her chair in. "You should know that I didn't make a reservation."

"I know," the maître d' replied. "Asha made it for you."

Sierra grinned. "Really?"

"Really," he replied.

Sierra leaned back so the maître d' could place a cloth napkin across her lap. "Can I ask you a question?"

"Sure," he replied.

Sierra chuckled and straightened the silverware that was already perfectly placed. "I don't exactly know what Asha looks like. Would you mind describing her to me?"

The maître d' raised one eyebrow. "You haven't seen her yet?"

Sierra blushed. "No, I haven't."

The maître d' looked toward the piano. "My advice," he said, "is to be patient and enjoy the entertainment. I don't think you'll be disappointed."

"I don't mean to sound shallow," Sierra interjected quickly. "I don't care what she looks like. I'm just nervous. I feel like I'm on a blind date."

The maître d' bent down on one knee and looked into Sierra's eyes. "Miss Stanton, might I suggest a little red wine to relax you?"

Sierra placed her hand on his arm. "That would be wonderful."

The maître d' motioned for one of the waiters to join them. A young man who had to be no more than twenty-two years old hurried over. His red hair was combed back, enhancing the topaz color of his eyes. He seemed surprisingly awkward in his tuxedo. Sierra imagined that he preferred something a lot less formal and a snowboard instead of a serving tray.

"Darren, please get Ms. Stanton a glass of our finest red wine," the maître d' said.

"Yes, sir," Darren replied.

With a nod of his head, the maître d' acknowledged the party of seven that had just walked in. "Ms. Stanton, if I can be of any more service, please don't hesitate to ask."

"Thank you," Sierra replied. She watched him cross the room with the grace of a ballroom dancer.

At about a quarter after seven, the lights dimmed and a tall Indian woman stepped up next to the piano. Her silky black hair was pinned up and her skin tone was a rich, dark honey. She wore a very flattering black dress that was slit up one side and stopped just short of the upper part of her right thigh. Sierra recognized the woman almost immediately as the one who had assisted her at the elevator.

The woman sat down at the piano bench and poised her long, slender fingers above the keys. With a subtle tilt of her head as though she could already hear the music, she began stroking the ivory. The soothing melody hushed the dining audience. Sierra sipped at her wine and gazed at the talented creature in front of her. She started to take another sip of wine when the woman briefly looked up. Their eyes met and the woman's lips parted revealing a brilliant white smile.

It can't be. Sierra almost let go of her wine glass as it tipped toward her lips. She grabbed the stem and rescued the little bit of wine that had spilled over the edge of her glass with a flick of her tongue. She looked back up to find Asha's eyes fixed on her and an amused grin tugging at her full lips.

Asha motioned for an older gentleman with thinning gray hair that had been standing off to the side to join her at the piano. He strode over to the bench, flipped out the coat tails of his black tuxedo, and sat down next to her. Within seconds, Asha removed her hands from the keys and the gentleman continued playing, pulling off a seamless transition. The restaurant patrons clapped and cheered in appreciation of Asha's performance. In return, Asha offered an infectious smile and a wave.

Sierra took another quick sip of wine as Asha approached. "Is this seat taken?" Asha asked, touching the only other chair at the table.

"No," Sierra said.

Asha pulled out the chair. "Do you mind if I join you?"

Sierra drank the rest of the wine in her glass and set it off to the side. "Of course I don't mind. You were sweet enough to make the reservation."

Asha scooted closer to the table and waved Darren back over to the table. "What it'll it be?" he asked cheerfully.

"Bring me a glass and a bottle of whatever Sierra is drinking," Asha replied.

"Right away," Darren said. He turned on his heel and hurried toward the kitchen.

Asha removed the cloth napkin from the plate in front of her and draped it across her lap. "I'm sorry about having to cancel yesterday."

"It's okay," Sierra replied, unable to keep from smiling. "I'm just glad you're here now."

Asha leaned forward and placed her hand on top of Sierra's. "I'm glad I'm here, too."

Darren returned to the table with a glass and a bottle of red wine. He poured a small amount into the glass and handed it to Asha. Asha slowly removed her hand from

Sierra's and took the glass. She gazed into the red liquid.

Sierra cocked her head to the side. "What are you doing?"

Asha swirled the wine and brought the glass up to her nose. "Being the owner's granddaughter does have it perks, but it also has its fair share of responsibilities. You've already tasted the wine and know that's its good, but I have to inspect it like I'm some sort of wine connoisseur or no one who's watching right now will even try it."

"Oh, the pressure," Sierra teased, glancing up at Darren and rolling her eyes. "I don't know how she does it."

Darren laughed. "Me either."

Asha took a sip of the wine, rolled it around her tongue for a minute, and swallowed. "It's a tough job, but someone has to do it."

Darren refilled Sierra's glass and grinned. "I think I'll go check on your order."

"Good idea," Sierra replied with a wink.

Asha waited for Darren to gain some distance before shifting her attention from the wine to Sierra. "So, tell my why a nice southern girl comes to this state all alone during the holidays?"

Sierra took only a second in considering telling Asha the truth. "I just needed time to myself."

Asha held Sierra's gaze. "Well, we all do from time to time."

"True," Sierra said. "How do you know that I'm from Florida?"

Asha pulled out the pins holding up her hair. The lustrous black locks fell onto her shoulders curling almost instantly. Her dark eyes gleamed with mystery. "Let's just say that I know people."

Sierra's lips curled. "What else do you know about me?"

Asha leaned forward and touched Sierra's hand. "Not as much as I want to."

Sierra blushed and briefly looked away. Darren approached with her order of blackened Mahi-mahi and fingerling potatoes. She was thrilled that Asha didn't let go of her hand. "Thank you, Darren."

"Will there be anything else?" Darren asked.

Sierra glanced at Asha. "Are you not having anything?"

"No, but thank you for asking," Asha replied. "Darren, please give me the check."

"No problem," Darren said. "I'll be back in a little while to see how everything is."

Sierra picked up her fork. "You don't have to do that. I'm completely capable of paying for my meal."

Asha's eyebrows furrowed. "It has nothing to do with you being capable and everything to do with me wanting to."

"You're too much," Sierra said, raising a bite of fish up to her lips. "Do all guests get such special treatment?"

"I don't know what you're talking about," Asha replied with a sly grin.

"Well, my lips are sealed," Sierra said. "I'm not sharing you with anyone." The words were out of her mouth before she could stop herself. She blushed and took another sip of wine.

• • •

Sierra slid the keycard into the lock and waited for the green bubble to illuminate before turning the handle. She pushed open the door and flipped on the entryway light. Her intestines felt as though they had turned into a rollercoaster track with butterflies as passengers strapped into the moving cart, fluttering their wings wildly as they barreled over the first drop-off. She took a deep breath and turned around, daring to look into the chocolate pools that were Asha's eyes. "I had a great time."

"Me, too," Asha replied. "I hope we can spend some more time together."

"I'd like that," Sierra said. "It's been a long time since I've sat down and enjoyed someone's company."

"Maybe we can make this the start of a very good habit," Asha said. She leaned over and kissed Sierra on the cheek. "Good night, Sierra."

Sierra's entire body trembled. "Good night, Asha."

Asha held Sierra's gaze for a second longer before striding back down the hallway. Sierra watched until Asha had descended the staircase out of sight. She closed the door and fell back against it. *What am I doing?*

CHAPTER FOUR

Sierra reluctantly opened her eyes to the darkness that enveloped the room. She had grown accustomed to the restless nights of sleep that had been the norm for the past year. Feeling surprisingly refreshed, she figured only a few hours had passed since climbing into bed after her evening with Asha. After all, what benefits she gained by sleeping peacefully were countered by the brevity of time that accompanied it.

She raised her head from the pillow to confirm her suspicions. "It can't be!" Throwing off the covers, she stumbled into the bathroom and switched on the light. After her eyes had adjusted to the brilliance of the fluorescent bulbs, she grabbed her wristwatch off the counter and checked the time. The short hand was almost over the eleven, with the long hand trailing slightly behind it.

"I can't believe it," Sierra said. "I actually slept through an entire night." She studied her reflection in the wall-length mirror and noticed that her eyes were bright and clear.

Almost bouncing out of the bathroom, she strutted over to the French doors and pulled back the drapes. The frigid air that had seeped through the crevice between the two doors and which the heavy material had kept at bay swept over her. She hugged her arms around her chest as she shivered and peered outside. Though the sky was slightly overcast, she could see the ski lifts were soaring over blankets of snow. Each swaying chair carried two to three passengers up to the skiers' selected run.

I'm going to have to try that out someday, Sierra thought. She turned away from the window and scanned the room. Her eyes lingered on the mahogany desk and the luxurious leather chair nestled up against it. She walked over and ran her fingertips across the chair's high back before pulling it out. She sat down and placed the palms of her hands down on top of the desk feeling its smooth, cool surface. *I just need one good idea to run with.*

Sierra tried to conjure up a more definitive direction in which the characters in the outline to her new mystery could go, but every idea was overshadowed by the desire she felt for Asha. Goosebumps came in waves as she remembered the warmth of Asha's kiss on her cheek and the soft touch of her hand. She couldn't get over how hearing Asha's laughter was like hearing music for the first time. It was completely uplifting and mesmerizing.

An idea suddenly popped into Sierra's head. She opened her eyes, sprang out of the chair, and hurried over to the closet. She pulled open the closet door, removed the laptop bag, and set it on the end of the bed. The bag unzipped easily, as though happy to rid itself of the stale air that had been trapped within its cushiony walls.

Sierra removed the relatively new laptop and the power cord from within the bag. She rushed back over to the desk and plugged the cord into the outlet beneath it. The light on the rectangular power box glowed green. She opened up the laptop and pressed the "on" button in the right-hand corner of the keyboard. The computer screen came to life.

"Patience is a virtue," she whispered, drumming her fingers on the desk while the computer booted up.

When the hourglass icon on the screen had finally transformed into a tiny arrow, Sierra guided it to the Microsoft Word icon and clicked on it. In less than two seconds, a window opened, revealing a clean electronic sheet of paper in which Sierra could write. Taking a deep breath, she slowly plucked at the keys until she had written an entire paragraph. Her stomach growled, but she ignored it. *Breakfast can wait,* she thought. *I just need to get this down.*

At about a quarter till two, Sierra's head felt as though someone had placed it in a vice. She reluctantly pulled herself away from the computer to go find something to eat. She dressed and headed down to the recreation room. To her disappointment, the lunch buffet had ended at one o'clock. She walked back into the lobby and spotted Jack at the registration desk.

Jack looked up and smiled. "Good afternoon, Ms. Stanton. How are you today?"

"Starving," Sierra replied. "Do you have any suggestions on where I might find a quick bite to eat around here that isn't fast food?"

"There's a deli around the corner," Jack said. "They have really good French dip sandwiches."

Sierra felt someone step up behind her. "That sounds perfect, thanks."

Jack grinned. "No problem." He shifted his gaze to the person standing behind her. "So, did they have frostbite?"

"Of course not."

Sierra recognized the singsong quality of the voice immediately. She turned around to embrace the beauty that went along with it. Asha smiled at her.

Jack crossed his arms in front of his chest. "I can't believe you had to go all the way up there."

"What happened?" Sierra said.

Asha's eyes visibly softened as she looked into Sierra's. "A guest and her two children were stuck up in one of the ski lifts for a few minutes while the lift's operator assisted another rider. The woman felt that they had been subjected to more adverse effects by the wind at that altitude and they possibly had frostbite."

"Oh," Sierra replied. "Can you get frostbite that quickly?"

"Maybe in Antarctica with no shoes on," Jack said sarcastically.

Asha shot Jack a cold stare. "Our guests' concerns are always a high priority and we address each with the utmost respect."

"Whatever you say," Jack said with a shrug. "You're the boss."

"You're lucky we're friends," Asha replied, her eyes sparkling. "Otherwise I would have to write you up for your lack of professionalism."

Jack feigned shock. "We're friends?"

Asha looked at Sierra and winked. "Not for long at this rate."

"That's just harsh," Jack said. He resisted smiling as he turned toward the computer and went back to work.

Asha took Sierra by the hand. "So you're off to get something to eat?"

"Yeah," Sierra said, seizing the opportunity. "Would you like to join me?"

"I'd love to, but I have to work today," Asha replied. "Are you free this coming Friday?"

"I can be," Sierra said.

"I don't want to intrude on any previous engagements," Asha replied.

Sierra squeezed Asha's hand. "You're definitely not intruding. Just call me later this week."

"I will," Asha said, slowly letting go of Sierra's hand. "See you soon."

"Yes, you will," Sierra confirmed, turning around so that Asha wouldn't see the big, goofy grin on her face. She crossed the room without looking back and breezed past a group of teenagers as they walked in through the door.

The pain in Sierra's stomach was no longer tolerable and she wasted no time in descending the snow-covered steps to find the deli that Jack had told her about. A wicked grin tugged at the corners of her mouth though as she thought about what she was really hungry for. *Indian.*

● ● ●

Sierra typed "Chapter Five" on the top third of the electronic sheet of paper in Microsoft Word before moving the arrow up to the save icon. Four days had passed since the last time she had been in Asha's presence. The flu had hit the lodge's staff hard and Asha had been forced to work double shifts. Sierra had kept busy with writing except during the evening hours when Asha would call. On a couple of nights, they chatted for well over an hour. Tonight, though, was Asha's night off.

Shutting down the computer, Sierra was surprised that Asha hadn't arrived for their planned evening yet. She walked over to the nightstand and picked up the phone to call the front desk. *Maybe I should wait a few more minutes,* she thought. She dropped the receiver back onto the cradle and fell onto the bed. A subtle knock on the door brought her back up onto her elbows. The next knock had her on her feet. She hurried over to the door and looked out the peephole. A woman dressed in blue jeans and an unbuttoned black pea coat stood outside her door patiently waiting. *Asha.*

Sierra opened the door and grinned. "Hi."

"Hi. I'm sorry I wasn't able to call earlier," Asha said, leaning against the door frame. "It's been one hell of a day."

"I think it's been one hell of a week for you," Sierra replied. "Would you like to come in?"

Asha didn't move. "Well, I was wondering if you still felt up to going out."

"Of course I do." Sierra said, leaving the door open as she went to the closet. "Just let me grab my jacket."

"You'll also need these," Asha said, stepping into the room and removing a pair of leather gloves from her jacket pocket.

Sierra was momentarily speechless as she accepted the gloves. "Thank you," she whispered, unable to meet Asha's eyes.

Asha stepped around Sierra and sat down on the edge of the bed. "Well, I wouldn't wear them snowmobiling or skiing or anything, but they should work just fine for tonight."

"I can't believe you remembered that I didn't have gloves," Sierra said, removing her jacket off the hanger. She closed the closet door, slipped on the jacket, and looked over at the bed. Asha was stretched out across it with her legs straddling one corner of the mattress. *She's trying to kill me*, Sierra thought. "So where are we going?"

Asha grinned. "It's a surprise, but it isn't far. You won't need your gloves until we get outside."

Sierra tucked the gloves into her jacket pocket and grabbed her room key. "Will I need my wallet?"

Asha shook her head. "I asked you out, remember?"

Sierra grinned. "I remember."

Asha took Sierra by the hand. "Good, because I would never accept money on an evening I initiated."

"I'll keep that in mind," Sierra said, reaching for the door.

Asha stopped for a moment and looked down at Sierra's shoes. "Do you have an extra pair of socks that you can bring?"

"Sure," Sierra said hesitantly, but unwilling to question Asha's motive. She hurried over to the dresser and removed one of the pairs that she had just purchased. "Will these work?"

Asha took a closer look. "Perfect." She took Sierra's hand and led her back to the door. "I'm really glad that I met you."

"Me too," Sierra replied. "I'm having a great time so far."

Asha opened the door and stepped into the hallway before releasing Sierra's hand. "You sound as though you expect something disastrous to happen."

Sierra pulled the door closed and jiggled the handle to make sure it was locked. "It usually does."

"Well, I'm no fortune teller," Asha said, "but I know for a fact that nothing disastrous will happen on my shift."

Sierra looked into Asha's brown eyes, swimming in the possibilities that lay hidden behind them. "I'm counting on that."

Asha's eyes were unflinching. "You have my word."

Sierra had a sudden urge to throw her arms around Asha's neck and kiss her, but she resisted. "I guess I should let you lead the way since I have no idea where we're going."

Asha's lips turned upward. "And I'm not giving you any hints."

Sierra tucked the socks into the opposite jacket pocket that her gloves were in. She couldn't resist smiling as they headed toward the elevator. "You like being mysterious, don't you?"

"Mysterious? Not really," Asha said. "I just really like surprising someone I'm interested in."

The little girl Sierra had once remembered being suddenly reemerged and her heart seemed to skip a beat. "And I'm someone that you're interested in?"

Asha pressed the button for the elevator. "You're one of the few genuine people that I've ever met. Of course I'm interested."

The sliding doors opened and they stepped into the elevator. Sierra had to know more. "How interested?"

Asha pressed the button for the lobby as her cheeks subtly reddened. "Very."

Sierra looked over at Asha. "That's a good thing."

Asha offered a shy grin.

Sierra returned the smile as painful memories flashed in her mind like exploding firecrackers. For an instant, she saw similar pain ripple across the surface of Asha's eyes before being interrupted by the parting elevator doors.

"Come on," Asha said, taking Sierra's hand. "Let's do a little celebrating."

"What are we celebrating?" Sierra replied, following Asha across the lobby.

"Here at the lodge, we have a little celebration every Friday night through the month of December," Asha said. "You missed our kick-off, but it was cut short due to a mild snow storm anyway. It's just our way of saying thank you to the guests who spend the holidays with us."

Sierra followed Asha though a maze of people mingling in the large recreational room. "So what's on tonight's agenda?"

"You'll see," Asha replied. She led Sierra over to a makeshift counter that had been set up just in front of the Christmas tree.

Jack sat behind the counter with fake reindeer antlers on his head. "Hey, ladies, how are the two of you this evening?"

"We're just fine," Asha replied. "Is everyone having a good time?"

"Yep," Jack said. "It's the best celebration we've had so far and the turnout seems to be larger than last Friday's."

"Good," Asha replied. "I think a lot of people were just wiped out from their travels."

"Will you need two tickets tonight?" Jack said.

Asha squeezed Sierra's hand before letting go. "You are correct, sir."

"What do we need tickets for?" Sierra asked.

"We're going ice skating," Asha replied exuberantly.

Sierra felt like she was suddenly thirteen again. She could barely contain her excitement. "Really?"

"Yes, really," Asha said. She accepted the tickets Jack gave her and turned to Sierra. "We use tickets to see how many guests take part in our celebrations. Each year, more and more people participate."

"I have always wanted to go ice skating," Sierra said excitedly.

Asha took a hold of Sierra's hand again. "Well, here's your chance."

• • •

The festival was situated a good fifty yards away from the back side of the lodge and twinkling white lights consumed every tree. The ice rink was the main attraction, the hot chocolate station running a close second with comparable lines. Just beyond that was a Nativity scene with real people and animals performing hourly reenactments. To the right of the rink was a very large, red sleigh with nine animated reindeer in front of it. The leading reindeer had a red nose. One of the lodge's employees was dressed up in a Santa suit and sat in the sleigh holding the reins. Some of the other employees were dressed as elves and helped children who wanted their pictures taken with Santa get on and off the sleigh.

Sierra finished tying up her skate and accepted Asha's outstretched hand. "I'm so glad you told me to bring an extra pair of socks."

"Well, I couldn't very well be responsible for you getting blisters," Asha said, helping Sierra over to the rink's entrance gate. "You might not forgive me for that."

Sierra stepped very cautiously onto the ice. "I'm sure you would think of something."

Asha's eyebrow shot up. "Is that so? Did you have an example that you'd like to share?"

Sierra felt the muscles in her legs working to keep her feet from sliding apart. "Well, for starters, you could teach me how not to fall down on these things."

Asha laughed and took Sierra's other hand. "Have you ever roller-skated?"

"Yeah, a long time ago," Sierra replied.

"Do you remember how you would push off with one skate and then the other?" Asha said.

Sierra nodded and pushed off with her right foot. Asha skated backwards, holding onto both of Sierra's hands. Neither of them spoke as they made their way around the rink. When they reached their starting point, Asha let go of Sierra's right hand and swung out to the left to skate beside her. They skated around a few more times, listening to the holiday music playing from the speakers strategically hidden throughout the festival grounds.

"What do you think?" Asha said.

Sierra giggled. "I just can't believe that I'm actually doing this. I feel like a little kid."

"There's nothing wrong with that," Asha said.

Sierra hit a groove in the ice and started to lose her balance. Asha swung around to the front and grabbed her waist, trying to keep the inevitable from happening. They spun around a couple times before Sierra's legs finally collapsed as though the puppet master had cut the strings to his puppet. Both she and Asha fell to the ground laughing as other guests darted by shaking their heads.

Asha got back up on her skates and helped Sierra to her feet. Sierra suddenly lost her balance again and fell forward into Asha. Asha caught her around the waist again, but this time they didn't fall. They stood hip to hip, staring into each other's eyes.

"Thanks for catching me," Sierra said almost breathlessly.

"I'll catch you any time you fall," Asha replied.

"I almost believe that," Sierra said, moving her mouth a little closer to Asha's.

Asha moistened her lips. "What can I do to convince you?"

Now Sierra's lips were less than an inch from Asha's. "I'll think of something."

"Hi," a chipper voice interrupted. "I hope I'm not intruding, Asha."

Sierra witnessed the dismay that flashed across Asha's face. *This can't be good*, she thought.

Asha turned to face the woman who could have easily been on PETA's most wanted list with her full-length mink coat. "Hello, Vivian. Are you having a nice evening?"

"I'm having a great time," Vivian replied. "I just wanted you to know that I was here so maybe we can catch up when you're not busy with your new friend."

"I'll let you know when I have a free moment," Asha said, flexing her jaw muscle.

Vivian placed her hand on Asha's arm. "I remember how busy you were last season," she said, giving Asha a wink. "It hasn't been that long."

"Long enough," Asha replied, her voice faltering.

A smug look came over Vivian's face as though she had accomplished what she had set out to do. Sierra knew this was the moment to intervene. "Asha, dear," she said. "Can we head up to our room now? I'm a little chilly and no amount of hot chocolate can warm me up the way you do."

Vivian's mouth dropped open.

Asha blinked hard before gazing over at Sierra. "I'm sorry, baby."

Even though Sierra knew that Asha was just playing along, it felt amazing to hear her say those words. "It's okay."

Asha looked back over at Vivian. "I'll call you later on this weekend. Have a good night." She took Sierra by the hand and helped her over to the edge of the ice skating rink. Vivian skated off in a huff.

"You okay?" Sierra asked, looking over at Asha.

Asha pulled off one of her skates. "I'm with you so I'm better than okay."

"Do you want to talk about it?" Sierra asked, tucking the laces of her skates into each boot.

"And ruin this perfect evening?" Asha replied with an easy smile. "I think not."

Sierra slipped on her tennis shoes and waited for Asha to put on her boots. "Are you in the mood for some food?"

"Sure," Asha replied, taking Sierra's skates. "Do you have something in mind?"

Indian food, Sierra thought, grinning. "No, but I'm open to suggestions."

Asha's eyes sparkled. "What were you just thinking about?"

"Nothing," Sierra said too quickly.

Asha bent down to pick up Sierra's skates. As she stood back up, she gazed into Sierra's eyes. "For some reason, I think you're bluffing."

Sierra struggled to find something to say as her cheeks reddened. "I, uh, just don't know this area well enough yet to make an informed decision."

Asha's eyes dropped to Sierra's mouth before darting over to the counter where she needed to return the skates. "Let me get rid of these," she said, holding up the skates. "Then we can decide."

"Sounds like a plan." Sierra's heart pounded in her chest, as though trying to break through the brick wall of betrayal that had been built around it.

"I'll be right back," Asha said.

Sierra allowed her mind to wander and her eyes to indulge Asha's beautiful body as she walked away. *My God, she's incredible. What I wouldn't do to feel those long legs wrapped around me and those hips rising and falling with anticipation of orgasmic release.*

"Let me give you some words of advice," a voice growled.

Sierra snapped her head around stunned by the person's closeness. "Excuse me?"

Vivian glared at her from the other side of the railing that surrounded the ice rink. "Asha's not into you for the long haul. You're not her type."

"And how would you know that?" Sierra replied, standing up.

Vivian pursed her lips. "Take a guess." She glanced over at Asha, who was making her way back over to them. "On the other hand, why don't you just ask Asha yourself?"

Sierra watched Vivian skate away.

Asha eased up next to Sierra. "What was that about?"

"Nothing," Sierra replied, noticing the concern in Asha's eyes. "There just seems to be a lack of holiday spirit in some people."

"Is that so?" Asha said, reaching out to take Sierra's hand. "Did she say something mean?"

"Not to worry," Sierra replied. She avoided Asha's touch by tucking her hands into the pockets of her jacket. She needed time to think. "It's so cold out here."

Asha allowed her hand to fall to her side. "What did Vivian say?"

Sierra turned toward the lodge. "Nothing worth discussing."

Asha grabbed Sierra gently by the arm. "I'll be the judge of that."

"Not here, okay?" Sierra said. She felt the cold bricks of self-preservation building a new wall around the feelings that she had started to develop for Asha. There was no more room for heartache or drama in her life. Either would totally destroy her.

Asha dropped her arm. "Let me at least explain my relationship with her."

"So, the two of you are together," Sierra replied, feeling the blow of disappointment stronger than she had anticipated.

Asha pulled Sierra closer. "No, but we were at one time."

Sierra noticed a few people watching them. "Let's go talk."

"Where would you like to go?" Asha said, allowing her hand to travel down the length of Sierra's arm.

Sierra accepted Asha's hand into hers. "Well, I think this might warrant a little more privacy than any restaurant can offer."

"I'll go anywhere that you want," Asha said, following Sierra toward the lodge.

Sierra felt the twist of uncertainty knotting up her stomach. There was only one place she could think of. "Follow me."

● ● ●

Sierra set the receiver down on the cradle. "It'll be about ten minutes before our burgers get here."

"That's all right," Asha replied, sitting down on the edge of the bed next to Sierra. "It's worth the wait. The burgers are fantastic. Besides, it'll give us some time to talk about Vivian."

Sierra felt the butterflies whirling in her stomach. They created an emotional tornado that tore across her heart. "Listen, I have no right to intrude in your personal life. I'm barely your friend."

Asha's eyes flickered with hurt. "So you do look at me as just a tour guide while you're here on vacation."

Sierra grabbed Asha's hand as she started for the door. "Please, I didn't mean to hurt you. You have to understand that we're just getting to know each other and I can't be hurt again by a friend or a..."

"Lover?" Asha said, dropping to her knees between Sierra's legs.

Sierra fell silent for a moment and avoided looking into Asha's eyes. "I can't afford to get involved with you."

"But you want to," Asha replied, cupping Sierra's chin.

Sierra shifted her eyes to gaze into Asha's. She felt her breath catch in her throat. "Yes."

Asha traced Sierra's lips with her finger. "I want that, too."

Sierra saw Asha's eyes drop to her mouth once more. The power to know how it would feel to have Asha kiss her was almost unbearable. She reached over and tucked a dark strand of hair behind Asha's ear. Asha caught her hand and pulled her close. Anticipation had quickened their breath. Sierra closed her eyes and leaned forward, waiting for the soft pillows of Asha's lips to grace her own.

CHAPTER FIVE

Asha's warm, wet kiss melted all reasons to resist further exploration from Sierra's mind. She dipped her tongue between Asha's lips and Asha responded by opening her mouth a little wider. At first, their tongues barely brushed by each other, but it only took their subtle moans to instigate a flurry of tantalizing strokes.

"My God," Sierra gasped between kisses. "Your lips are so soft."

Asha opened her eyes and moved her lips so that they brushed Sierra's. "And so are yours. I can't get enough of them." She brought her lips back to Sierra's.

Sierra's heart pounded in her chest and echoed in her ears. Her entire body trembled. There was a familiarity in Asha's kiss and she didn't have to stretch her imagination to understand the significance. For the first time in her life, she was being kissed the way she had always dreamt.

The joy that this realization invoked was short-lived as Vivian's vicious gaze materialized in Sierra's mind. She tried to resist the insecurities that anchored into her heart and dragged her happiness beneath the depths of pain and regret, but she pulled away as Asha tried to kiss her again.

Concern spread across Asha's face. "What's the matter?"

"Tell me about Vivian," Sierra replied, unable to meet Asha's eyes. "And please tell me the truth."

The muscles in Asha's jaw flexed. "Why would I lie?"

"I wasn't trying to insinuate that you would," Sierra said. "I just want you to know that I can handle whatever you tell me."

Asha shook her head and pushed herself off the floor. "Exactly what would I gain from lying?" she said, her voice cracking slightly. "Can you tell me that?

Sierra got to her feet. "I'm sorry. I'm just not the type who wants a one-night stand or to be the other woman while two people are trying to work out their relationship."

"Is that the kind of person you think I am?" Asha said, crossing her arms in front of her chest. "Do you really think because I happen to find you attractive that all I want from you is a one-night stand?"

"You've just met me," Sierra replied.

Asha shook her head. "Whatever."

"None of what I'm saying is coming out right," Sierra said, reaching out to Asha. "You just don't know what kind of year I've had."

"So why don't you tell me?" Asha said, taking a step back to avoid Sierra's touch. "I assumed it had to be something quite horrible to bring you here at the holidays."

Sierra looked up in surprise. "Why would you think something like that?"

"You're so full of life, Sierra," Asha said, lowering her voice along with her arms. "But every time I see you smile, it's overshadowed by the pain you think no one can see in your eyes."

"I don't have to take this crap from you," Sierra said, brushing past Asha as memories bombarded her. "Yes, I've been hurt worse than I could have ever possibly imagined. Yes, I know I keep my guard up, but you have no right to give out lectures, Asha. It's obvious you still have feelings for Vivian. The look on your face was a dead giveaway!" She yanked open the door just as Darren was raising his hand to knock.

"Good evening, Ms. Stanton," Darren greeted, his smile fading instantly. "You ordered two entrees?"

Sierra tried to find her voice. "Uh, yes, yes I did."

Darren leaned toward the left to try to see into the room. "Is everything all right?"

Sierra blocked his view by partially closing the door. "Everything's fine. I just stubbed my toe on the way to get the door."

"But I hadn't even knocked," Darren said.

"I've been checking every few minutes," Sierra replied. "You have no idea how hungry I am."

Darren studied Sierra for a minute longer. "Are you sure everything's okay?"

"I'm sure," Sierra said, digging in her pocket for some tip money. She smoothed out a five-dollar bill and handed it to Darren. "Thanks for the quick service," she said, taking the tray.

"No problem, Ms. Stanton," Darren replied. He dropped his voice to a whisper. "If you need anything, anything at all, don't hesitate to ask."

"I promise," Sierra said, flashing her best smile.

"Have a good night," Darren said, tucking the money into his pocket.

"I will," Sierra said. She slipped back into the room and closed the door.

"Thank you," Asha said. "That might have been messy."

Sierra walked over and set the tray down on the table. "And why's that?"

Asha walked up behind Sierra. "Because I don't want to have to tell my grandmother that I've upset the only person who's been able to get to me since Vivian."

Sierra turned around. "What?"

"It's a long story," Asha replied, taking Sierra's hands. "But one that I didn't want to share with you until we'd had the opportunity to get to know each other a little better. Can you understand that?"

Sierra dropped her eyes and nodded. She felt ashamed by how she had treated Asha. There was no excuse for her self-righteous attitude except for a heartache that Asha knew nothing about. "I'm sorry. This past year has made me cynical."

"I'm sorry, too," Asha replied. "I wasn't prepared to have someone like you enter my life. It's thrown me for a loop."

"Scared?" Sierra said, chuckling nervously. "Because I know I am."

Asha wrapped her arms around Sierra's waist. "It's more like terrified."

Sierra laid her head on Asha's shoulder and peered into her eyes. "I'm only here for a few weeks."

Asha placed her finger on Sierra's lips. "I don't want to think about that right now."

Sierra kissed the tip of Asha's finger. "So what do you want to think about?"

"Spending as much time as possible with you before you leave," Asha replied.

"And how much time will that be?" Sierra said, taking Asha's hand.

Asha sighed. "There's a lot of work around here that I'm responsible for. Every once in a while, I'll take a day off during the week but that depends on my workload. I usually have the weekends off, though."

"I think that'll work out perfectly," Sierra replied. "I can keep focused on a project that I need to tackle as well."

Asha pulled out one the two chairs at the small dining room table for Sierra. "Is there anything I can help with?"

Sierra sat down. "You've already helped me."

"I did?" Asha said, taking the other seat and scooting up to the table. "When did I do that?"

Sierra grinned and removed one of the plates from the tray. "The moment you offered to take me snowmobiling."

Asha took the other plate and placed the tray on the floor. "I don't understand."

"Trust me on this," Sierra replied, picking up her hamburger. "You've helped me more than you know."

• • •

"I should probably get going," Asha said, getting up from the table and tossing her napkin on the empty plate. "My grandmother will want to go home soon."

Sierra tried to hide her disappointment. She had been so caught up in their conversation that she had stopped eating almost an hour before. Now the half-eaten hamburger was cold and unappealing. She pushed it to the side and got up to follow Asha over to the door. "It's been a long day for her."

Asha took Sierra into her arms and hugged her tightly. "Thanks for being so understanding about Dee. She and Devi are all I have. I try to look after them the best I can."

"I think you do an amazing job," Sierra replied, resisting her desire to know more.

"I don't know about that," Asha said. "By the way, is tomorrow too soon to ask if I can see you again?"

Sierra gazed into Asha's tired eyes. "It isn't soon enough."

Asha pressed her lips firmly against Sierra's before grabbing her coat. "You always know the right things to say. How is that possible?"

Sierra grinned. "I'll never tell."

Asha leaned her head down and started kissing Sierra's neck. "Is that so?" she mumbled.

"That's not fair," Sierra said, arching her head back. "Besides, you weren't very forthcoming at the elevator last week."

Asha pulled her mouth away. "I don't know what you're talking about."

Sierra raised an eyebrow. "Well, let's see if I can refresh your memory. I was standing at the elevator with my shopping bags. You came up and pressed the button for me."

"It's starting to sound familiar," Asha said, avoiding Sierra's gaze and leaning down to kiss her neck again.

Sierra tipped Asha's chin upward. "Not so fast, Sparky."

"Ooh, a nickname," Asha said with an ornery grin. "What do I get after our next date?"

"Nothing if you don't tell me why you didn't say anything at the elevator," Sierra replied.

Asha dropped her eyes and stared at the floor. "I didn't want you to base your decision on whether to go out with me or not by how I looked."

"I don't understand," Sierra said softly. "You're beautiful."

"That's just it," Asha replied, looking away as a subtle hue of red settled in on her dark honey coloring of her cheeks.

"I see," Sierra said. "So you have had your share of superficial people too, then?"

Asha's eyes locked on Sierra's. "Yes."

"Well, I'm definitely not one of them," Sierra replied. "In fact, I judge a book by its contents, not by its cover."

"That's so strange," Asha said, furrowing her eyebrows.

"What is?" Sierra said.

Asha kissed Sierra's forehead. "One of my favorite authors said that very same thing on a radio interview a couple weeks back."

"Oh, really," Sierra said, swallowing hard. "What are the odds?"

"Maybe you've heard of her," Asha said. "Her name is S.A. Webb."

"Ah, the lesbian mystery writer," Sierra replied.

"That's the one," Asha said.

Sierra glanced down at her wristwatch. "I can't believe how fast time passes when I'm with you."

"What time is it?" Asha said, pulling Sierra even closer.

"It's almost eleven," Sierra replied. "What time does Dee usually call it a day?"

"About now," Asha said.

Sierra's heart fell. "I know you can't, but I wish you could stay a little while longer."

"Me, too," Asha replied. "I really enjoy learning everything about you."

"The feeling is mutual," Sierra said. She leaned forward and kissed Asha on the lips.

Asha reluctantly pulled away. "I'll see you tomorrow, right?"

"Just tell me what time and I'll be ready," Sierra said, holding onto Asha's hand.

"Does noon work?" Asha replied.

"It's perfect," Sierra said. "What's on the agenda?"

Asha pretended to seal her lips with a lock and key.

"Fine, don't tell me," Sierra spat playfully. "You won't get any more kisses until then."

Asha pushed out her bottom lip in a pout. "That's not fair."

"You're really cute when you do that," Sierra said, wrapping her arms around Asha.

"Does that mean I get another kiss?" Asha said, her eyes pleading.

"How could I resist?" Sierra replied. She pressed her lips firmly against Asha's. "Now you'd better get going."

"All right," Asha said, opening the door and stepping into the hallway. She turned back toward Sierra. "Is it strange that I already miss you?"

Sierra felt as though a large chunk of ice suddenly slid from her heart. She hadn't been prepared for that admission. There was nothing she could say. Her tongue suddenly felt glued to the bottom of her mouth. She peered into Asha's dark, gentle eyes, knowing that tears were starting to pool in her own.

Asha took Sierra into her arms. "It's all right, Sierra."

"I'm okay," Sierra said, her voice catching in her throat. "You're just so sweet."

Asha cocked her head to the side. "Why, because I say what's on my mind?"

Sierra nodded. "It's a nice change, that's all."

Asha's voice softened. "Someone really hurt you."

Sierra's eyes were unflinching as she stepped away. "That's an understatement."

Asha reached for Sierra's hand. "You can talk to me."

Sierra caught movement out of the corner of her eye. "Another time perhaps."

"Hi, girls," Dee greeted cheerfully as she approached. "I thought I might find you up here."

Asha held Sierra's gaze for a second longer before turning to Dee. "I'm sorry if I kept you waiting."

"Nonsense, dear," Dee said, waving her hand dismissively. "There's always something to do. In fact, I was checking the vending machines to make sure they were stocked when I noticed the two of you in the hallway. I thought that now was the opportune time to see if I needed to ask Jack to take me home or not. I know how frisky young people can be."

"Grandma!" Asha replied, shaking her head in disbelief.

Sierra laughed. "Actually, Asha was on her way down to see if you were ready to go."

"Oh, I see," Dee said, taking Asha's hand. "I have such a sweet granddaughter."

"Yes, you do," Sierra replied, looking at Asha.

Asha held Sierra's gaze. "See you tomorrow."

Sierra noticed the desire burning in Asha's eyes. It was unmistakable. It penetrated her soul and moistened the valley between her legs. "Twelve o'clock sharp," she replied.

"Good night, Ms. Stanton," Dee said. "Sleep well."

"I will," Sierra said, before shifting her attention back to Asha. "Thanks for tonight."

"My pleasure," Asha said. "I enjoyed it immensely."

"Me too," Sierra said.

Asha squeezed Dee's hand. "Let's get you home. It's late."

With a tired smile, Dee allowed Asha to lead her down the hallway. Sierra waited until they had reached the elevator before closing the door. Moving over to the bed, she fell into its billowy softness. She raised her hands up to her face and inhaled. Asha's scent tantalized her imagination. *This is going to be one hell of a long night.*

• • •

At just two minutes till noon, Sierra heard a soft knock at the door. "Just a sec," she said, resisting the urge to skip from the desk to the door. She made a detour into the bathroom and checked her appearance. The dark circles beneath her eyes had completely disappeared. The laugh lines at each corner on the other hand seemed to be more defined and she knew exactly who was responsible. She opened the door and found Asha holding mistletoe above her head. "Why Asha, I do believe you need to be kissed."

"That's what I was hoping for," Asha replied, wrapping one arm around Sierra's waist.

Sierra closed her eyes. "If there were ever a sweeter indulgence than chocolate it's your lips."

"There you go again," Asha said. "I can never think of something that sweet to say."

Sierra reached up and touched the side of Asha's face. "Just kiss me."

Asha closed her eyes and leaned forward, meeting Sierra's luscious lips with her own. They broke off the kiss just long enough to gaze into each other's desire-filled eyes before passion evaporated the separation and they pressed their lips back together. Each intense kiss led to a deeper one. Their hips locked together and rotated to a needful rhythm. Sierra moved backward past the open door, never disengaging from Asha's lips.

Asha kicked the door closed and backed Sierra up against the wall next to the bathroom door. After tucking the mistletoe into her pocket, she held Sierra's hands up against the wall and left Sierra's lips to nibble on her neck. "I want you."

Sierra arched her head back as Asha made her way further down her neck. "I want you, too."

Asha lifted Sierra off the ground. "Hold on."

Sierra wrapped her legs around Asha's waist. "My God, you're strong."

Asha carried Sierra over to the bed and sat her down on the edge of the bed. She brushed aside the strands of blonde hair that had fallen in front of Sierra's eyes. "And you're breathtaking."

Sierra noticed that Asha seemed to have been suddenly struck by temporary paralysis. She made no move to touch her. "Tell me what you're thinking," Sierra whispered.

Asha smiled and shook her head. "It's nothing."

Sierra's heart pounded in her chest. Every part of her body cried out for Asha, but none as loud as her heart. "I was thinking that maybe we should slow down."

The relief that surged into Asha's eyes was unquestionable. "Are you sure?"

Sierra kissed the tip of Asha's nose. "I need the pleasure of your company more so now than your body if that makes any sense at all."

"It makes complete sense," Asha said, pulling Sierra close. "There's so much more I want to know about you before we make love."

"I feel the same way," Sierra replied still trying to grasp the depth of Asha's words.

Asha kissed Sierra on the lips. "Are you still up for what I had planned for today?"

Sierra grinned. "Definitely."

● ● ●

The Eagle Bahn Gondola out of Lion's Head Village offered spectacular views of Vail Mountain. Sierra embraced them with a trembling heart. A week prior, she would have sworn to anyone listening that God himself couldn't get her up that mountain. It had taken only one look into Asha's brown eyes and the ear-to-ear grin that had spread across her face to change her mind. Now, with only seconds to go before reaching the top, she released her death grip on Asha's hand and slipped on her gloves.

"Are you sure you're okay?" Asha said, shaking out her hand as the gondola came to a stop.

"Of course I am," Sierra replied, stepping out of the gondola. "I've never been better."

Asha tucked her hands into her jacket. "Why do I get the feeling that you're not telling me the whole story?"

Sierra took Asha's hand and pulled her over to the side so not to interfere with other passengers exiting the gondola. She touched the side of Asha's face. "Don't look so concerned."

"I have to be," Asha said. "I don't want to miss anything."

"You're not," Sierra replied, kissing Asha on the lips. "I'm not a huge fan of heights."

Asha's eyes widened. "You should have told me! I feel terrible."

Sierra threw her arms around Asha's neck. "Don't feel terrible. I'm glad that we're here. I might have never done this otherwise."

Asha brightened. "You mean it?"

Sierra rubbed her hands together. "Of course I mean it. Now, are you going to tell me about this place or not?"

"This is the famous Adventure Ridge, my dear," Asha replied, opening her arms to their full expansion.

"Adventure Ridge?" Sierra said. "What type of adventure are you going to take me on?"

Asha smiled. "Well, I figured since this is probably one of the few times you have experienced a winter wonderland of this magnitude, we should try a few things before I get you up on a pair of skis."

"You really think you can convince me to go skiing?" Sierra replied, turning her face away from the wind.

"I think I might be able to convince you," Asha said with ornery grin.

Sierra studied Asha's face. "What do you have in mind?"

"I'm not giving all my secrets away," Asha replied. "You just have to trust me."

The word "trust" echoed in Sierra's mind and pain rolled down the banks of her memory. This time, however, she ignored the pain and concentrated on Asha's brilliant smile. "I trust you."

"Good," Asha said. "Now let me tell you a little about this place. First, Adventure Ridge is like a smorgasbord for the winter enthusiast. It has ice skating, which we've already done. It also has snowshoeing, ski-biking, snowmobiling tours and tubing."

"Tubing?" Sierra replied, following Asha past a group of teenagers. "What's that?"

Asha chuckled and squeezed Sierra's hand. "You'll see."

CHAPTER SIX

Sierra rushed into her room and collapsed onto the bed. "Oh my God, that was so much fun!"

Asha closed the door and unbuttoned her coat. "I'm so glad you liked it."

Sierra sat up, pulled off her jacket, and tossed it over the bed onto the recliner. She leaned back onto her elbows and patted the space beside her. "Come here."

Asha dropped her coat onto the floor and stepped over to the bed. She grinned. "Am I in trouble?"

Sierra reached up and traced the outline of Asha's lips. "You're only in trouble if you don't kiss me."

Asha didn't need additional coaxing. She brought her lips to Sierra. Slowly, Sierra lay back on the bed, with Asha on top of her. Their hips rocked into each other's. Asha pulled away and grinned. "How was that?"

"On a scale of one to ten," Sierra said, stroking her chin. "I give it around a nine."

Asha pursed her lips. "A nine?"

An ornery grin tugged at the corners of Sierra's mouth. "If you think you can do better..."

Asha pressed her lips against Sierra's. Sierra felt a soft nibble on her bottom lip and the tantalizing flick of Asha's tongue. When she slipped her tongue into Asha's mouth, Asha gently sucked on it and stroked it with her own tongue. Within seconds, Sierra was dripping wet and thrusting her hips urgently into Asha's.

"I guess from that reaction that was more along the lines of a ten?" Asha said, kissing the tip of Sierra's nose.

Sierra opened her eyes. "Ten? That was more like a twenty!"

Asha rolled back on to the bed and placed her hands behind her head. She took a deep breath. "It's a tough job, but someone has to do it."

Sierra propped herself up on one elbow and peered down at Asha. "I'm glad you're the one who volunteered."

"Am I the only one who's volunteered?" Asha said, staring into Sierra's eyes.

Sierra held Asha's gaze. "Are you asking me if there's someone else in my life that I'm interested in?"

Asha's jaw muscle flexed. "Yes, that's exactly what I'm asking."

Sierra ran her finger along Asha's jawline. The truth clung to the tip of her tongue and though she knew admitting it would be painful, she could not fathom lying to Asha. She took a deep breath and allowed the air to escape her lungs slowly. "There hasn't been anyone for a long time."

Asha cupped Sierra's face with her hands. "I haven't been with anyone for almost a year. Now I'm starting to fall for someone who's going to leave in three weeks and I might never see again."

"You're falling for me?" Sierra said, unable to control the quiver in her voice.

Asha glanced away. "Like I said, I wasn't prepared for you to walk into my life."

Sierra felt the happiness that bubbled within her heart explode into a rush of energy. She threw her arms around Asha and hugged her so tightly that she worried she might actually break Asha's ribs. Asha returned her hug. They lay in each other's arms for over five minutes without saying a word. Finally, Sierra pushed herself up and reached for Asha's hand. "I can't think about having to leave you, so we need to keep our minds preoccupied."

Asha accepted Sierra's hand and sat up. "What do you suggest?"

"Well, I saw a flier for a sleigh ride dinner," Sierra replied. "How does that sound?"

"It sounds wonderful," Asha said. "Let's see if there are any openings left."

• • •

"I'm sorry we had to settle for pizza," Asha said as she walked Sierra back to her room.

"It's all right," Sierra said, squeezing Asha's hand. "There's always tomorrow."

"Speaking of tomorrow," Asha said. "I was wondering if you'd like to go skiing."

Sierra laughed out loud. "You're just not going to give me a rest, are you?"

The hopefulness in Asha's face began to dwindle. Even her eyes seemed to dim. "I'm sorry. I just assumed..."

Sierra interrupted Asha's statement with a kiss. After a couple of seconds, she pulled her mouth away. "I'm just giving you a hard time. I had a great time tubing today. It was just a little scary the first time."

"What about the second time?" Asha said, following Sierra a little further down the hallway before reaching Sierra's room.

"It was a little less scary," Sierra said. She slid the keycard into the lock and waited for the green light. When it was illuminated, she turned the handle and propped open the door to her room. "Do you want to come in?"

Asha shifted from one foot to the other. "Of course I do, but I'm not sure if that's a good idea."

Sierra reached out for Asha's hand. "Just for a little while, perhaps? I'll take you up on your skiing offer."

Asha took Sierra's hand and kissed it. "Okay, you've got yourself a deal." She followed Sierra into the room and closed the door.

Sierra took off her jacket and hung it in the closet. Asha walked past the bed and sat down in the recliner without taking off her coat. "Should I put mine back on?" Sierra teased.

Asha's lips parted into a grin as she pushed herself back out of the recliner to unbutton her coat. "You're quite the smartass, aren't you?"

Sierra waited as Asha walked toward her, swaying her hips from side to side. "Well, you took it off, didn't you?"

Asha handed Sierra the coat. As Sierra reached for it, Asha dropped it on the floor and grabbed Sierra's hand and pulled her close. "You're irresistible," she whispered.

Sierra felt Asha's hot breath against her lips. "How irresistible?"

"Do you want me to be completely honest?" Asha replied, wrapping her arms around Sierra.

"Yes," Sierra said, barely audible enough for Asha to hear it.

Asha closed her eyes and inhaled a quivering breath. "I want to undress you, deliberately taking my time, like I envisioned in my dreams last night. I want to memorize every freckle, every birthmark and every curve. I want to caress every part of you, first with my hands and then with my tongue."

"My God," Sierra gasped, brushing her lips against Asha's. "You make it feel like it's a hundred degrees in here."

"I'm sorry," Asha said.

"Don't apologize," Sierra replied, kissing Asha gently on the lips. "I wasn't complaining. I just wish I could give you that tonight."

Asha kissed the tip of Sierra's nose. "I would only want to make love with you if it were, in fact, making love. We haven't known each other long enough to harbor such an intense feeling for one another, but I'd be lying if I said there wasn't a possibility for it either. Well, at least from where I stand, that is."

Sierra searched Asha's eyes for a twinge of deceit lurking within the brown depths, but there wasn't any. "I don't know what to say."

Asha hugged Sierra. "You don't have to say anything. I just wanted you to know how I feel."

Sierra laid her head on Asha's shoulder. "I think the possibility is there for me, too."

• • •

Sierra swiveled the alarm clock back to where she could see it. Only ten minutes had passed since the last time she had checked. It was still a little over three hours before daybreak and an additional two before she met Asha for breakfast. *This is ridiculous,* she thought. *I have to stop thinking about her.*

Tossing the covers aside, Sierra climbed out of bed and shuffled across the room to the desk. She opened up her laptop and ran her fingers along the top of the keypad. Finding the rectangular power button, she pressed it gently. The computer screen brightened and a short wave of sound followed.

Sierra sat down in the chair and absentmindedly reached over to her left hand to play with the ring that no longer graced her finger. Realizing what she had done, pain erupted from deep within her soul and radiated throughout her body causing her to tremble. Tears followed, cascading down her cheeks and plummeting onto the keys. Her heart swelled and seemed to crack open slightly as though a fault line had developed across it. She waited for the usual wretched feelings of hopelessness to rip it open the rest of the way.

A few more breathless seconds passed and Sierra hesitantly lowered her hands away from her chest. The gut-wrenching despair she had grown accustomed to every time she remembered the past year didn't impact her quite the same way. In fact, it had been ousted by the joy she now felt simply by imagining Asha's 1,000-watt smile. As the pain diminished, passion surged through her heart; just like a hundred lightning bolts all at once, it electrified her soul, revitalizing her.

Sierra rested her hands on the keypad and began typing feverishly in Microsoft Word. She wanted to get her thoughts down and quickly before they were swept away in her need to stare into the chocolate pools that were Asha's eyes and melt in their reflection. An hour turned into two, then four. When she finally looked down at the bottom right-hand corner of the computer screen she had less than forty-five minutes to get ready for her morning rendezvous with Asha.

• • •

The moment Sierra stepped outside onto the snow-covered porch, she felt the shroud of warmth that the lodge had provided dissipate. Stumbling toward the wooden bench to her right, she tried to maintain both her balance in the rented ski boots and the grasp she had on the skis, which Jack had just fitted for her. She set the skis along the back of the bench and pulled her gloves on. *I'm so going to regret doing this,* she thought.

Sitting down in front of her skis, Sierra practiced buckling and adjusting her boots as Asha had encouraged her to do during their engaging conversation over breakfast. She also remembered that Asha had stressed the importance of her boots being comfortably snug, but not too tight. "Well, here goes nothing," Sierra muttered under her breath. She pushed herself back up onto her feet and trudged back and forth in front of the bench.

After a few minutes, she checked her watch and wondered what was taking Asha so long. Her mind inevitably flashed to an imaginary scene of Vivian coming down the spiraling staircase and pretending to sprain her ankle on the bottom step. Of course, Asha would rush over, being the wonderful person that she was, and scoop Vivian into her arms. As Asha carried her over to the first available chair, Vivian would press her lips against Asha's, sealing their fate and her own.

Sierra shook head, trying to clear the image from her mind. Abruptly pivoting to make another pass in front of the bench, she was startled to see Asha standing directly behind her. "You're looking good, Ms. Stanton," she said, balancing a pair of skis over her shoulder.

"Thanks," Sierra said, feeling her cheeks get hot. "I was starting to worry about you."

"Sorry," Asha said, stepping closer to Sierra. "After I got my gear, Jack asked me to approve some scheduling changes real quick. Unfortunately, it took longer than I anticipated."

"It's okay," Sierra said. "I used the time to get more acquainted with my boots." She clicked her heels together for emphasis.

"Does that mean you're ready for your first thrilling ski lesson?" Asha said, reaching for Sierra.

"I sure hope so," Sierra said with a slight nervous chuckle as she took Asha's hand.

Asha raised Sierra's gloved hand to her lips and kissed it. "You'll be fine," Asha said, raising her eyebrow. "You have the best instructor around."

"I'm counting on that," Sierra said, releasing Asha's hand to gather up her skis.

Asha laughed. "Come on, brave one. Let's hit the slopes."

Sierra swallowed hard. "Slopes?"

• • •

Sierra leaned on Asha's shoulder as they worked her other boot into the binding. With one final shove, it snapped into place. Asha stood back up and brushed the snow off her knees. "First things first," she said, reaching into her jacket pocket and removing two pairs of sunglasses. "Which one of these fit better?"

Sierra tried on both pairs of sunglasses. "These do," she said, holding up one pair and handing the other to Asha.

"Wow," Asha replied. "You have great taste."

Sierra slipped the sunglasses on. "What do you mean?"

"They're Armani," Asha replied.

Sierra reached up and touched the sunglasses. "Do you want them back?"

"No, silly," Asha said. "You look absolutely stunning."

Sierra lowered her head and peered over the lenses. "Thanks," she said softly, "so do you."

Asha slipped the other pair of sunglasses on. "Thank you."

"Are you blushing?" Sierra teased, leaning forward to poke Asha in the ribs. She realized her mistake a little too late as she started to fall forward.

Asha grabbed Sierra and held her for a moment. "I guess this means you're falling for me, huh?"

Sierra tried to think of some smartass remark, but it was useless. She was lost in the desire to kiss Asha.

"Should I take your silence as a good thing or a bad thing?" Asha said.

"It's definitely a good thing," Sierra replied, regaining her balance with Asha's help.

Asha kissed Sierra on the lips. "I love that."

Sierra blushed. "All right, Sparky, let's get to it."

"Okay, there are a few things you need to remember when you're skiing," Asha replied. "First, try to stay in control."

Sierra chuckled. "Oh yeah, that won't be a problem."

"Don't worry," Asha said. "I'll teach you everything you need to know to keep from running into other skiers and trees."

"Trees?" Sierra exclaimed. "I have to worry about crashing into trees?"

Asha laughed. "You'll be fine."

"Uh, huh, sure I will," Sierra said, unconvincingly. "Let's hear rule number two."

"Skiers and snowboarders who are in front of you have the right of way, so it's your responsibility to avoid them," Asha said. "If you have to stop, don't obstruct the trail or stop where you're not visible from above. That can be quite dangerous."

"Are you sure I can do this?" Sierra said, breathing warm air into her cupped gloved hands

"I know you can," Asha said. "It appears a lot harder than it really is."

"I don't know," Sierra replied. "This is extremely intimidating. I'm so nervous I could be sick."

"Don't be nervous," Asha said. "We're going to take this nice and slow."

"I like that plan," Sierra replied. "Oh, and thanks for letting me borrow some warmer gloves."

"No problem," Asha said. "Okay, the thing we need to work on is balance and maneuverability. I want you to try moving to your left."

Sierra laughed. "Tell me you're joking."

"We'll take it slow," Asha replied. "Now take my hand."

"Gladly," Sierra replied, smiling.

• • •

"Okay, last time," Asha shouted. "You can do it! Just keep your focus."

Sierra planted each ski pole into the snow. She wasn't sure if the poles that Asha had insisted getting really helped with balance, but they were essential in unlatching the binding surrounding her boots and getting back up on her feet. Bending at the knees, she pushed off and skied down the small incline toward Asha. A few seconds later, she threw her arms up in triumph. "Woo-hoo! I did it!"

"Yes, you did!" Asha said, throwing her arms around Sierra. "Now, we can try the green runs together!"

Sierra dropped her poles onto the ground so she could wrap her arms around Asha's neck. "You're insane!"

Asha grinned. "Maybe a little."

"Well, you're going to have to do a lot of smooth talking to get me to do that," Sierra said. "I'm quite content staying on the bunny slope."

Asha kissed Sierra passionately. "How's that for starters?"

"I'm still not convinced," Sierra said dreamily. "You should probably try that again."

"Is that so?" Asha said, tucking a strand of Sierra's hair back into her knitted hat.

"That's so," Sierra replied.

Asha brought her lips once again to Sierra's. "Better?"

"Third time's a charm, I think," Sierra said, her body trembling from the cold.

Asha leaned in and kissed Sierra. She pulled back abruptly. "You're freezing."

"Maybe a little," Sierra said. "I'm a southern girl, remember?"

"I remember," Asha said. She rubbed her nose against Sierra's in an Eskimo kiss. "Let's get some hot chocolate to warm you up."

"That sounds good," Sierra replied. "Back to the lodge?"

Asha picked up Sierra's ski poles and used one of them to undo her boots from their bindings. "No, I thought I'd take you to Belle's Camp. It serves some great hot cocoa."

Sierra picked up her skis and took her poles back from Asha. "Why don't you lead and I'll follow?"

"How about if I just walk beside you," Asha said, taking Sierra's skis and hooking them together so they would be easier to carry.

Sierra nodded. "I'd like that."

"Oh, there's just one thing about Belle's Camp," Asha said, walking alongside Sierra.

"Which is?" Sierra replied.

Asha glanced over. "It's at the top of an 11,840-foot peak at the top of Blue Sky."

Sierra's mouth dropped open. "What do you say we try something a little more..."

"Grounded?" Asha interjected with a genuine smile.

Sierra nodded. "Would that be all right?"

"It's perfect," Asha replied. "I know just the place."

• • •

Sierra took a seat at a two-person table as Asha stood in line to place their order at the Vail Coffee Company's counter. Almost instantly, her attention was drawn to a rather boisterous man on her right. He held nothing back as he recanted a tale to four of his friends about an unfortunate spill down one of the slopes that landed him in a body cast for six months. Sierra was unable to continue listening without fear of chickening out of skiing, and turned her attention to a small group of teenagers huddled together in one corner of the room. They all sat on the edge of their seats, listening intently to the advice that their apparent ski instructor was dishing out. Sierra took mental notes as the older man instructed the group to take long, deep breaths, hold it, and exhale slowly if they started to panic during the skiing lessons.

Sierra started the exercise almost immediately. She was inhaling for the fourth time when she noticed a woman staring at her from across the room. When their eyes met, the woman excused herself from the other women at the table and made a beeline to where Sierra was sitting. "Excuse me," she said, approaching the table. "I hate to intrude, but I'm a huge fan of your work."

Sierra smiled graciously as she kept Asha in her periphery. "Thank you."

The woman knelt down next to Sierra. "I was wondering if I could get your autograph?" she whispered. "The only writing instrument my friends and I could come up with is the permanent marker we use to mark our gear. Will that work?"

"Of course," Sierra said, taking the black marker the woman held up. "Do you have a napkin or something for me to sign?"

"Would you mind signing the back of my jacket?" the woman said, turning around.

"Are you sure?" Sierra said.

"Oh, yes," the woman replied. "Could you make it out to me? My name's Gloria."

Sierra took the permanent marker. "I'd be delighted to, Gloria."

Gloria turned around after Sierra finished and smiled. Her soft, rounded features reminded Sierra of an overstuffed teddy bear. "Thank you so much," Gloria gushed. "I've wanted to meet you for so long!"

"I'm glad you introduced yourself," Sierra said, shaking Gloria's hand.

"Well, I don't want to draw any more attention to you than I already have," Gloria replied. "I'm sure you and your partner are enjoying the little peace and quiet that this place has to offer."

Sierra didn't flinch. "Yes, we are."

"Take care," Gloria said.

"You too," Sierra replied. She watched Gloria walk back over to her friends, where they each took turns looking at her jacket.

"Is everything okay?" Asha said, setting the two cups of hot chocolate down on the table.

"Of course it is," Sierra replied. "Why?"

"I noticed that woman talking to you," Asha said. "Do you know her?"

"No," Sierra said. "Worried?"

Asha leaned back in her seat. "I wouldn't blame anyone for hitting on you."

Sierra blushed. "She wasn't hitting on me, but I'm flattered you noticed."

"Who wouldn't notice the most beautiful woman in this place?" Asha replied, before taking a sip of her hot chocolate.

Sierra's cheeks got even redder. "You have to stop. You're embarrassing me."

"And I'm guessing that's a bad thing?" Asha replied.

"Not really," Sierra said, taking Asha's hand. "I'm enjoying it immensely."

CHAPTER SEVEN

Sierra rolled over and looked up at Asha. "Tell me that was the green run."

Asha laughed and looked back at the tiny hill leading away from the ski lift. "Nope, but at least you didn't fall until you were out of the way of the other skiers."

"Now, there's a bright side," Sierra said, accepting Asha's outstretched hand.

Asha pulled Sierra up to her feet and helped her angle her skis in a forward direction. "You just have to remember what I showed you."

Sierra peered down the slope and almost threw up. How could she be so naïve? She was deathly afraid of heights, so what the hell was she doing? The answer came instantly as she glanced over at Asha. *You're in love with her,* she thought. *And you won't even know what it could've been like to make love with her because you're going to die!*

Asha placed a firm hand on Sierra's shoulder. "If you don't feel comfortable doing this, or if you're having second thoughts, just tell me."

Sierra heard the disappointment in Asha's voice and somewhere deep in her being it drowned out her fear. "I'm fine," she said calmly, forcing a reassuring smile.

Asha's face brightened. "Just remember what I've told you and you'll glide down that mountain like an Olympic contender."

Sierra looked over at Asha. "You really expect me to believe that?"

"It was worth a try," Asha said, patting Sierra on the butt.

"I'll say," Sierra said, taking a moment to find her balance. "Do you want to go first?"

"Nah," Asha replied. "I can keep better track of your progress if you're in front of me."

Sierra planted the ski poles into the ground. "Well, I guess it's now or never." She pushed off gently in the hopes that it would minimize the snowball effect that she envisioned happening if she went head over heels.

"Be strong!" Asha shouted.

Sierra's skis sliced grooves into the snow as she barreled down the slope. Panic set in just as quickly. Her mind tried to list in the matter of importance each rule that Asha had stressed and incorporate them into her situation. She kept her hands out in front and her elbows flush with the front of her stomach. She even tried to keep her shins in constant contact with the front cuff of her boots. The noise rushing by her ears, however, began drowning out her thoughts and in the darkest recesses of her mind she remembered Asha telling her to snowplow if she started going too fast.

Sierra pigeon-toed her skis, bent her knees, and forced her eyes to stay open, but the strength in her legs couldn't keep her skis from crossing over one another. Suddenly, her legs twisted into a scissor-like embrace and the ground rushed toward her with astonishing speed. A couple seconds later, she rolled onto her back with her face caked in snow and stared up into the blue sky, unable to move.

Asha raced over. "Are you okay? Is anything broken?"

Sierra wasn't sure how to answer. Her body felt as though Santa's sleigh and all of his eight reindeer had plowed into her, leaving not one incriminating red mark to be found. When she attempted to separate her skis, the muscles in her legs refused to generate any motion. "Where's the nearest exit?"

Asha removed her skis and shoved them into the powdery snow along with her poles. "A little further down the slope," she said, untangling Sierra's skis so she wouldn't injure herself further when she tried to get up. "I could try to carry you, but I don't think that would be advisable."

Sierra shook her head and slowly got back up. "I actually believe that getting down on my own is probably the safer bet."

"Probably," Asha replied. She picked up Sierra's ski poles and handed them back to her. "Race you?"

"To the bottom of this snow-packed insanity?" Sierra replied incredulously. "Are you crazy?"

"Just about you," Asha said, sliding Sierra's other ski beneath her foot.

"You haven't known me long enough to make that claim," Sierra replied, snapping her boot down into the binding. "After a couple weeks of me, you'll be driving me to the airport yourself."

"I seriously doubt that," Asha said. "Actually, I don't see me ever getting enough of you."

"You'd be the first," Sierra said. She forced a smile to keep from tearing up. "Now, enough about that. Let's go."

Asha did a slight bow. "After you, my dear."

Sierra shoved the ski poles into the ground and pushed off. In a valiant attempt to stay upright, she kept her skis parallel with one another and watched the other skiers below. As she careened down the final stretch, she began mimicking their movements just in time to miss sailing over an embankment and into some trees. Approaching the bottom of the slope, she sliced both skis sideways, creating a small wave of snow and coming to a miraculous stop.

Asha skillfully skied up beside her. "Wow, you were awesome! What a recovery! Are you sure you've never done this before?"

"I'm sure," Sierra said.

Asha bounced up and down on her skis. "Do you want to go again?"

Sierra gazed back up the slope. "I'll sit this next one out, if that's okay."

Asha's eyes grew wide with concern. "Did you hurt yourself on that fall?"

"My body feels a little sore," Sierra replied, feeling as though the muscles in her legs had been subjected to a blender.

Asha removed her sunglasses. "Do you hate it?"

"I need to try it again before I can give you an honest answer," Sierra replied. "And that means I need to rest for a little while first."

"Okay," Asha said. "I'll stay with you."

Sierra touched the side of Asha's face. "You go ahead and I'll wait for you."

"Are you sure?" Asha said.

"Yes," Sierra replied. "When you get back, we'll go again together."

"You're on!' Asha said. She blew Sierra a kiss and headed back toward the ski lift.

• • •

Sierra dragged herself over to the bed and collapsed. Her muscles twitched and jerked at the sudden release of responsibility in keeping her upright. Asha laid down next to her and grasped her hand. "Are you alright?"

"I've never been better," Sierra said. "Can't you tell?"

"Oh, yeah," Asha replied, playfully sarcastic. "Your words are dripping in excitement."

Sierra rolled onto her side and placed the palm of her hand on Asha's cheek. "Seriously, I had a wonderful time."

"I'm glad," Asha replied.

"I don't know how you do it, though," Sierra said, forcing her eyes to stay open as exhaustion slowly stole the rest of her energy.

"How I do what?" Asha said.

"Keep going the way you do," Sierra said. "I'm wasted and you look like you're ready to take on the world."

Asha gazed into Sierra's eyes. "Well, my parents had been phenomenal skiers, so it seemed only natural that I follow in their footsteps. I had my first lesson when I was thirteen and I've been skiing for over twenty-three years now."

Sierra noticed the deep regret which flashed across Asha's eyes. "Do you mind telling me what happened to them?"

Asha lay back on the bed and clasped her hands behind her head. "There's no doubt you've noticed that Dee and I aren't related by blood."

Sierra jabbed Asha gently in the ribs. "I would have never guessed."

Asha smiled. "My parents met while they were attending college in Michigan. They were surprised to learn that they were from the same area in India and had never crossed paths. The more they talked the more they liked each other. After two years of dating, they were married."

Sierra laid her arm across Asha's waist. "So you were born in the U.S.?"

"Three years after my parents were married." Asha replied. "My sister was a surprise about six years after that."

"So how did your parents meet Dee?" Sierra asked.

"Her husband, Bill, gave my father his first job," Asha said. "After a while, Bill started treating my father like his own son. Apparently, Bill and Dee couldn't have kids, so they basically adopted my parents. They helped my parents buy their first house, their first car, and put me through a private school. I grew up loving them as though they were my flesh and blood."

"That's amazing," Sierra said.

"You're telling me," Asha replied. "There weren't many people back then who would have given an Indian couple a chance in hell. Bill and Dee were different though. They never judged my parents by the color of their skin, just by how hard they worked for a better life and the morals they lived by."

"So what happened to your parents?" Sierra asked softly.

Asha took a deep breath as she stared up at the ceiling. "Right after my twelfth birthday, my parents went to Aspen for their fifteenth wedding anniversary. Bill and Dee watched over Devi and me while they were away."

"That was very kind of them," Sierra said.

"They have always been kind," Asha replied. "Anyway, I was the one who answered the phone a week later when the police called to say my parents were missing after a winter storm had moved in unexpectedly. Bill and Dee had all of us leave that very night to aid in the search. My sister and I were too young and we didn't know how to ski, but Bill and Dee assisted the search party for another grueling week until they were found."

Tears pooled in Asha's eyes before spilling down onto her cheeks. "I'm here," Sierra said, pulling Asha into her arms.

Asha nuzzled her face into Sierra's shoulder. "They were found side by side, holding onto one another for warmth, but the storm had been too much for their bodies to endure. The authorities predicted that they had probably held on for over forty-eight hours with their only shelter being a cluster of trees before the elements became too much for them."

"I'm so sorry," Sierra whispered, kissing Asha on the forehead.

Asha wiped her eyes. "I need to get some tissues."

"I'll get it," Sierra replied. She slipped her arm out from underneath Asha and hurried into the bathroom. When she returned Asha was sitting up on the edge of the bed.

"Thank you," Asha said, taking the tissues. She dabbed at her eyes before lightly blowing her nose.

Sierra sat down beside her. "So how did this place come to be?"

Asha stared down at her hands. "Bill and Dee had always wanted to open a ski lodge and I guess losing my parents felt like they had lost their own children. Within the year following my parent's death, they had obtained official custody of Devi and me, started searching for land to build on, and hired an architect to design everything the way they wanted it. The rest is history."

"I remember you mentioned having your first skiing lesson at thirteen," Sierra said. "I can't imagine how hard that must have been for you."

Asha's eyes were red and swollen. "I kept thinking that had I known how to ski, I might have been able to save them."

"Your parents death wasn't your fault," Sierra replied.

"But you don't understand how it felt seeing the ones that were supposed to be searching for my parents come back to the resort every night and complain about how bitterly cold it was outside," Asha said softly. "I would have kept searching even if it had killed me."

Sierra placed her hands on Asha's face. "Is that why you come out during the winter season?"

"I don't understand the question," Asha replied, dropping her eyes.

"The way I see it," Sierra said, tilting Asha's chin upward until their eyes met again. "Bill and Dee built this place to honor your parents."

"How do you figure?" Asha said.

"Well, it's simple," Sierra replied, taking Asha's hand. "Bill and Dee had the money to build this place the entire time they knew your parents. Had they really wanted to, they would have built this lodge long before their deaths. I think building the lodge helped repair their hearts and keep your parents' love for each other alive. You come here every year because when you're out there skiing or rescuing someone, you feel closer to them."

"Don't tell me," Asha said, kissing the top of Sierra's hand. "You're a psychologist, aren't you?"

Sierra chuckled. "Not even close."

"You should be," Asha replied. "You're a great listener."

"My mom used to tell me that same thing," Sierra said, hugging Asha tightly.

"Tell me about her," Asha said. "What's she like?"

Sierra released her embrace on Asha and struggled to keep her voice from trembling. "She was wonderful, absolutely wonderful, all the way to the very end."

Asha stood up and took Sierra into her arms. "I'm so sorry. I didn't know."

"What do you say we don't talk about any more sad stuff for today?" Sierra said. "Instead, let's discuss where we should go for dinner."

Asha kissed Sierra softly on the lips. "That sounds like a great idea."

Sierra batted her eyelashes. "Well, I'm going to have to work on coming up with a whole lot more of these great ideas and see what that gets me, won't I?"

"I guess you will," Asha replied, her words dripping with desire.

Sierra placed her hands on Asha's hips before sliding them up to her ribcage. She wanted to feel Asha's skin beneath her fingertips and the warmth of her touch. "Asha, we need to go before I give in to what I really want."

"And what would that be?" Asha said, moving her mouth next to Sierra's ear.

Sierra's breath quickened. "I want to get closer to you."

Asha used her tongue to trace the outside of Sierra's earlobe. "How close?"

Sierra slowly slid her hands up toward Asha's breast. "However close you'll let me be."

"Do I get to be that close to you?" Asha replied, pulling Sierra's shirt away from her jeans.

"Yes," Sierra managed as her fingers glided over Asha's hardened nipples.

The phone on the nightstand rang, but neither of them acknowledged it. Asha slid her hands up Sierra's back and unsnapped her bra. With one motion, Asha removed Sierra's shirt and bra over her head and brought her mouth to Sierra's nipples. Sierra threw her head back and moaned as Asha sucked gently, alternating between breasts. "I need this off," she said, clawing at Asha's shirt.

Asha removed her warm mouth from Sierra's nipples and quickly discarded her shirt and bra. She brought her lips to Sierra's and they kissed passionately. Sierra grabbed Asha's belt loops and pulled her toward the bed. They fell onto the mattress as their hips grinded urgently into one another's. Sierra felt Asha's hardened nipples brush against her own and the valley between her legs grew even wetter.

"I don't think I can stop," Asha whispered, kissing down Sierra's neck. "I want to taste you."

"Oh my goodness, I want that to," Sierra gasped, fumbling to unbutton her jeans.

"Please let me," Asha said, sitting up slightly.

"I want yours off, too," Sierra replied.

Asha climbed off the bed and started to unbutton her jeans. A loud knock resonated in the room. "Asha?" Jack shouted from behind the door. "Are you in there?"

Sierra looked up disbelievingly. "This can't be happening."

Asha's face fell. "Let me see what he wants." She grabbed her shirt off the floor and quickly put it back on. Stepping up to the door, she flipped her hair away from her collar and cracked open the door. "What!"

"Sorry, Asha," Jack said. "I tried to call you first."

"I was a little busy," Asha growled.

Jack dropped his voice. "There's been a report of a small avalanche near where a couple of snowboarders were practicing. They're staying at another lodge but they haven't come back yet. We've been asked to help in the search."

"Get the team assembled," Asha said. "I'll be down in two minutes."

"You've got it," Jack replied.

Asha closed the door, stripped off her shirt, and grabbed her bra off the floor. "I'm so sorry, Sierra."

"I understand," Sierra said, pulling her shirt back on. "I'll be here if you need anything."

Asha slipped her boots back on. "I'll probably not be back for quite some time, so just get some sleep and I'll call you in the morning."

Sierra followed Asha to the door. "Be careful."

"I will," Asha replied. She opened the door to leave, but hesitated. "I'll make tonight up to you," she said softly. "I promise." She kissed Sierra one more time before escaping out the door.

Sierra closed the door and walked back over to the bed. The sheets were crumpled where she and Asha had lain and she envisioned the two of them making love. The throbbing between her legs intensified and so did the wetness. Sierra knew exactly how to remedy her need for release, but she turned from the bed and headed to the shower. She didn't want to pretend Asha was touching her; she wanted the real Asha.

• • •

The telephone rang a little after midnight. Sierra swiveled away from the desk and dove across the bed. She snatched the phone off the cradle. "Asha?"

"Who the hell is Asha?" the tired voice replied.

"Dana?" Sierra said. "What in the world are you doing up at this hour?"

"What time is it here?" Dana chuckled. "Oh, shit, it's just after two in the morning."

"You're insane," Sierra replied.

"Sorry if I woke you," Dana said. "I was starting to worry and you know I hate that."

Sierra yawned. "Well, you didn't wake me if that makes you feel better."

"There are only two things that will make me feel better at this point."

"Which are?" Sierra replied.

"You weren't sleeping because you're having incredible sex with some young hottie and if so, hang up right now." Dana paused for a moment. "Are you still there?"

Sierra chuckled. "Yes, I'm still here."

"Too bad," Dana replied.

"Are you going to ask if I'm over the writer's block?" Sierra said. "Or do I need to overnight the manuscript I've been working on to you?"

"I knew sending you on this trip would be good thing," Dana said, congratulating herself.

"It's definitely been good for me," Sierra replied.

Dana remained quiet for a couple of seconds. "What's her name?"

"What?" Sierra said evasively. "I don't know what you're talking about."

"As your agent, I demand answers," Dana replied. "Is she cute?"

Sierra took a moment and envisioned Asha's face. "Beautiful."

"Single?" Dana continued.

"Yes," Sierra said.

"Slept with her yet?"

Sierra straightened. "Hey, give me some credit!"

Dana laughed. "I am."

Sierra felt as though her heart had suddenly sprouted wings. "We did get pretty close tonight."

"What happened?" Dana pressed.

"She's on the search and rescue team," Sierra replied. "She had to go search for some missing snowboarders."

"Does this superwoman have a name?"

"Asha," Sierra said dreamily.

"Tell me more about her," Dana said with motherly concern.

"What's wrong?" Sierra replied.

"I don't want you getting hurt," Dana said. "You've already had such a rough couple of years with your mom and everything."

Sierra winced. "I don't want to talk about that, okay? I need you to be my friend right now."

"You've got it," Dana replied. "I'm sorry."

Sierra laid back on the bed. "It's okay."

"Do you have feelings for this woman?" Dana asked.

Sierra sighed. "To tell you the truth, I think I'm falling in love with her."

"My goodness," Dana replied. "This is serious."

"I'm so scared," Sierra confided. "I have no idea if I'm ready to have my heart broken again. I mean, aren't I just asking for it to happen? We live on different coasts for crying out loud."

Dana said nothing.

"Hello?" Sierra said into the receiver.

"Look, Sierra," Dana replied. "You have to stop thinking that everything that happens in your life is your fault and start believing in divine intervention."

"Divine intervention?" Sierra repeated angrily. "I lost my mother, my lover and my best friend all in the same month. Oh, wait the same week! Don't talk to me about divine intervention."

Dana cleared her throat. "Look, you never told me why you and Tori broke up, but it was pretty obvious to everyone that she was sleeping around with your best friend."

Sierra felt sick. "I don't want to talk about this."

"You went from the best-seller list to Miss Homebody," Dana continued. "You stopped mentioning both their names simultaneously and you stopped wearing your ring. I even told you that I had seen them out together."

"Enough," Sierra said bitterly. "I know everyone but me was aware of what was going on. Stop rubbing it in."

"You knew as well, Sierra." Dana said bluntly. "If you didn't think something was up the two of you wouldn't have stopped having sex."

"I never said we weren't making love," Sierra shouted angrily.

"You told me last September that you were thinking about going on a diet to look sexier for Tori, as I recall," Dana said, keeping her tone nondefensive. "But you were already so thin."

"I was taking care of my mom," Sierra whispered. "It was a full-time job. It was my fault Tori cheated."

"No, it wasn't," Dana replied. "She let you down and betrayed you. She wasn't there for you when you needed her the most. If you want my opinion, the two of them deserve each other."

Sierra wiped away the tears streaming down her face. "I guess, but they're no longer a part of my life, so can we stop talking about them?"

"Sierra, you're the one still holding onto them," Dana replied gently. "You can't spend the rest of your life afraid to love someone because the two of you live on opposite coasts. If you think you're falling for Asha, just fall."

"That's easier said than done," Sierra said, checking the time.

"You once told me that you love writing," Dana said through a yawn.

"I do love writing."

"I know you do," Dana said. "But you write from the heart. If it's hurting, your creative ability is suffering, too."

Sierra shook her head. "Remind me why it is I put up with you?"

"Because you deserve the best," Dana said.

Sierra laughed.

"And because you help me afford the finer things in life," Dana continued.

"Which is?" Sierra said.

Dana cleared her throat. "I don't know how it happened. A new jag just appeared in my driveway out of nowhere."

"You're too much," Sierra said. "When did it get beamed down?"

"Funny," Dana replied. "But if you must know, the aliens delivered it a few days ago. I figured my prize-winning novelist will make sure I can keep up with the insurance payments."

"You have too much faith in me," Sierra said.

"Who said I was referring to you?" Dana teased. "Now, get some sleep and call me if things get interesting with Asha."

"I will," Sierra replied. "Thanks for calling."

Dana was momentarily silent. "That's what real friends are for."

"I know," Sierra said, before setting the receiver down. She wiggled underneath the covers and stared at the alarm clock.

The minutes ticked by and soon it was after one in the morning. Sierra paced back and forth across the floor. She had tried counting sheep and bottles of beer. She had tried naming everyone she could think of in her high school class, but all their faces had transformed into Asha's. *I have to sleep,* she thought.

Back in bed, Sierra kicked the rest of the blankets onto the floor. She was burning up and it wasn't due to a faulty thermostat. "This is insane!" she cried out softly.

The phone rang and Sierra sat straight up. "Please let it be her," she whispered, picking up the phone. "Hello?"

"Hi." Asha's voice was sullen. "I'm sorry if I woke you."

"I wasn't asleep," Sierra said. "Is everything alright?"

Asha didn't speak for a moment. "I know this place that serves really good coffee twenty-four hours a day."

Sierra tossed the covers to the side. "I'll be down in five minutes."

CHAPTER EIGHT

Sierra reached across the table and took Asha's hand. "You did everything you could."

"I know," Asha replied, staring at what was left of the dark liquid in her coffee cup. "It's just never enough, you know?"

"What more did his parents want you to do?" Sierra asked, furrowing her eyebrows. "I mean, you're the one who fucking found them! You're not a doctor! They can't hold you responsible if their son can't walk again. He's the one who took up his buddy's dare to go explore uncharted slopes."

For the first time in over an hour, a smile tugged at Asha's lips. "How is it that when you cuss it sounds sexy?"

"Because I am sexy," Sierra said with a smile.

"Yes, you are," Asha replied. "You're the sexiest woman I've ever laid eyes on."

Sierra dropped her gaze to the table. "You're very sweet."

"Did I embarrass you?" Asha said, squeezing Sierra's hand.

Sierra looked up. "A little."

"Well, it's the truth and I'm not apologizing for it," Asha replied, pushing her chair back. "I'm going to get some more coffee. Do you want some?"

Sierra covered the top of her mug with her hand. "I think I'll pass this time."

Asha walked around the table and knelt down beside Sierra's chair. She stared into Sierra's green eyes before kissing her.

"What was that for?" Sierra said, feeling slightly intoxicated by Asha's passionate kiss.

"For being here," Asha said, standing back up.

"I wouldn't want to be anywhere else in this world than right here with you," Sierra replied.

Asha glanced at Sierra's left hand. "Not even Florida?"

Sierra got up from the chair and met Asha's lips with her own. "There's no one back there that you need to worry about."

"Who said I was worried?" Asha said, kissing the tip of Sierra's nose.

"Your eyes did," Sierra said.

Asha pulled Sierra even closer. "What are they saying now?"

Sierra met Asha's gaze and for a moment, the entire world disappeared. She was completely captivated by the desire which cascaded over her like a chocolate waterfall and filled the valley between her legs with warm nectar. "I hope they're saying that they want me."

"If you only knew how much," Asha whispered.

"Show me," Sierra replied.

Asha moved her mouth next to Sierra's ear. "You'll just have to wait."

"Until when?" Sierra said as Asha took a step toward the counter to refill her cup.

Asha looked back over her shoulder. "Until you realize that I'm worth falling head over heels in love with."

• • •

Sierra flipped up the collar of her jacket and followed Asha out of the coffee shop. "What time is it?"

"You don't want to know," Asha replied, holding Sierra's hand.

Sierra laid her head against Asha's shoulder as they walked back toward the lodge. "I wish it was Friday."

"And why's that?" Asha said, leaning her head gingerly on top of Sierra's.

"I was hoping you might be free to spend more time with me," Sierra replied.

Asha stopped in the middle of the sidewalk and pulled Sierra into her arms. "I was hoping you would say yes to dinner at my place on Friday."

Sierra moved her body closer to feel Asha's warmth. "I would love to, but isn't your place a little far away for dinner?"

Asha laughed. "I own a cabin a few miles away, so we can skip the detour to California for now."

"I just assumed that you stayed with Dee," Sierra replied, secretly thrilled at this discovery. "What time would you like me there?"

"My dear," Asha said. "I thought I'd pick you up about seven o'clock. Will that work?"

"Of course that works," Sierra said. "Do I need to bring anything?"

"Just your appetite," Asha replied.

"I can do that." Sierra kissed Asha on the lips. "I can't wait to spend more time with you."

"The feeling is mutual," Asha said.

Sierra shivered. "I swear it's getting colder."

"It always does just before dawn," Asha said, taking Sierra by the hand again.

"It's almost morning?" Sierra asked, falling into step alongside Asha.

"I told you that you didn't want to know what time it was," Asha replied.

Sierra didn't reply. She stared straight ahead, lost in thought.

"What is it?" Asha asked nervously. "You're not upset, are you?"

Sierra gave Asha a sideways smile. "I'm definitely not upset."

"Then what?" Asha said, letting Sierra take the steps up to the lodge first.

Sierra pulled open the entryway door. "This is our first all-nighter and we didn't even take our clothes off."

Asha grinned. "More relationships would last longer if they followed our formula."

Stepping into the lobby, Sierra waved at the young woman working behind the registration desk and walked over to the elevator. She pressed the up button and turned to Asha. "Are you saying that you consider us in a relationship?"

Asha reached over and pressed the elevator button again. "Come on already."

Sierra grabbed Asha by the arm. "Are you avoiding the question?"

"Is it working?" Asha replied with an ornery grin.

Sierra slipped in between the parting elevator doors. "No, not really, but maybe if you tried to convince me it would help."

Asha stepped onto the elevator and pressed the button to close the doors. Then she backed Sierra up against one wall. "What do you suggest?"

A flurry of ideas whirled through Sierra's mind, but only one stuck out. "Will you hold me until I fall asleep?"

Asha wrapped her arms around Sierra. "I would love to."

• • •

Sierra flipped on the light and held the door open for Asha. "Make yourself at home."

"Thanks," Asha replied, tossing her coat over one arm. She crossed the room and made a beeline for the recliner.

Sierra watched as Asha sank into the chair in complete exhaustion. "Can I get you anything?"

Asha raised her eyes to meet Sierra's and offered a tired grin. "I'm fine," she said. "I just need to get a little sleep before my shift starts."

"When is that?" Sierra replied, taking off her jacket.

"Around nine o'clock, give or take a few minutes," Asha said, tilting her head back.

Sierra hung her jacket in the closet. "That's less than four hours away."

"Uh-huh," Asha replied, barely keeping her eyes open.

Sierra walked over to the bed and pulled the covers back. "Why don't you go ahead and lie down for a bit?"

"What are you going to do?" Asha said, kicking off her shoes.

"I need to shower," Sierra replied. "I don't want to get into bed feeling this grungy."

Asha pushed herself out of the recliner and looked down at her clothes.

"You wouldn't possibly have something that I could borrow to sleep in, would you?"

Sierra's stomach seemed to stir with a thousand butterflies, now awakened. "Does that mean you're staying until your shift?"

Asha slid her hands into her back pockets. "Only if it's okay with you."

"It's definitely okay with me." Sierra wondered if her feet were actually touching the ground as she walked over to the dresser. She pulled out the bottom drawer and removed a pair of navy blue sweatpants and a white T-shirt. She tossed them over to Asha. "The pants might be a little short, but I think they'll work."

"It's perfect," Asha replied. "You don't happen to have a sweater or something that I could borrow for work, do you?"

Sierra pulled out another white T-shirt and a pair of flannel pajama bottoms. "Help yourself to anything you find," she said, striding toward the bathroom with her selected sleeping apparel. "I think that everything in the dresser will fit you."

"I will, thanks," Asha said.

Closing the bathroom door, Sierra flipped on the light. She set her clothes on the counter and stared at her reflection. Her eyes sparkled with a mischievous gleam. *Oh, the evil thoughts one has when one is completely...*

Sierra blinked hard as her heart pounded ferociously in her chest. She shook her head as though the thoughts she was having about Asha had somehow become tangible and she could shatter them. *My God,* she thought, sitting down on the toilet seat for support. *I am falling in love with her.*

Reaching over and turning on the shower, Sierra waited a few minutes before getting undressed. Her heart felt as though a battle had been waged between her mind and her soul. Old wounds resurfaced and painful memories bombarded her mind. They healed just as quickly, though, by imagining the sound of Asha's laughter and the trust so evident in her eyes. Sierra stepped underneath the spray as tears rolled down her cheeks. "I do love her," she whispered.

• • •

Sierra tiptoed over to the bed and gazed down at the beautiful woman curled up on one side. "Asha?"

Asha struggled to lift her eyelids. "I'm sorry," she mumbled. "I'm just so tired."

"It's okay," Sierra replied, switching off the light. She slid beneath the sheet and turned onto her side facing away from Asha.

Asha moved her body closer to Sierra's and draped her arm around Sierra's waist. "Thanks," she whispered.

"For what?" Sierra replied, scooting her butt back slightly so their bodies merged together in perfect symmetry like yin and yang.

Asha yawned. "For letting me stay."

"You're welcome," Sierra said sleepily, pretending to succumb to exhaustion. The truth was she could have screamed it or run the Boston Marathon waving a banner that read "Really, I should be thanking you," but she knew Asha needed her sleep. Her bouncing up and down with joy would not help the situation nor extinguish the fire raging between her thighs.

For over ten minutes, Sierra lay quiet and listened to Asha's rhythmic breathing. When Asha rolled onto her back, Sierra turned over and strained to see Asha's brown eyes through the darkness. "Are you still awake?" she said. When there was no answer, she nuzzled her head against Asha's shoulder and laid her hand on Asha's stomach where she could feel the heat of her skin through the T-shirt. She tried to stay awake, but the need for sleep overwhelmed her.

Asha, on the other hand, stayed awake for almost an hour too afraid to open her eyes and ruin the moment. In her arms, a beautiful woman slept and it was all she could do to keep breathing.

• • •

The relentless ringing of the phone roused Sierra from her tranquil dreams. She buried her head beneath the pillow to drown out the noise. Silently she cursed whoever had the audacity to be so insistent until it dawned on her that it might be Asha. Almost knocking the phone off the nightstand with the pillow she had hurled aside, Sierra scooped up the receiver. "Hello," she answered, struggling to sound awake.

"I had almost given up on you," Asha replied.

"I was just getting up," Sierra said, covering up the receiver's mouthpiece to yawn.

Asha laughed. "Sure you were."

Sierra swung her legs off the side of the bed and struggled to sit up. "Oh, my God," she moaned.

"What's the matter?" Asha replied, immediately alarmed.

Sierra leaned forward slightly and tried to massage out her spine by moving from side to side. The muscles in her body screamed in agony as though they had been twisted and stretched over and over again with a pulling hook like saltwater taffy. "I feel like I was in a car accident."

Asha sighed with relief. "You almost gave me a heart attack."

"Sorry," Sierra said, collapsing back onto her pillow. "I didn't expect to hurt this much."

"Skiing will do that to you," Asha said. "Even people in top physical condition are usually sore for a day or two after trying it for the first time. Is there anything I can do?"

Sierra closed her eyes and allowed her mind to wander. "I could think of a few things."

"Well, I get a dinner break from seven to eight o'clock," Asha replied. "How about we explore some of those options then?"

"I'd love to," Sierra said. She moved her shoulders in a circular motion, trying to loosen the stiffness, but it felt more like she was grinding gears. "Although, I'm not sure I'll be able to move at all by that time."

"I'm sure we can figure something out," Asha said. "But for now, I have to go."

"I'm glad you called," Sierra replied.

"I hated leaving you this morning," Asha said. "You look like an angel when you sleep."

Sierra blushed. "Thank you."

"You're nibbling at your bottom lip, aren't you?" Asha said confidently.

Sierra released her lower lip. "No," she said, her guilt evident in her tone.

"Don't worry, I love when you do that," Asha replied. "Oops, I have a guest at the counter. I'll see you tonight."

"Okay," Sierra said. "Bye." She waited until the line went dead before hanging up the receiver.

There was only one thing on the day's agenda and that was writing. Sierra staggered over to the desk and fell into the leather chair. She pressed the laptop's power button. Her imagination came alive, as did the computer screen. Within minutes, her fingers found their rhythm and they transformed her thoughts from an imaginary world to a written one that she could share with those ready to quench their thirst with good literature.

• • •

At five minutes after seven, Sierra called down to the front desk. "Front desk, this is Alexandria. How can I help you?"

Having expected that Asha would be the one answering, Sierra took a second to gather her thoughts. "Hi, is Asha Amin available?"

"I'm sorry, ma'am," Alexandria said. "She's assisting another guest. Is there something I can help you with?"

Sierra gazed across the room at the laptop. "No, that's all right. Will you just let her know that Sierra called?"

"Of course," Alexandria replied. "Will there be anything else?"

"No, that should do it."

"Have a good evening then," Alexandria said.

"You do the same," Sierra replied before hanging up the phone. She walked back over to the desk and picked up her wallet. Thumbing through the bills, she removed a handful of one dollar bills before tossing it back onto the table. She grabbed her keycard and proceeded out the door into the hallway.

The vending machines were in a small room catty-cornered from the elevator and the staircase. Sierra quickly made her dinner selection of a Coke and a Snickers bar and headed back toward her room. As she approached the stairs, she heard a familiar voice that made her skin crawl. Vivian was on her way up and she sounded wasted.

Sierra knew there was no way she could make it to her room without Vivian spotting her. Hurrying back into the small vending room, she held the door slightly ajar with her foot. She needed to keep tabs on Vivian and know when it was safe for her to venture back out. Of course, if Vivian decided to grab a soda, the night would indeed get interesting.

Vivian's voice grew steadily louder. "Don't you remember how good it was between us?"

"I remember."

Sierra recognized the other person's voice instantly and her heart felt as though it had been flung upon a sword. *Asha.*

"Do you remember how you would call out my name?" Vivian said. Her tone was thick with drunken desire. "I want to hear that again."

Sierra covered her mouth afraid she might be ill at any moment. *This can't be happening.*

"We're over," Asha replied, her voice low and emotionless. "What you did was unforgivable."

"Are you sure about that?" Vivian said seductively. "I'll bet one kiss would change your mind."

"You're unbelievable," Asha said. "Come on, knock it off."

Sierra peeked into the hallway and watched as Vivian brought her lips dangerously close to Asha's.

"What's the matter?" Vivian said, rubbing her hips against Asha's. "Having second thoughts?"

Asha grabbed Vivian by the arms. "I said I would help you to your room, but that's it."

Vivian glared at Asha. "You'll be back begging me to fuck you," she said angrily. "That tramp you're so interested in probably hasn't even put out for you, has she?"

Sierra's head felt like a jackhammer was strapped to the back of it.

Asha visibly trembled as she stepped over and punched the button for the elevator. "This conversation is over," she growled.

"It isn't over until I say it's over," Vivian shouted.

The elevator doors parted. "Get in the elevator," Asha replied, reaching in and selecting the fourth floor. "I think we've walked off enough of your drunken stupor so this is where we part ways."

Vivian staggered past Asha and stepped onto the elevator. "Just one more thing."

A middle-aged man approached with a towel wrapped around his neck. "Hold the elevator."

"What is it?" Asha said, sounding defeated as she blocked the doors from closing.

"Come closer," Vivian replied. "I don't want the whole world to hear."

Asha leaned inward. Vivian pressed her lips against Asha's as the man squeezed past them to get into the elevator. When their lips separated, Vivian licked hers suggestively. "You know where I'll be if you get lonely later."

Asha glanced at the man taking great interest in Vivian's display of public affection. "I'll keep that in mind," Asha said. "Have a good night."

"I will," Vivian replied.

As soon as the elevator doors closed, Asha's face fell and tears sprung from her eyes. She tried to wipe them away, but it was a futile attempt. Sierra wanted more than anything to rush over and comfort her, but that would only cause the situation to go from bad to worse. Instead, she waited in silence for Asha to make her next move.

Asha wiped away another tear and tossed her hair back from her face. She looked down at her watch. "Shit," she whispered.

The elevator doors reopened and Asha looked up. She took a step back as Vivian emerged from the elevator.

"It's going to be okay, baby," Vivian said, reaching for Asha. "I know what you need."

Sierra looked away as Vivian caressed Asha's face and kissed her lips. She looked back in time to see Asha once again push Vivian away. "You're married!" Asha hissed. "You lied to me."

Vivian held up her hand. "I'm not married now."

Asha shook her head. "Don't you mean you're not married tonight?"

"Look, my husband has his flings and I have mine," Vivian said matter-of-factly. "I could get anyone to go to bed with me, but I want you. It's a win-win situation."

Asha crossed her arms in front of her chest. "For whom?"

"For both of us," Vivian replied, looking Asha up and down. "I need a great fuck tonight and you definitely won't get one with little Miss Sunshine State."

Sierra gritted her teeth. She wanted nothing more than to spring into the hall and wing the soda she held in her hand at Vivian. Instead, she squeezed the candy bar in her right hand so tightly that the wrapper fused with the chewy caramel inside.

"How do you know so much about her?" Asha asked angrily.

"Don't get upset," Vivian said, laying her index finger against Asha's lips. "I had to learn as much as I could about my competition."

Asha took another step back. "There's no competition."

"I'm glad to hear you say that," Vivian said, turning around and pressing the button for the elevator. "I'll be upstairs waiting."

"I didn't mean it like that," Asha said.

Vivian stepped onto the elevator and selected her floor. She blew Asha a kiss as the doors slid closed. Asha placed her hands on top of her head kicking her foot against the elevator. She whirled around, checked her watch, and shook her head. "Damn it."

Sierra swallowed hard. *Go downstairs. Come on, go downstairs to call.*

Asha threw her hands back down at her sides and headed down the hallway. Sierra leaned her head back and sighed. *What am I going to do?* She opened the door just a crack and listened. Slowly stepping out into the hallway, she walked cautiously over to where the two corridors intersected and peeked around the corner. She watched as Asha knocked again and again on her door.

Slipping out of sight, Sierra looked down at her sweatpants and tennis shoes. She raced back into the vending room and tossed the soda and candy bar into the trash. Feeding the Coke machine another two dollars, she selected water and didn't bother with the change. With a quick twist of the top, she splashed the water onto her face and neck. She threw the bottle into the trash and quickly stepped back into the hall. "Okay," she whispered, taking a deep breath. "I can do this."

CHAPTER NINE

Sierra rounded the corner and conjured up her best smile as she walked up to Asha. "Hello, stranger."

Asha turned from the door. "Hi, yourself. What have you been up to?"

Sierra kissed Asha on the cheek. "When you didn't call, I thought I would go for a quick run. I hope I didn't make you wait long."

Asha pulled Sierra into her arms. "I had to deal with a rather unruly guest. I'm sorry that I'm late"

Sierra gazed into Asha's eyes. "It's okay, you're worth the wait."

Asha kissed the tip of Sierra's nose. "I missed you today."

"I missed you too," Sierra replied, turning to unlock the door. "Did anything out of the ordinary happen?"

"Not really," Asha said flatly.

Sierra opened the door and took Asha by the hand. Her mind replayed the exchange between Asha and Vivian over and over again. "Would you like to come in?"

"I'd love to," Asha replied, following Sierra into the room.

"Have you eaten today?" Sierra asked, moving over to the bed to take off her shoes.

"I had a granola bar," Asha replied, leaning her back against the wall opposite from where Sierra was sitting.

"I don't think that counts," Sierra said, getting to her feet. "We only have about a half hour. I'm not sure that's enough time to have dinner before you have to go back to work."

Asha grabbed Sierra by the hand. "I'm glad you're feeling better."

"What do you mean?" Sierra replied.

"Earlier, when you mentioned how sore your body was, I thought you might not be able to move around for a day or two," Asha said. "I'm impressed by your determination to run today."

Sierra forced a smile. "I'm resilient if you didn't notice."

"Oh, I noticed," Asha said. "I notice everything about you."

Sierra pulled Asha toward the bed. "Have you noticed the need I have for you to kiss me?"

Asha waited for Sierra to stretch out across the bed before climbing on top of her. "I did notice."

Sierra wrapped her arms around Asha's neck. "I know we don't have a lot of time, but maybe we could spend it kissing. What do you think?"

"That's a great idea," Asha replied. She brought her lips to Sierra's and rocked her hips seductively downward.

Sierra felt the valley between her legs flood with desire. She rocked her hips in responsive need. "Asha?" she gasped.

"Yes, baby," Asha replied, kissing down the side of Sierra's neck.

Sierra took a deep, nervous breath. "Are you over Vivian?"

Asha jerked her head up. "What?"

"I need to know," Sierra said, tracing Asha's lips with her fingertips. "I need to know that you're completely over her."

"Why are you asking this now?" Asha said incredulously.

Sierra fought off the urge to tell her the truth. "I just need to know if there is a chance the two of you might get back together. I can tell you still care about her."

Asha rolled off of Sierra and onto her side. "It's so strange that you brought her up."

"Why?" Sierra replied, hating her deception.

"I had to take her up to her room tonight," Asha said distantly. "She drank too much, not that it's a shock to anyone who knows her. She's usually drunk by six o'clock."

"Did anything happen?" Sierra said.

Asha blinked back tears. "No," she said softly. "Vivian really wanted it to and she can be quite convincing, but all I could think about was you."

"I'm so glad," Sierra replied.

"Would it surprise you to learn that she's married?" Asha asked.

"Yes," Sierra replied, shaking her head. "How can she live with herself?"

Asha shrugged. "She made a series of bad choices trying to live up to her parents' expectations. Now she lives out her true desires whenever she's on vacation with any woman she can sink her claws into."

"She sunk them pretty deep into you, didn't she?" Sierra said, kissing Asha on the cheek.

"You have no idea how deeply," Asha replied.

Sierra thought about the recent tragedies in her own life. "I'm sorry that she hurt you. I know how difficult losing the person you love can be."

Asha reached over and touched Sierra's cheek. "I know you do. I can see it every time you look at me."

Sierra laid her head on Asha's chest. "As they say, that which does not kill us only makes us stronger."

Asha chuckled. "That saying sucks."

"I couldn't agree more," Sierra replied with a laugh.

Asha's brown eyes grew serious. "I'd be lying if I said I didn't want to come back by after my shift and sleep with you."

"But?" Sierra said.

"But, I don't want to just sleep with you," Asha replied.

Sierra shifted nervously under Asha's intense stare. "What *do* you want then?"

"I want you to tell me the truth," Asha said. "I want to know who hurt you so deeply that it made you terrified to love anyone else."

Sierra's mouth went dry. "That's all in the past. Why do we need to dredge it up?"

"It's not in the past," Asha replied. "You carry it around with you."

Sierra sat up and turned her back to Asha. "I do not."

Asha placed her hand on the center of Sierra's back. "Yes, you do. It's obvious with all the questions you ask about Vivian."

Sierra stood up and glared at Asha. "You have no right to talk to me that way. I saw you with Vivian tonight."

Asha's eyes widened. "You saw us?"

"Yes," Sierra replied hotly. "I was in the vending room when the two of you had your lovers' spat. I'm not sure why you didn't take her up on her invitation."

"What invitation are you talking about?" Asha said defiantly.

"The invitation to fuck her," Sierra shouted, tears spilling from her eyes. "I overheard the whole thing."

Asha's body visibly tensed. "Why didn't you tell me?"

"Because I wanted you to tell me," Sierra replied. "I can't handle any more heartache. My ex-girlfriend cheated with my best friend the day of my mother's funeral and that was truly enough for me. I have to know that you're over Vivian or I can't make love with you."

"Hold on," Asha said, reaching for the phone. She dialed quickly. "Alexandria? Yeah, everything's okay. See if you can find someone to cover the rest of my shift. Oh, it's until midnight. That's great. You're a lifesaver. Thanks."

"What was that about?" Sierra asked weakly as Asha hung up the phone.

Asha walked around the bed and took Sierra into her arms. "Let's get out of here."

"Where do you want to go?" Sierra replied.

"I want to take you home and cook you dinner," Asha said. "Then you can tell me more about this stupid woman who broke your heart."

"You cook?" Sierra said, attempting to change the subject.

Asha led Sierra over to the closet. "I'll cook you the best meal you've ever had."

Sierra grabbed her jacket. "Do I need anything else?"

"Only if you plan on staying the night," Asha said.

Sierra walked into the bathroom and grabbed her toothbrush. She held it up for Asha and shrugged. "Just in case."

• • •

Asha held open the passenger side door to her black Nissan Pathfinder. "Thank you," Sierra said, sliding into the passenger seat.

"You're quite welcome," Asha replied before closing the door. She rushed around to the other side and climbed behind the wheel. When she saw that Sierra was blowing warm air into her hands, she switched on the engine and let it idle for a few minutes. "I'll have the heat on in no time."

"I'm not that cold," Sierra said, her teeth chattering.

Asha shook her head. "You're so stubborn."

"I prefer to think of myself as set in my ways," Sierra said with a smile.

Asha held her hands up to the air vents before switching them on high. She pointed all of them in Sierra's direction. "It only takes about ten minutes to get to my place, so you should be thawing just as we're getting there."

Sierra laughed. "You're wonderful."

Asha steered the Pathfinder down a narrow road where piles of snow were deposited on each side. Sierra gazed through the window as the lights of Vail disappeared behind them and gave way to towering pine trees, undisturbed snow drifts and tranquil silence. After about five miles, they rounded a blind curve and a very quaint log cabin came into view. Twinkling white Christmas lights surrounded the door, windows, and railing around the front porch.

Asha slowed and pulled into the drive. "This is it."

"You have to be kidding," Sierra said astonished.

Asha's mouth twitched. "Do you not like it?"

"Like it?" Sierra replied, opening the passenger side door. "I absolutely love it!"

Asha smiled and switched off the engine. She unbuckled her seatbelt and stepped out of the SUV as Sierra shuffled up the steps to the front door. With a quick press of a button, all the doors in the vehicle locked and the alarm was activated.

Asha hurried up the steps and unlocked the cabin door. "After you," she said, holding the door open for Sierra.

Sierra stepped past the foyer into the living room as Asha closed the door and locked it. "This place is beautiful."

"Thank you," Asha replied. "Why don't you let me take your jacket and then have a seat on the couch while I get us something to drink?"

Sierra unzipped her jacket and allowed Asha to take it off her shoulders. "Do you have any hot cocoa mix?"

Asha raised an eyebrow. "It wouldn't be home without it. I'll be right back with two steaming cups."

Sierra watched Asha slip off into the other room, presumably the kitchen, before taking the two steps down into the sunken living room. As she journeyed to the couch, she scrutinized every detail for lingering signs of another woman. *Old hurts die hard,* she thought, collapsing onto the couch that was distanced perfectly from the fireplace. Her body sank into the plush cushions before she could even take off her boots.

Asha walked back into the room carrying a bundle of fire wood. "I thought it might be nice to have a fire."

"That sounds wonderful," Sierra said. "Do you need any help?"

Asha gave her a quizzical look. "No thanks. I just want you to relax."

"I'm not going to argue with that," Sierra said. She snatched a TV guide off the coffee table and flipped it open.

"See anything good to watch?" Asha asked over her shoulder as she fed the small fire she had going with kindling.

Sierra looked up with a mischievous grin. "Well, that depends on what you're referring to."

Asha blushed. "I was referring to the television."

"Oh," Sierra said, shifting her desire-filled eyes back to the pages of the TV guide. "I don't watch television enough to know what's good. Do you?"

Asha brushed the soot off her hands from the poker onto her jeans. "Not really. I'd rather read. Oh, that reminds me. Devi went to the store and picked up a new book for me."

Sierra slipped off her boots. "Which one?"

A loud whistle sounded. "Oh, that's the milk for the cocoa," Asha said. "I'll be right back."

Sierra set her boots beneath the coffee table and curled up in one corner of the couch. Asha returned with a tray of sliced summer sausage and pepper-jack cheese with round, buttery crackers on the side. She hurried back to the kitchen and returned with two steaming cups of hot cocoa. "I thought this might be a nice appetizer before dinner," she said, sitting on the opposite end of the couch.

"I love it," Sierra replied, stacking a slice of cheese and summer sausage onto a cracker. "So tell me about this new book that Devi got for you."

Asha crossed her legs beneath her and took a sip of hot cocoa. "It's the new one by S.A. Webb called *Screaming Silence*."

Sierra almost choked on her cracker and countered it by coughing violently. Asha jumped up from the couch and sprinted into the kitchen returning with a glass of water. "Are you okay?" she asked, kneeling down beside Sierra.

Sierra took a sip of water. "I'm fine. It just went down the wrong pipe."

"Are you sure you're okay?" Asha said, her eyes wide with worry.

Sierra leaned forward and kissed Asha gingerly on the lips. "I'm fine. Go on and tell me about this book."

Asha got up and walked over to the bookshelf. She selected *Screaming Silence* from the plethora of other lesbian titles and sat back down on the couch. "I can't wait to read it."

"Why don't you, then?" Sierra said.

"Are you serious?" Asha replied, excitement dancing in her eyes.

"Of course I am," Sierra said. "You can kick your legs out and rest your head on my lap while you read."

Asha stretched out the rest of her body over the length of the couch, her head on Sierra's lap, and began reading the first chapter; her pronunciation was precise and eloquent. Sierra ran her fingers through Asha's hair, enjoying the silkiness of every strand. She continued to listen, despite the fact that she knew the story by heart. She'd never had anyone read a book to her before, much less her own, and she loved it.

At the start of chapter four, Sierra noticed Asha's words were starting to slur, but she said nothing. Asha struggled to stay focused with valiant effort. Finally, she looked up at Sierra with tired brown eyes. "I'm sorry. I'm so exhausted."

"It's okay," Sierra replied. "We can finish some other time."

Asha gave Sierra a weary smile. "You can't stop reading mid-chapter. It's like switching off a movie in the middle of a scene. I just need to get some coffee and I'll be fine."

Sierra laid her hand on Asha's forehead. "What if I read the rest of the chapter?"

"Really?" Asha asked, handing the book to Sierra.

"I can read, you know," Sierra teased.

"I know that," Asha said, nuzzling her head in Sierra's lap. "What do you think is going to happen to the main protagonist? Do you think her girlfriend is going to be the next victim?"

Sierra pondered her answer for a second. "I'd rather not guess," she said finally. "Now close your eyes and relax."

As each sentence rolled off her tongue, Sierra took note of the subtle changes occurring with Asha's body as she fell asleep. When at last her breathing had eased and the almost undetectable twitching of her muscles had ceased, Sierra carefully folded the upper right hand corner of the page down to save their spot and closed the book. She switched off the table lamp and watched Asha sleep until the glow from the fire died off with the last of the embers.

Sierra laid her head against the back of the couch and closed her eyes. She tried her best to get comfortable. Suddenly, the shrillness of the telephone broke the silence. Asha shot forward and fell onto the ground.

"Are you okay?" Sierra said, switching back on the lamp.

"I'm fine," Asha chuckled, getting to her feet. "Whoever is calling this time of night might not be when I'm through with them, though."

Sierra waited as Asha went into the kitchen to answer the phone. A few minutes later, she came bounding back into the room. "Guess what?"

"You won the lottery," Sierra said with a grin.

"I wish," Asha said. "But it's almost as good in my book."

"Out with it, woman," Sierra said, taking Asha's hand and pulling her down onto the couch.

"I don't have to be back at work until ten o'clock tomorrow morning," Asha replied. "So if you decide to stay over, I can fix you breakfast!"

"I wasn't going to get breakfast otherwise?" Sierra teased.

Asha pulled Sierra into her arms and kissed her passionately. When their lips parted, Asha gazed into Sierra's eyes. "I'm sorry I fell asleep, but I'm wide awake and ready to take on the world."

"What do you want to do?" Sierra said innocently.

Asha flashed a wicked smile. "What are my options?"

Sierra crossed her arms in front of her chest. "Nothing if I don't get a little bit of sustenance."

Asha jumped to her feet. "How does baked chicken and a garden salad sound?"

"Delicious," Sierra replied. "Can I help you with anything?"

"Would you mind setting the table?" Asha asked, nodding toward the dining room.

"Not at all," Sierra replied. "Where might I find the plates and stuff?"

"Come on, I'll show you," Asha said, taking Sierra's hand. "Besides, you can help me pick out a bottle of wine."

"Ooh, you have a deal," Sierra said, following Asha into the kitchen. "Do I get the grand tour after our feast?"

"There isn't much more to see, but I'd be delighted to show you the rest of it," Asha replied, opening up one of the dark wood cabinets.

Sierra accepted the two plates Asha handed her and walked back into the dining room. There was only one room that she truly wanted to explore. She placed the plates on the table and chuckled nervously. "Oh, how I want to explore," she whispered.

● ● ●

Asha refilled Sierra's wine glass. "So tell me about Florida."

"There isn't much to tell," Sierra said. "What do you want to know?"

Asha reached across the table and took Sierra's hand. "Do you live close to the ocean?"

Sierra ran the tip of her finger around the lip of the wine glass. "Yes," she said. "I live across the street from the beach."

Asha took a sip of her wine. "Have you ever had to evacuate because of an impending hurricane?"

"Quite a few times," Sierra said, lifting the wine glass up to her mouth. "I've had to replace the windows quite a few times as well."

Asha laughed. "I bet it gets crazily expensive even with insurance."

Sierra nodded and took a sip of wine.

"Have you ever thought about living anywhere else?" Asha asked.

Not until recently, Sierra thought. "Not really."

Asha drank the last of her wine. "Will you tell me about your mother?"

Sierra grabbed the wine bottle and poured the remainder of the red liquid into Asha's glass. "In a word, she was awe-inspiring. She had iron-clad faith that love conquers all."

"Do you not share that sentiment?" Asha asked.

"I encountered some heartache that skewed my belief in love," Sierra said, surprised by her honesty. Suddenly, her defenses collapsed and a tsunami of emotion crashed onto her heart, flooding her body with tears. She turned away from Asha and covered her face with her hands.

Asha knocked over her chair as she rushed to Sierra's side. She placed her hand on Sierra's shoulder. "I'm here," she said compassionately.

The last wall of pride with which Sierra had surrounded herself crumbled and she buried her face in Asha's chest. Her hot tears saturated the thin material of Asha's dress shirt. "I'm so sorry," she said.

Asha helped Sierra up from the chair and into the living room. "Everything is going to be okay," she whispered, sitting down beside her on the couch.

Sierra lifted her head. "It was so horrible."

Asha pulled Sierra into her arms. "Tell me what happened."

"My mother passed away from breast cancer last November after battling it for two years," Sierra said, struggling to keep her voice from cracking. "I stood by her side throughout the entire ordeal, including the chemotherapy and the failed attempts to surgically remove all the infected tissue. It was a tough road, but my mother smiled every day, and every day I wanted to be there to see that smile. I never knew if it would be the last one or not."

"That's understandable," Asha replied.

"Not everyone saw it that way," Sierra said, taking a deep, quivery breath.

Asha brushed Sierra's hair away from her forehead. "Who didn't see it that way?"

"My ex," Sierra replied solemnly. "The day of my mother's funeral, she said she couldn't get off work."

"What?" Asha said. "Does this woman have a piece of coal where her heart should be?"

Sierra chuckled through her tears. "It gets better."

"Oh, I can't wait to hear this," Asha said sarcastically. "If we were in Florida right now, I would have to go visit your ex and see if I could knock some sense into her."

"Well, that would take you knocking sense into her and my former best friend."

Asha remained silent; the look on her face spoke volumes.

Sierra wiped the back of her hands across her eyes. "My best friend had told me that she would be at the funeral and I was grateful. When she didn't show up I got worried and left after the funeral to check on her."

"What did you find?" Asha asked.

"Her car was in the driveway, which I thought was rather odd, since she almost always parked in the garage. I knocked on the front door, but didn't get an answer. When I tried the door, it was unlocked."

"Tell me that you didn't go inside," Asha said.

Sierra shrugged. "I couldn't walk away without being sure, so I poked my head into the living room and noticed the television was on. I knew she would never leave the house without switching it off, so I made my way toward the kitchen, hoping to find her in there. When I heard noises coming from the direction of her bedroom, I started to panic. I called out to her as I raced toward the bedroom door."

Sierra fell silent as her body began trembling uncontrollably. Asha pulled her closer. "Go on," she whispered.

"I thought she was in trouble," Sierra said.

"But she wasn't?" Asha replied.

"No," Sierra said, drawing a ragged breath. "When I snatched open the door, I was prepared to fight with everything I had to save her against a rapist or burglar, but when I saw who was in the room with her, I felt like I'd been sucker punched. No, it was more like being stabbed in the heart. Twice."

"Who was in the room?" Asha asked, already knowing the answer.

"My girlfriend," Sierra said, her voice dropping to a mere whisper. "She was frantically trying to get her pants on while my best friend made the bed."

Asha wiped her sweating palms on her jeans. "What did you do?"

Sierra shrugged. "I closed the door and walked away. When my girlfriend came home a short time later, she blamed me for her infidelity."

"On what grounds?" Asha replied.

"She said I left her alone too often," Sierra said, looking down at the pale circle around her finger.

"You know that's bullshit, right?" Asha said heatedly. "It wasn't your fault. You were doing the right thing. She should have been there to support you."

Sierra patted Asha's hand. "What's done is done. Can we change the subject now? I'm exhausted."

Asha nodded. "Why don't I show you where you're sleeping tonight?"

"I'd like that," Sierra said, pushing herself up off the couch. She followed Asha past the dining room and into the master bedroom. A large, king-size bed dominated the room.

"I hope this will work," Asha said, walking over to her dresser. "I have some pajamas that you can wear, if you want."

"That really isn't necessary," Sierra replied. She walked over to the bed, removed her bra from beneath her shirt, and slid off her jeans.

"Can I get you anything else, then?" Asha said, averting her eyes.

"Will you just stay with me?" Sierra said. "I don't want to sleep alone tonight."

"Of course," Asha replied, moving over to the door. "I need to make sure everything is locked up and then I'll be back."

"I'll be right here," Sierra said sleepily. "Don't be too long."

"I won't," Asha replied, switching off the light. "I'll be back before you can miss me."

"I already miss you," Sierra mumbled, before falling asleep.

"I've missed you my entire life," Asha replied. "And now, it will never be the same."

CHAPTER TEN

The unmistakable aroma of freshly brewed coffee pervaded Sierra's dreams. She inhaled deeply, tasting the richness of the beans as though she had taken an actual sip of the invigorating liquid. Her eyelids battled her body's refusal to embrace the morning. They fluttered from open to closed repeatedly until at last she used her fingers like tiny crowbars to pry them apart.

Reality rode in on the rays of light that filtered into the shimmering green of Sierra's eyes. Her heart thundered in her chest. She lay in the middle of Asha's bed, enveloped by her scent that fragranced the pillows, sheets and blankets. *This is too good to be true,* she thought, snuggling her head down into one of the pillows.

The bedroom door eased open and Asha came into the room carrying a small wooden tray. She wore a semi-tight, white T-shirt that outlined her breasts in perfect detail and a pair of faded jeans. "Good morning," she said, noticing that Sierra was awake. "How did you sleep?"

"Like a rock," Sierra replied, unable to avert her eyes before Asha caught her staring at her breasts.

Asha blushed and a shy smile tugged at her lips. She placed the tray on the dresser. "Do you take your coffee black or with cream and sugar?"

"It depends on how good the coffee is," Sierra said with a hint of orneriness. She propped herself up against the headboard and avoided Asha's gaze. She knew the desire moistening the valley between her legs would no doubt be reflected in her eyes.

Asha carried over two mugs and handed one to Sierra before sitting down next to her on the edge of the bed. "I think you'll like it straight up, then."

Sierra took a careful sip. "Wow, I'm impressed."

"You don't have to just say that," Asha said.

"Believe me," Sierra said, taking another sip. "When the coffee is good, it's the only thing I'll have straight up."

Asha grinned. "I feel very fortunate in that regard."

"So do I," Sierra replied.

Asha leaned in and kissed Sierra softly on the lips. "How fortunate?"

Sierra set her coffee mug down on the nightstand next to the bed. "I wish I had all day to show you."

Asha stared at Sierra from over the rim of her coffee mug. "What does an hour get me?"

Sierra scooted over to the other half of the bed. "Will a thousand kisses work?"

"I think that'll do," Asha said, setting her mug down and sliding beneath the covers

Sierra brought her lips to Asha's and ignored the painful memories attempting to steal the immense joy that kissing Asha ignited in her. She wasn't going to let her past ruin the moment. The need for Asha was undeniable. Her entire body ached for release as if another woman's touch had never graced her skin.

Asha's brown eyes were backlit by flames of desire as she pulled her lips away. "I want you."

Sierra took a deep, quivering breath. "I want you, too."

Asha brought her lips back to Sierra's, easing her onto her back. Their kisses deepened as their tongues entwined, mimicking the pleasures that each of them wanted to bestow upon the other. Sierra grasped the ends of Asha's shirt and pulled it free from her jeans. "I want this off."

"Take it off, then," Asha replied, pulsating her hips steadily into Sierra's.

Sierra pulled the shirt over Asha's head and tossed it onto the floor. Her eyes settled on the beige bra that impeded her view of what she longed to wrap her lips around. As if reading her mind, Asha sat up and slid each bra strap from her shoulders, peeling away the silky material covering her breasts. She lowered back down and brought her breasts dangerously close to Sierra's lips. "Is this what you wanted?"

Sierra didn't hesitate as she hungrily accepted one of Asha's breasts into her mouth and tantalized the already hardened nipple with gentle strokes of her tongue. Asha's breathing quickened and the steady pulse of her hips erupted into an urgent need. Sierra flicked her tongue faster and softly bit down. She sensed that Asha was as close as she was to an orgasm.

Asha threw her head back. "Don't stop!"

Sierra bit down a little harder and a cry of pleasure slipped through Asha's lips.

"Oh, my God!" she screamed, her body shuddering in orgasmic release.

Sierra was overwhelmed by her own orgasmic tidal wave. Her body trembled beneath Asha's and she pulled her mouth away to keep from biting down too aggressively on Asha's breast. It had been a while since she had experienced so much passion and she wanted more— a lot more.

Asha collapsed and rolled onto her back. Her chest rose and fell as she tried to regain control of her breathing. "That was amazing," she said, a satisfied grin spreading across her face.

Sierra turned onto her side and took Asha's hand. "I'm so glad you enjoyed it."

Asha gazed into Sierra's eyes. "Was it all right for you? I mean, were you able to..."

"Yes," Sierra said, her cheeks reddening.

Asha rose up onto her elbows. "Can I feel?"

Sierra swallowed hard. "What?"

"I want to feel how wet you are," Asha replied, laying her hand on Sierra's thigh and massaging it suggestively. "Please let me."

Sierra felt Asha slide her hand toward the inner part of her thigh. "I'm just so wet," she said, placing her hand on top of Asha's. "Perhaps we should wait."

Asha moved her hand closer to Sierra's moist valley. "I need to touch you."

Sierra felt one of Asha's fingers slip between her thighs and stroke the thin material of her underwear that covered her private garden. Her clitoris throbbed for attention. Without further hesitation, she parted her thighs for Asha.

Asha ran her finger back across the material. "You're so wet," she whispered, tracing the outline of Sierra's underwear.

"I want to feel your touch," Sierra moaned, gazing up at Asha.

Asha brought her lips down to Sierra's and simultaneously slid her hand beneath the cottony underwear. Her fingers were immediately immersed in warm, thick nectar as they separated the walls guarding Sierra's sanctuary.

Sierra arched back and spread her legs even further. "You feel so good," she said, clawing at Asha's back.

Asha followed the warm nectar to its source and penetrated it with two of her fingers. She curved them upward, searching for that certain ridge where she could play her masterpiece and hopefully hit a high "G" note. As soon as Sierra dug her nails into her back, she knew she'd found it.

Sierra felt her impending orgasm stealing energy from every part of her body. Her feet and hands tingled and her face felt numb. The moisture in her mouth had evaporated. The muscles in her lower back burned as her hips jerked up and down. Each stroke from Asha's fingers fueled another blast of intensity by the physiological reactions her body hadn't enjoyed in quite some time. "Oh, Asha!" she cried as her body erupted.

Asha waited until Sierra's body stopped shuddering before removing her fingers. She raised them to her lips and licked each one. "My God, you taste amazing."

"I'm glad you think so," Sierra said, suddenly feeling extremely vulnerable. She pulled the covers up around her shoulders. "What time do we have to leave?"

Asha looked across the room at the clock on the dresser. "We'll need to get up in a few minutes."

Sierra sighed, but said nothing.

"What's wrong?" Asha asked, pulling Sierra closer.

"I just don't want this moment to end," Sierra said.

"Who said it has to end?" Asha replied. "Maybe it's just the beginning, with a scheduled intermission."

Sierra tilted her head upward to gaze into Asha's eyes. "I hope so."

"I know so," Asha said. "You have to believe that we were destined to meet."

"How do you know we weren't destined to have a fling and that's it?" Sierra replied.

"Do you consider what's going on between us a fling?" Asha said, her words catching in her throat.

Sierra traced the outer edge of Asha's lips with her finger. "No," she said softly.

"Good," Asha replied. "I would have been heartbroken had you said otherwise. Now let's get up so I can fix us some breakfast. I'm starving and since I don't have time to have what I really want I'd better get to cooking."

"What do you really want?" Sierra asked, watching Asha slip from beneath the covers.

Asha's gaze traveled down to Sierra's pelvic region. "Something I'm willing to wait for."

"Is that so?" Sierra replied. "How long are you willing to wait?"

"As long as it takes," Asha replied. "I'm a very patient person."

• • •

Sierra stepped into the foyer of her suite and closed the door. It was exactly as she had left it the night before, but something seemed amiss. She dropped her jacket beside the closet and walked over to the bed. The digital clock on the nightstand displayed the time as eight minutes after ten o'clock in the morning. Fifteen minutes had passed since she and Asha had arrived back at the lodge. Five of those minutes had been spent enjoying each other's lips in the cab of Asha's truck, with an additional five discussing her current, hectic schedule. They'd shared one last, lingering kiss before entering the lobby and reluctantly parting ways.

Lying down across the bed, Sierra stared up at the ceiling. She didn't need to investigate what seemed off about her return; she already knew the answer even if she didn't want to admit it. It was her heart. It was on the mend and she could sense a little faith trickling back into her way of thinking. She glanced at her ring finger and for the first time in months didn't see a failed commitment. She saw that it hadn't been the right commitment.

Overwhelmed by the revelation, Sierra felt the demons of guilt release their chains on her soul. She got up, walked over to the French doors, and slung back the curtains. Shadows were banished from the room by the natural light that flooded in. I'm free, she thought, embracing the sun's rays.

She rushed over to the desk and plopped down into the leather chair. Her heart thumped in her chest. She booted up the laptop and closed her eyes as Microsoft

Word loaded onto the screen. Her every thought now revolved around her early morning escapade with Asha. She opened her eyes and began typing furiously. The oasis between her legs steadily grew wetter by the stream of warm nectar that poured from her own honey pot with every word.

Around three o'clock, Sierra arched back and stretched her arms high above her head. Hunger gnawed at her stomach, but satisfaction filled her mind. She had succeeded in completing another chapter although it would go through quite a few more revisions before sending it off to Dana. Still, she was halfway through a book that a few months before she hadn't believed would ever exist.

A loud knock at the door startled Sierra so much so that she almost flipped over backward in her chair. "Hold on," she shouted, regaining her balance.

A large bouquet of white Stargazer lilies was arranged perfectly in a vase just outside the door. Sierra looked up and down the deserted hallway before plucking the small envelope, on which her name was inscribed, from a clear plastic, fork-like holder. She removed the card from within and read the simple message aloud as her immense joy revealed itself in tears; "I loved waking up with you this morning." She ran her fingertips over the card's closing: "Love, Asha."

Sierra looked up and down the hallway one more time before picking up the vase. It was surprisingly heavy. She stepped back into the room and walked over to the small dining table. It was cluttered with her writing outlines, wadded-up ideas that had led to dead ends, and character profiles. Clearing off a section in the middle, she set the vase down and positioned it so the lilies would receive ample sunlight. She hurried over to the phone and dialed "0."

"Is Asha available?" Sierra asked after Alexandria had finished her "this is the front desk" spiel.

"Yes, she is," Alexandria replied. "Hold for one moment, please."

Sierra drummed her fingers.

"Hi, this is Asha."

"Has anyone ever told you that you're amazing?" Sierra said, her heart feeling as though it was doing back flips.

Asha chuckled. "Yes, one person in particular has mentioned that a few times, ma'am."

"Well, what if that one person wants to see you later if you're able to spare a few minutes and thank you properly with a kiss?" Sierra replied.

"I believe that can be arranged," Asha said, keeping a professional tone. "I'll look at the evening schedule and see if I can personally address that issue."

"You do that," Sierra said. "You know where I'll be."

"I do," Asha replied. "Have a good rest of the day."

Sierra dropped the phone on the cradle and fell back onto the bed. The springs from the mattress caught her weight and bounced her a few times. She giggled at her desire to do it again. *What would it hurt*, she thought. She stood back up and threw her body even harder onto the bed. Her laughter resonated against the bedroom walls as she bounced even higher.

Exhausted and starving, Sierra slid down the side of the bed and onto the floor. *That took so little energy when I was kid*, she thought. She picked up the phone and dialed room service. As she waited for someone to answer, she thought about her favorite meal as a kid, grilled cheese and tomato soup.

"Hello, Ms. Stanton," Darren greeted her. "What can I get for you this afternoon?"

"I was wondering if a grilled cheese sandwich and tomato soup happened to be on the in-room dining menu," Sierra replied.

"I'm afraid not," Darren said. "There isn't a huge demand for it."

"That's a shame," Sierra replied, contemplating whether anything else sounded good.

"We do whip that up for Asha from time to time, though" Darren continued. "I'm sure she wouldn't mind if we did the same for you."

"Are you sure?" Sierra said, elated that she and Asha had something so insignificant in common. "I don't want you to get into any trouble."

Darren laughed. "I'd get into more trouble if I denied you a grilled cheese sandwich and Asha found out about it."

"Is that so?" Sierra said.

"You have no idea," Darren said emphatically. "Last year, she got so mad at me that I thought I was going to get fired for denying one of her seasonal flings a drink."

"Seasonal flings, huh?" Sierra said.

"Uh, I didn't mean it like that," Darren replied apologetically.

"It's okay," Sierra said. "I wasn't offended."

"You don't understand," Darren said, his voice dropping to a whisper. "Every year, Asha seems to hook up with these superficial hotties. No matter how many times I've warned her, she still goes all out and gets crushed in the end."

"I see," Sierra said.

"I couldn't tell you how many nights Asha spent pining after this one chick last year," Darren continued. "Everybody tried to warn her, but she didn't want to listen. She fell hard. I'm not sure if she hadn't met you that she would have recovered."

"Does she have anyone back in California?" Sierra said, unable to resist asking the question she had purposefully refused to entertain until now.

"Asha?" Darren said incredulously. "Nah, she spends all her time working to build her business."

"How do you know this?" Sierra said.

"She gave me this job a few years ago while I was attempting to secure my place on the Olympic team for downhill skiing," Darren replied. "In return I've made it my mission to see that she finds happiness."

"Wow, that's very noble," Sierra said.

"Not really," Darren said. "Asha treats me like a younger brother. She's always looking out for me. In fact, she contacted a retired downhill ski instructor who taught some of the previous Olympic contenders and convinced him to take me under his wing."

"That's wonderful," Sierra replied.

"No, that's Asha," Darren said. "I have to go now, but I'm always around if you need anything. Your grilled cheese and tomato soup should be up in about twenty minutes."

"Thanks," Sierra said. "I really appreciate...everything."

• • •

The afternoon faded into the evening with the temperature plummeting in the wake of the setting sun. Sierra ended her writing marathon and selected the "hibernate" feature from the drop-down menu. She closed up the laptop and rubbed her eyes. They were tired and blurry and she had a wicked headache. It was time to face the cold, hard truth that she was undoubtedly getting older. She needed to get her eyes examined and it needed to be sooner rather than later.

She walked over to the balcony and looked through the small windowpanes that resembled a checkerboard pattern on each French door. The town was still buzzing with activity as families rushed out to grab a bite eat and holiday shoppers lugged recently purchased gifts back to their cars or hotel rooms. The trees were still hidden beneath their cold, white coats. The wind continued to stir up the top layer of snow, creating an effect which reminded Sierra of the snow-globes her mother used to collect.

A tear rolled down Sierra's cheek and then another. This was as close as she had ever been to experiencing the wonderful Christmas stories her mother had read to her as a child. After her mother's death, she had spent countless hours trying to recall what her favorite memory had been of the two of them. Staring at this wintry paradise, the answer came as swiftly as if it had arrived on the wings of a dove.

Gazing into the clear night sky, Sierra pressed her hands against her aching heart. "It was every Christmas morning," she said, almost sobbing. "There was never a twinkling light or a brightly colored package that outshined the joy sparkling in your eyes at being able to spend the day with me." Collapsing to her knees, she wept in front of the world. "I missed you last Christmas, Mom, and every day since. It's been tough traveling this road all alone."

Sierra felt the warmth from an embrace deep within her soul. She wasn't a religious fanatic, far from it, but she understood the significance of what she had experienced. The truth was she had never been alone. Her mother had always been there in spirit, guiding her, and always would be. This thought helped Sierra stand back up again. Now it was up to her to take the reins and explore the infinite possibilities that life had to offer.

Closing the curtains, Sierra hurried into the bathroom and splashed her face a few times with warm water. She squeezed a couple of drops of Visine into her eyes and followed them up with the covering magnificence of makeup. When she looked back into the mirror, there wasn't a single hint of her prior distress. She combed and straightened her hair and dabbed some perfume behind her ears before turning off the bathroom light.

From within the closet, Sierra selected a fitted pair of jeans and a cream-colored sweater. She was careful not to mess up her hair or get any makeup on the collar of the sweater as she pulled it over her head. The black boots she had selected to wear with her ensemble added an extra inch to her height. Her goal was to turn every head in the room and make one in particular fall head over heels in love with her.

Sierra checked the time as butterflies swarmed in the pit of her stomach. Asha would be taking her break in the next few minutes to come see her, but that plan was about to change. *There's no time like the present*, she thought.

• • •

As Sierra neared the bottom of the stairwell, she peered over the railing toward the registration desk. A mob had surrounded Asha and Jack as each guest tried to unload their rented skis, poles and snowboards as fast as possible. Asha was checking the equipment in as Jack raced back and forth, putting the stuff away to eliminate clutter and confusion. Alexandria, on the other hand, was addressing a variety of questions ranging from the nightly skiing conditions to the best place for dinner, all while intermittently answering the phone.

Sierra weaved through the maze of human chaos to the other side of the room. She noticed a few of the supposed bachelors watching her as though she had the potential of being their main course for the evening. The thought absolutely sickened her. *Mission accomplished, though*, she thought. *Now let's see if Asha notices.*

A rather skittish-looking woman, who found herself caught up in all the pushing and shoving that was occurring around her, finally snapped. She started swinging her ski poles around like a madwoman and shouted that her personal space was being invaded. A few of the guests moved aside in fear, but some of the younger crowd armed themselves with their own poles and moved in as though they were about to slay a beast.

Asha jumped over the check-in counter and rushed in. "Give me those," she said, ripping the poles out of the woman's hands.

The woman shrunk away as embarrassment set in. Asha handed the poles off to Jack and climbed up on the counter. "That's enough," she shouted at the crowd. "Where's your holiday spirit? Now I want everyone to form one line and be patient. The flu has hit our staff hard, so we're a little short-handed, but we will get to you. There will be no additional fees charged for equipment not returned on time."

Sierra moved through the crowd and ignored the slanderous remarks from people assuming she was cutting in front of them. She approached Asha, who had her head bent over a receiving log. "Is there anything I can do to help?"

Asha glanced up and did a double-take. "Wow, you look incredible."

"Thank you," Sierra replied. "I was hoping I'd get that reaction."

"Trust me," Asha said. "There's a reaction all right."

"Ooh, I'm intrigued," Sierra said. "Anything you'd like to share?"

Asha's eyes saddened. "Unfortunately, I'm glued to this chair until the next shift arrives at midnight."

"If they show up," Jack interjected, taking a pair of skis from Asha.

Sierra leaned over the counter to keep from having to shout. "Do you need an extra set of hands?"

"That would be awesome," Asha replied. She nodded her head toward Alexandria. "Would you mind helping with the phones?"

"No problem," Sierra replied, giving her a wink.

"You're the best," Asha said. "Alexandria will love you for it."

She's not the one I want to love me, Sierra thought. She walked over and informed Alexandria of Asha's request. Alexandria almost jumped up and down with joy and probably would have if not for her heels. She showed Sierra how to work the phones and told her what to say, then left for a restroom break. About ten minutes later, she returned with two cups of coffee and nonstop chatter.

Around ten-thirty, Sierra took one final call from a guest wanting an additional couple of towels brought up. She scribbled his room number down on a Post-It and handed the request off to Jack, who immediately set out to fulfill the man's wishes. Alexandria excused herself to grab another cup of coffee, leaving Sierra and Asha alone for the first time all evening.

"How are you holding up?" Asha said, looking up from a stack of paperwork.

"I'm beat," Sierra said with a tired grin. "I can't wait to crawl into bed."

Asha put down her pen and rubbed her eyes. "I wish I could be there to tuck you in, but I have so much paperwork to get through."

"It's okay," Sierra replied, getting to her feet.

Asha pushed the chair she was sitting in away from the desk and walked over to Sierra. "Could I have a kiss before you go?"

"Only if you walk with me back to my room," Sierra said.

"You've got yourself a deal," Asha said, taking Sierra by the hand.

Alexandria came back around the corner. "Where are the two of you off to?"

"I'm going to take a short break," Asha said over her shoulder as Sierra led her toward the elevator. "I'll be back within ten minutes."

Alexandria rolled her eyes. "I won't hold my breath."

"Keep it up," Asha teased. "I know who signs your paycheck, remember?"

"How could I forget?" Alexandria said. "You mention it every year."

"I'm persistent," Asha said, pressing the button for the elevator.

Alexandria shook her head. "Whatever you say, boss."

Sierra stepped into the elevator and looked over at Asha. "How persistent?"

Asha pressed "3" on the control panel. "You're going to have to wait and find out."

As soon as the elevator doors closed, Sierra and Asha rushed into each other's arms. Their kisses were frantic but passionate. When the elevator arrived on the third floor, they raced down the hall hand-in-hand to Sierra's room. Sierra barely got the keycard into the slot to unlock the door before Asha had scooped the hair away from the back of her neck and began kissing it.

"My God," Sierra gasped, falling into the room.

Asha closed the door behind them and pushed Sierra up against the wall. "I can't stay, but I really want you to know how much you're driving me insane looking as good as you do."

Sierra arched her head back as Asha kissed down her throat. "I just want to make sure no other woman turns your head."

"Not a chance," Asha replied. She brought her lips back to Sierra's.

Sierra grabbed hold of Asha's belt loops to keep from undressing her. "When do I get to see you again?"

"Not soon enough," Asha said. "I need to go home tonight and get some things done around the house. I have to be back at work tomorrow morning at eight o'clock sharp."

"That's insane," Sierra said. "When will you sleep?"

"I'll get a few hours tonight," Asha replied. "I have a feeling the next couple of days will be repeats of tonight's fiasco. What do you say to going out on Friday evening?"

"I'd love to," Sierra said. "Any chance I'll get to see you before then?"

Asha kissed Sierra softly. "I didn't plan otherwise."

"That's good," Sierra replied. "I'll be around almost every day working, so feel free to call me when you can spare a few minutes."

"Are you eventually going to shed some light on what you're working on or should I start guessing?" Asha said, pressing her hips into Sierra's.

Sierra placed the tip of her finger on Asha's lips. "When it's finished, I'll let you see it. I promise."

"I'm going to hold you to that," Asha said, gazing into Sierra's eyes.

"Well, you'd better get going," Sierra said. "Before I make you hold your body against me."

Asha pressed her lips one more time against Sierra's. "I don't want to leave you tonight."

I don't want you to ever leave me, Sierra thought. "I don't want you to go, either."

Asha wrapped her arms tightly around Sierra. "Will you call me when you wake up in the morning?"

"I planned on it," Sierra said. She kissed Asha again before reluctantly letting her slip out the door.

CHAPTER ELEVEN

Sierra's feet landed squarely on the revolving track and beads of sweat rolled down her face. She stared intently at the wall-length mirror, but was unaware of her reflection. From the start of the run, she had allowed her mind to transport her into the midst of the African Jungle. Her only purpose was salvation. A Siberian tiger was gaining on her. She could feel its breath on her neck, the rush of air from its mighty claws as it swiped at the lean, white muscle on her legs, and she could hear the sound of its razor-sharp teeth snapping down with each missed bite.

"Almost there," Sierra gasped. She envisioned Asha waiting for her along the shores of the Nile in a powerful speedboat. If she could keep this pace for a few more seconds and make a giant leap, she would escape certain death by landing in Asha's loving embrace. "I can make it," she huffed, stretching out her stride.

"To where?" a voice hissed.

Sierra's eyes narrowed as she registered the reflection of the person standing beside the treadmill. "Hello, Vivian," she growled.

"I'm sorry to have interrupted your mind trip to wherever," Vivian said, tossing her hair back from her shoulders. "But I was wondering if you knew of Asha's whereabouts on this glorious Friday afternoon."

Sierra slowed down the pace of the revolving track. "Sorry, I don't."

"I guess I'll have to go find her," Vivian replied.

"I guess so," Sierra said, maintaining her icy gaze.

"It's a good thing that you're working out," Vivian said, giving Sierra the once over.

"And why's that?" Sierra replied.

"Because Asha doesn't do big," Vivian said viciously.

"She did you," Sierra said, offering an equally vicious grin.

Vivian's eyes flashed with anger. "You'll regret that comment." She pivoted on her two-inch pumps and strutted out of the gym.

Sierra maintained a watchful eye on the doorway. She wanted to make sure there wasn't a surprised ambush in her immediate future. After a five-minute walk to cool down and slow her heart rate, she stepped off the treadmill, completely at ease. She patted her face with the small hand towel that she had brought from the bathroom and looked around to see what she wanted to do next.

The gym was furnished with every type of aerobic equipment and free-style weight combination anyone could possibly need. Sierra walked over to the solitary weight bench, adjusted the amount on the bar, and slid beneath it. She positioned her hands directly in line with her shoulders and lifted the bar off its perch. "One," she whispered, after completing the rep.

As Sierra brought the bar to her chest again, Vivian appeared beside her. "Hello, Sierra," she sneered.

Sierra attempted to lift the bar back to the top, but Vivian intervened by placing both of her hands on the bar and forcing it downward. A desperate struggle ensued with Sierra finding that she was no match for the weight being thrust upon her. The bar inched its way downward. She could feel Vivian's breath on her face as she leaned even harder on the bar. "I will crush you if you don't stay away from Asha," she hissed.

Sierra was terrified, but she knew she would rather be crushed than give Vivian the satisfaction of seeing it. "If you don't get the hell off of me, you'll regret it."

An evil smirk developed on Vivian's face. "Okay, tough girl, what are you going to do about it?"

"It's not Sierra that you should be concerned with," Asha interjected, striding into the room.

Vivian immediately released the bar and casually stepped away as though she and Sierra had just finished up a friendly chat about the benefits of working out. Asha rushed over to the bench and assisted Sierra in raising the bar back onto its perch. She wrapped her arms around Sierra and helped her to sit up. "Are you okay, baby?" she said, hugging Sierra tightly.

"Yes," Sierra replied. Exhaustion plagued her arms, sending her muscles into spasms.

"What in hell were you trying to do?" Asha hissed, glaring menacingly at Vivian.

"She was just on her way out," Sierra interjected.

"That's right," Vivian said, eyeing Sierra curiously.

"I guess you'd better start walking, then," Asha said.

Vivian's smile was villainous as she turned to leave. "I'll see myself out," she replied nonchalantly.

Asha turned back to Sierra, her eyes wide with disbelief. "Are you sure you're okay?"

Sierra conjured up her best smile. "I'm fine," she said. "I just want to know how you knew I was in trouble."

"The surveillance camera," Asha said, pointing toward the far right corner of the gym. "I'm the one monitoring them today. When I saw Vivian come in, I had a feeling she would do something stupid. I never expected that she would physically try to hurt you."

Sierra shrugged. "She just seems to take a very unhealthy interest in your love life."

"I still can't believe you're letting her off the hook like that," Asha replied, shaking her head. "You could file an assault and battery charge against her and there would be surveillance video to back up your claim."

"Everything comes full circle," Sierra said, laying her head on Asha's shoulder. "Look on the bright side, it makes my stay here a little more interesting."

"If she tries something like that again," Asha said, her voice trembling with anger. "I'll call the police and file the report myself."

"I'm sure it won't come to that," Sierra said, feeling the burning sensation in her arms lessen slightly.

Asha glanced up at the wall clock. "I have to get back to the security office, but I'd love to walk you back to your room."

"I'm going to try to finish my workout," Sierra replied, getting up from the bench.

"Are you sure that's such a good idea?" Asha said worriedly.

"I'll be fine," Sierra said, glancing toward the direction of the surveillance camera. "Besides, I know where you'll be if I need you."

Asha chuckled. "Yes, you do and you know I'll be paying close attention."

"Ooh," Sierra said, swinging her hips from side to side. "I like that type of motivation."

Asha kissed Sierra on the forehead. "I thought you might."

"I'm sorry I'm all sweaty," Sierra said, noticing Asha licking her lips.

"No need to apologize," Asha replied. "I lack the adequate salt intake my body needs to survive anyway." With that, she kissed Sierra's forehead again. "I think that'll hold me over until dinner."

Sierra crossed her arms in front of her chest and tried to keep from smiling. "Exactly what does your doctor prescribe for this inadequate salt thing?"

Asha pulled Sierra into her arms and kissed her passionately on the lips. "Well, under his advisement, I should be getting at least two kisses every hour to sustain normal activity."

"Whatever will you do until dinner?" Sierra said, walking with Asha over to the door.

"Hmm..." Asha said, tapping a finger against her chin. "Let's see, we have almost five hours till our scheduled rendezvous and probably an additional hour until we eat. That's a total of six hours, which equals twelve kisses."

"That's a lot of kisses," Sierra replied, brushing her lips against Asha's. "Whatever should we do?"

Asha traced the outside of Sierra's lips with her tongue. "I could think of a few things."

"You could?" Sierra said, an erotic shiver radiating from her spine and causing goose bumps to explode all over her body. "Like what?"

"Well, I think for every five kisses missed we should have to repay it in one lump sum," Asha replied.

Sierra's eyebrow shot up. "What are you suggesting?"

Asha ran her fingers through Sierra's hair. "Maybe you should bring an overnight bag with you tonight."

Sierra pressed her lips together to keep from showing her excitement with a big, goofy grin. "Are you hinting around that you want a repeat of what happened Tuesday morning?"

Asha's eyes flared with desire. "No, I want more than that."

"How much more?" Sierra said, feeling her nipples harden without Asha even touching them.

Asha placed her lips next to Sierra's ear. "I want to explore every inch of your body with my tongue."

Sierra's mouth went instantly dry. "I think that can be arranged," she whispered.

Asha kissed Sierra one more time before opening the gym door to leave. "I want to know everything thing about you, Ms. Stanton."

Sierra moistened her lips. "I want that, too."

"Good," Asha replied. "Now, I'd better get back before someone notices I'm missing."

"If you have to," Sierra said, desperately needing to take a sip of water.

Asha squeezed Sierra's hand. "I'll meet you out front at seven o'clock sharp."

"I'll be there," Sierra replied. "I can't wait to have you all to myself."

"The feeling is mutual," Asha said. She stepped aside for two teenage boys and their father to gain access to the room. "I guess I should go."

"I'll come with you," Sierra said.

"I thought you were going to finish working out," Asha replied.

Sierra couldn't resist blushing. "I might be working out later and I wouldn't want to be too tired to give it my best."

Asha stepped into the hallway. "I think you might be on to something."

Sierra pulled the gym door closed and walked beside Asha toward the elevators. "Maybe we should do a little warming up for tonight between floors."

"Good idea," Asha said, pressing the button for the elevator. She pulled Sierra into her arms and kissed her. "I wish we could start this evening right now."

"Well, you know where I'll be if you get off work a little early," Sierra said, stepping onto the elevator.

"That's true," Asha replied, following Sierra onto the elevator and placing her hands on Sierra's hips.

The distance between them shrunk as the elevator doors closed. Sierra brought her lips to Asha's and their tongues began an exotic dance. Asha steadily worked her hands up each side of Sierra's shirt until they lingered just below her breasts. The elevator stopped abruptly on the fourth floor. An older, Middle Eastern couple hurried in as Asha flung herself against the back wall of the elevator. Sierra threw her hand in front of her mouth to keep from laughing. The couple shook their heads and kept their eyes forward. Asha grabbed the silver hand rail and hung her head, stifling laughter.

The elevator stopped again, this time on the third floor. "I'll see you tonight," Sierra said, moving past the couple and into the hallway.

Asha nodded and blew Sierra a kiss. Sierra reached out and pretended to grab it. Neither averted their gaze as the elevator doors closed. Sierra walked toward her suite, humming an old Aerosmith song. A smile crept across her face as she thought about the lyrics. *Love in an elevator. Livin' it up when I'm goin' down. Love in an elevator. Lovin' it up till I hit the ground.*

• • •

At five minutes till seven o'clock, Sierra emerged from the elevator carrying only her laptop bag. She held it tightly against her side and made a beeline for the front door. Her mind was a smorgasbord of what-ifs, the most prevalent being what to say if Dee called her over to the registration desk and asked what her and Asha's plans were for the evening. What could she possibly say? *Oh, Asha and I are going to have dinner and afterward we plan on skipping desert to explore more intimate sweets.* She could imagine Dee's deep blue eyes growing wide with ocean-size disbelief.

Sierra pushed open the lobby door and stepped onto the front porch. The outside temperature seemed to instantly freeze the moisture within her every breath. She zipped up her jacket and tucked her hands into its pockets. The relief that she hadn't crumbled under Dee's watchful gaze or been subjected to any probing of tonight's probabilities made the bitter cold a little more bearable.

It took a very short amount of time for the wind to strip away the warmth provided by Sierra's apparel. She walked the length of the porch a few times, trying to keep her extremities from becoming too cold. There was no way she was going back into the lodge. She had escaped unscathed and planned on keeping it that way, so she waited expectantly for Asha's truck to pull up.

The front door opened partially and Dee stuck her head out. "Sierra?" she said. "Don't you want to wait inside where it's warm?"

"It's okay," Sierra replied, her teeth chattering. "I'm sure Asha will be here any second."

"All right, dear," Dee said. "Don't stay out here too long and catch a cold."

"I appreciate your concern," Sierra said. "If she doesn't show up in the next few, I'll come in and warm up by the fire."

"That won't be necessary," Asha interrupted, trudging up the steps.

"Where's your truck?" Sierra asked, concern spreading across her face.

"Someone parked the damn snowplow behind it," Asha replied.

Dee opened the lobby door a little wider. "Come on in," she said, motioning them to hurry. "I'll get you both some hot cocoa to warm yourselves with while I find out who has the keys to the snowplow."

"That's okay," Asha said. "I already called Devi and we're going to swap vehicles. She should be coming around the corner any second."

Dee pinched Asha's cheeks. "I have such a resourceful granddaughter."

"Who won't have any cheeks if you pinch any harder," Asha chuckled.

Sierra saw a red Jeep Wrangler pull up beside the parked snowmobiles. "Is that Devi?"

"Right on time," Asha replied, hugging Dee.

Dee gazed over Asha's shoulder at Sierra. "Will you two be stopping by for dinner tomorrow night?"

Sierra's heart felt like it was catapulted into her throat. She opened her mouth to speak, but no words came but a single syllable word, "uh."

Asha stepped over to Sierra and took her hand. "That's the plan," she said nonchalantly.

"Am I intruding?" Devi asked, jogging up the steps.

"Not at all," Asha replied. "We were discussing dinner plans for tomorrow night."

"Ooh," Devi teased, addressing Sierra. "You should feel special. It isn't every day Asha brings someone home to dinner."

"Knock it off," Asha said, playfully slugging Devi in the shoulder. "Or you're uninvited."

"Where's the sisterly love in that," Devi replied, tossing her car keys to Asha. "Come on, Grandma, I know when we're not wanted."

Dee smiled at Sierra. "Pay them no attention, dear. They really do love each other."

Devi took Dee's hand and pulled her into the lodge. She looked back and stuck her tongue out at Asha before closing the door.

Asha shook her head and looked at Sierra's laptop bag. "Are you not staying over?"

Sierra's lips curled upward as her cheeks reddened. "I didn't know if Dee was aware I was spending the night with you, so I hid my clothes and everything in it."

Asha took Sierra's hand. "You should be a mystery writer."

"I'll keep that in mind," Sierra laughed. She followed Asha down the steps and over to the Jeep.

• • •

Sierra helped Asha clean off the table from their exquisite Indian feast of chicken curry, samosas and naan. "My God," she said, carrying their wineglasses into the kitchen. "Where did you learn to cook like that?"

Asha set their plates into the bottom rack of the dishwasher along with the rest of the larger dishes. "My mom gave me a few cooking lessons when she was alive and I've spent a lot of time since then expanding on that."

"Well, it's the best meal I've ever tasted," Sierra said. "Each bite was like an explosion of exotic spices satisfying all my taste buds."

"I'm so glad you enjoyed it," Asha replied. She took the wineglasses from Sierra and set them on the counter. "Would you like some more?"

"I'd love some," Sierra said.

Asha finished off the wine by filling each glass three-quarters of the way full. "Would you like to go sit by the fire and listen to some music?"

"That sounds perfect," Sierra said, taking her glass from Asha.

They moved into the sunken living room and sat down on opposite sides of the couch. Asha used one of three remotes to switch on the stereo system. She selected the five-disc CD changer and pressed play. The stunning voice of Sarah McLachlan filled the air with the first track from her *Wintersong* album.

"I love her voice," Sierra replied, taking a sip of her wine.

"Me, too," Asha said. "I have every one of her CDs."

"So do I," Sierra said. "There's something so soothing about her voice that the rest of the world melts away when I listen to her."

Asha set her wineglass down and stood up. She walked over to Sierra and extended her hand. "Dance with me?"

Sierra stared up at Asha. "I have absolutely no rhythm."

"Is that a no?" Asha replied.

Sierra took Asha's hand. "No, that's a warning," she said, chuckling.

"Well, I guess it's a good thing we're starting off with a very slow song," Asha said, leading Sierra over to the other side of the coffee table.

Sierra wrapped her arms around Asha's neck. "Yes, it is."

The title track from *Wintersong* began playing. Asha pulled Sierra close and their hips rocked gently from side to side. Sierra peered into Asha's softened eyes, the flames from the fireplace reflecting in the brown hues. She raised her hand and caressed the side of Asha's face. Asha closed her eyes and nuzzled her cheek against Sierra's hand. "Have you ever experienced a more perfect moment?" she said.

Sierra brought her lips to Asha's. "Never."

Asha opened her eyes. "Kiss me again."

"Gladly," Sierra said.

Their kiss ignited a passion hotter than the flames in the fireplace scorching the wood and causing it to crackle and pop. Sierra brought her hands to the top of Asha's shirt. One by one, she unbuttoned the dress shirt without the need to leave Asha's lips. Slipping it off her shoulders, it fell to the ground, leaving the beauty of Asha's skin and the silky white bra she wore glowing in the firelight.

Asha moved her hands beneath Sierra's sweater and massaged her fingers up Sierra's back until they reached her bra strap. A quick snap and the clasp unhooked, relaxing the see-through lace material. Pulling the sweater along with the bra over her head, Asha's gaze fell onto Sierra's chest. "You're beautiful," she said.

Sierra bit her lip and looked away. "Thank you," she whispered.

Asha cupped Sierra's face. "Don't be shy about the truth."

Green met brown as Sierra gazed into Asha's eyes. "You make me feel like I'm the only woman in the world."

"In my world," Asha said. "You are."

Sierra took Asha's hand and brought it up to her chest. "Take me to bed."

"I thought you'd never ask."

• • •

Sierra and Asha stumbled through the bedroom door. Both pairs of their jeans had been left behind in a heap in the middle of the hallway. Sierra fell back on the bed with Asha on top of her. Asha nibbled on her neck, tantalized each of her breasts with soft tongue strokes, and kissed down her stomach. She slid onto her knees and hungrily tore off Sierra's bikini underwear. "Please let me taste you."

Sierra widened her legs and felt Asha's hot tongue slip into her sanctuary with needful grace. "Oh my God," she moaned. "You feel so good."

Asha inched her hands up to Sierra's breasts and massaged her hardened nipples between her fingertips. Sierra gripped the comforter and arched back. Each stroke from Asha's tongue stirred a cataclysmic need to give her what she so desired. Sierra wrapped her legs over Asha's shoulders and thrust her hips upward.

A sudden release of orgasmic energy rocked Sierra's entire body and she screamed in ecstasy. Asha continued to drink the nectar flooding into her mouth until Sierra pushed her away. She moved up next to her and pulled Sierra's trembling body into her arms. "Come here, baby," she said softly.

"You're so amazing," Sierra whispered, laying her head on Asha's chest. "That was so intense my toes actually curled."

A smile developed on Asha's face. "Does that mean I get to do it again," she said.

Sierra chuckled. "You have to give me a little time to recover."

Asha kissed the top of Sierra's head. "You have all the time in the world."

Sierra looked up. "Do I have time for this," she said, flicking her tongue slowly against Asha's bottom lip.

Asha's hips jerked. "I think there's time for that," she said breathlessly.

Sierra rolled on top of Asha and pulsed her hips rhythmically into Asha's that were already grinding upward. She took her time exploring the means by which to cause Asha the greatest pleasure. She learned that flicks of her tongue on Asha's nipples caused Asha to squirm, but gentle sucking caused her to moan.

"Don't stop," Asha whispered, pressing Sierra's head down.

Sierra obeyed and worked her way down Asha's incredible body until her chin brushed against soft, damp hair. Nudging Asha's legs apart with gentle kisses on her inner thigh, Sierra slipped her tongue into Asha's oasis and gulped the sweetness pouring out of her lover's strong physique. Asha's body tensed and Sierra felt her try to pull away. Wrapping her arms around Asha's thighs, Sierra held Asha in place and sucked on her clitoris with gentle strokes from her tongue penetrating deeply into Asha every so often.

Feeling Asha's thighs tightened around her head, Sierra responded by sucking even harder and quickening her tongue strokes. Asha placed her hands on Sierra's head and pressed downward. Her body tensed and Sierra looked up just in time to see Asha bury her face into a pillow and bite down on its softness.

Asha lay breathless as Sierra kissed back up her body and laid down beside her. "I'm guessing that was okay."

Asha curled up on her side and nuzzled her head into Sierra's chest. "The best," she said softly. "I'm not sure I could even walk right now."

"That's a good sign," Sierra replied, exhaustion zapping her energy. "Why don't you close your eyes for a few minutes?"

"I think I will," Asha mumbled, already drifting off.

Sierra closed her eyes and let the peace of sleep steal her away.

CHAPTER TWELVE

The morning sun's rays warmed the mini-blinds surrounding the windows and brightened Asha's bedroom. Sierra had been awake for over an hour, listening contently to Asha's rhythmic breathing. She rose up onto her elbows and tried for the fourth time to see the alarm clock that was across the room on the dresser. She fell back on the pillow and sighed in disgust.

"Are you okay?" Asha mumbled, turning over and kissing Sierra's bare shoulder.

"I'm sorry if I woke you," Sierra replied. "I just want to know what time it is."

Asha looked over at the alarm clock. "It's almost eight-thirty."

Sierra rubbed her eyes. "I hate getting old."

Asha leaned over and kissed Sierra on the cheek. "You don't look a day over twenty-five."

A smile tugged at the corners of Sierra's mouth. "Are you trying to get me in bed?"

Asha pulled the covers away from Sierra's breasts. "You're already in my bed," she replied, raising an eyebrow. "And you look better than any twenty-something I've ever seen."

"How many have you've seen?" Sierra teased.

"Enough to know that they suffer in comparison to the woman next to me," Asha replied.

Sierra shook her head. "You're quite a smooth talker when you want to be."

"I have my moments," Asha said, raking her fingers across Sierra's stomach.

Sierra grabbed Asha's hand. "You can't do that right now."

"Why?" Asha said, with a mischievous grin spreading across her face.

"Because I already want you," Sierra replied, pulling the covers back over her hardening nipples.

"Is that a bad thing?" Asha asked. She brought her mouth beside Sierra's ear and traced the outline of it with her tongue.

Sierra's entire body shivered. "I didn't say it was a bad thing."

Asha kissed down Sierra's neck. "Why don't you turn onto your stomach so I can kiss your back?"

"I like the sound of that," Sierra replied. She turned over, laid her head down, and tucked her arms beneath the pillow.

Asha kissed across her back, outlining Sierra's shoulder blades with tantalizing tongue strokes. "Your skin is amazingly soft."

"Thank you," Sierra replied. She felt Asha's hand massaging the lower part of her back. "That feels good."

Asha worked her fingers in a circular motion over each of Sierra's vertebrae. "Still feel good?"

"Uh-huh," Sierra said dreamily.

Asha glided her hand over Sierra's butt a few times. Her fingers pressed downward, massaging the muscles evenly. "How's this feel?"

"Heavenly," Sierra replied. Her hips rotated subtly as she enjoyed Asha's strong fingers.

Asha placed one of her knees between Sierra's legs and moved her hips forward suggestively. She slowly slid her hand down between Sierra's thighs. "You're so wet."

Sierra moved her legs further apart. "Make me wetter," she whispered.

Asha didn't need additional coaxing. She slipped her fingers past the protective gates of Sierra's labia and penetrated deep into her inner sanctum.

Sierra's sexual energy sailed up the climatic ladder as Asha pulsated her fingers against the rungs of her G-spot. "Harder," she gasped.

Asha thrust her hips and pressed her breasts firmly into Sierra's back. "Come on baby," she said, sweat pouring down her face. "I want to feel you explode."

Sierra felt the walls of resistance disintegrate as the wrecking ball of orgasmic release thundered into it. "Oh, my God!" she screamed into the pillow.

Asha eased her fingers from Sierra and laid down beside her. "Was that okay?"

Sierra snuggled up into Asha's arms. "You couldn't tell?"

Asha grinned. "I could tell."

"Good," Sierra said. "Because I sure didn't know what I could possibly say to convince you otherwise."

Asha kissed Sierra on the forehead. "Why don't you try to close your eyes for a little while?"

"What are you going to do?" Sierra said dreamily.

"Hold you," Asha said. "I just want to hold you."

• • •

Sierra shuffled into Asha's kitchen, wearing a robe that Asha had left out for her. "Good morning," she said, covering her mouth as she yawned.

"Well, good morning, sleepyhead," Asha replied, covering the plate of sizzling bacon with a paper towel. She walked over and wrapped her arms loosely around Sierra's waist. "I was hoping the smell of a home-cooked breakfast might wake you from your slumber."

"It smells terrific," Sierra said, inhaling deeply. "I'm starving."

Asha kissed Sierra on the lips. "I wasn't sure what you liked, so I fixed a little bit of everything."

Sierra rubbed her nose against Asha's. "You didn't have to do that."

"I know," Asha said. "I wanted to."

"You're too much," Sierra said. "Remind me why you're not in a long-term relationship with someone?"

Asha released her embrace on Sierra and shrugged her shoulders. "You don't live on the West Coast," she said. "My story might different if that were the case."

Sierra held Asha's gaze. "I think my story might be different as well if that was indeed the scenario."

Asha nodded before glancing over at the plate of bacon. "Why don't you have a seat at the table? I'll start bringing out the various dishes that our appetites can dive into."

"Are you sure that there's nothing that I can help with?" Sierra said, taking Asha's hand.

"I'm sure, baby," Asha replied.

Sierra's heart pole-vaulted over an imaginary cloud. "I want you to know I love when you call me that," she said, smiling shyly.

Asha brought Sierra's hand up to her lips. "I love calling you that. Now, get your cute butt out to the table." She flipped Sierra lightly with a towel.

"I'm going. I'm going," Sierra huffed playfully. "You'd think we were married."

Asha's eyebrows raised, but she didn't say anything. Sierra hurried into the dining room and slapped herself in the forehead. *That was not one of my brightest moments,* she thought. She collapsed into one of the pillow-topped wooden chairs and clasped her hands together in front of her.

Asha came out carrying two large plates and placed them in the center of the table. "Are you okay?" she asked, giving Sierra a warm smile. "You look a little flushed."

"I'm fine," Sierra replied. She wiped the perspiration that had developed on her palms onto the soft, cottony material of the robe. "I'm still working on waking up."

"You're a night owl, aren't you?" Asha said, resting a large serving spoon on the edge of the platter that contained scrambled eggs.

"You could say that," Sierra said, scooting her chair closer to the table. She looked at the other dish set next to the scrambled eggs and licked her lips. "Are those homemade hash browns?"

"Yes," Asha replied. "I'm guessing that's a good thing."

"You have no idea," Sierra exclaimed. "You'd better hurry. I can't promise those will be here when you get back."

"Well, try not to eat the plate," Asha said, chuckling.

"What else did you fix?" Sierra asked. Her eyes were wide with expectation.

"Oh, you know, the usual," Asha teased. "I have the bacon, pancakes, and biscuits and gravy still to bring out."

"You're going to make me fat," Sierra said, patting her belly.

"I'm sure we'll figure out a way to work off some of those calories," Asha said, wiggling her eyebrows.

Sierra looked up and down Asha's body. "Don't tease."

"Who said I was teasing?" Asha said. "We have all afternoon until six o'clock tonight when we're expected at Dee's."

"Hmm," Sierra said. "I guess we should get to eating."

A mischievous grin spread across Asha's face. "That's the idea."

• • •

Sierra lay spread-eagle on top of the bare mattress with the fitted sheet covering her in the middle of Asha's bed. The top sheet was in a giant ball on the floor and the bottom of the comforter now hung off the right-side. One pillow had somehow managed to make it halfway across the room, but she hadn't the energy to rescue it. "I can't move," she said, staring up at the ceiling. "You're going to have to shower without me."

"Where's the fun in that?" Asha said, peeking out from the master bathroom.

Sierra propped herself up onto her elbows. "You have a point." She tossed the sheet aside and sat up slowly. "You do realize that you're a very wicked woman."

Asha stepped out from behind the doorway and leaned against the frame. "Why's that?"

Sierra's mouth went dry as she stared at Asha's beautiful, naked body. "You have an amazing mind, a great sense of humor, a kind soul, and a body that looks like it was carved out of the most expensive marble by the gods. How can I possibly survive dinner with your grandmother and sister when I know I'll be dripping wet all evening?"

"Do you really think the sole reason we're showering is to get cleaned up for dinner?" Asha said, wiggling her finger at Sierra with a come-hither look.

Sierra made her way over to Asha. "Why else would we be showering?"

Asha brought her mouth next to Sierra's ear. "Because I want to fuck you as hot water rains down on top of us."

Sierra's knees almost buckled. "I'm so there," she said breathlessly. "But only on one condition."

Asha tilted Sierra's chin slightly upward. "And what would that be?"

Sierra took a deep, quivering breath. "I get to fuck you at the same time."

Asha grabbed Sierra's hand and led her into the shower. They pressed their breasts into one another's as the warm water rained down onto them. Asha dipped her head into the water and brushed the dark locks away from her face. Sierra kissed her throat and nibbled on her earlobe. She placed her hands on Asha's hips and rocked her own hips into them. She was dripping wet and the need for release was building exponentially.

Asha pulled her head out from beneath the shower nozzle and gazed into desire-filled green eyes. "I want you." She grabbed Sierra tightly and slipped her hand between her thighs.

For a second, Sierra's thoughts were swept away by the flurry of passion bestowed upon her. Asha pushed her against the cool tiled wall and thrust her hips passionately. She pulled her fingers in and out of Sierra's sanctuary, all while stroking Sierra's clit with her thumb. Sierra contemplated succumbing to Asha's lust for her to climax, but she resisted. She brought her hand between Asha's thighs and used the abundant, naturally created lubricant to enter Asha's body.

Their breaths quickened and their hips collided, splattering the water on their stomachs. Sierra felt Asha's muscles tightened around her fingers as her own sexual release teetered on the brink of an orgasmic canyon. "I'm so close," she gasped.

Asha moaned and closed her eyes. "Oh, baby, I'm coming!"

They grasped onto one another to keep from crumpling as their bodies trembled like leaves from the thunder of their simultaneous orgasms. Sierra leaned back against the wall and braced her foot against the edge of the tub to keep from falling on top of Asha. "I can barely stand," she said softly.

"I can't even feel my legs," Asha replied.

"Gosh, is that a good sign," Sierra chuckled nervously.

"It's a great sign," Asha whispered, her eyes softening as she stared into Sierra's.

Sierra held Asha's gaze, unable to speak as she contemplated the subtle difference in the radiant brown pools. *Could it be love,* she thought, daring to hope.

Asha looked away. "We should probably finish showering before the water turns ice-cold."

Sierra swallowed the lump of possibility and grabbed the soap from the side of the tub. "I'll be quick."

Asha took the soap from Sierra's hand. "I'll be slow," she said. She rubbed the soap between her hands, creating a rich lather. "Now turn around so I can start with your back."

Sierra turned around and closed her eyes as Asha moved the soap in rhythmic circles across her back. *If this is a dream,* she thought. *I hope I never wake up.*

• • •

The exterior of Dee's house was built to reflect the Queen Anne Style of architecture with pastel yellow paint and angled bay windows. The interior was a blend of new and old. There was at least one grandfather clock on each of the three floors. The top floor had been converted into a fully equipped apartment for Devi, with its own entrance from a separate staircase accessed through the back of the house. The second floor had a room dedicated to Dee's knitting and on the opposite side, her expansive master bedroom with a walk-in closet the size of a small den. The adjoining master bathroom had dual sinks, a clawfoot tub and a glass shower.

Sierra turned in a circle and studied the custom-made cherry wood cabinetry in the kitchen. "Wow, what contracting outfit did such exquisite work?"

Asha tossed the hand towel she had used to dry off the dishes from dinner onto the counter. "Believe it or not, my grandfather built them. He also designed and built the staircase in the lodge."

Sierra walked over and wrapped her arms around Asha's neck. "Does anyone in your family not exceed expectation?"

"Where would be the fun in that?" Asha chuckled, kissing Sierra on the nose. "So are you ready to have a little more fun?"

"Somehow I don't believe you're referring to throwing me against the counter and having your way with me," Sierra said.

"I wish," Asha said, taking Sierra by the hand and leading her toward the living room. "Remember, they're harmless."

Sierra shook her head and followed Asha into the living room. "That's what you keep telling me," she whispered.

Devi looked up from her latest issue of *Outside Magazine* and immediately flipped it closed. She set it on the table beside the plush recliner she was kicking back in and smiled warmly as Sierra. "Thanks for washing the dishes. It was nice to be able to sit back and relax after all that food."

Sierra sat down next to Asha on the loveseat. "It was my pleasure after such a scrumptious meal."

"I'm so glad you liked it, dear," Dee said. She sat with her feet curled up on the couch and an afghan covering her legs. "There's something about having a warm slice of honey ham this time of year that's really fitting."

"My mother felt the same way," Sierra said, keeping her smile from faltering.

"Asha told me your mother passed away last year," Dee replied. "I'm so sorry to hear that. I'm sure you miss her something terrible."

"I do," Sierra said.

"Are you close to your father?" Dee said, pulling the afghan up over her arms.

"Not really," Sierra replied. "We see happiness differently."

"What does that mean?" Devi asked, leaning forward with interest.

"My parents divorced when I was seventeen," Sierra replied. "I'd always had a good relationship with my father until I brought my first girlfriend by to meet him. He totally flipped out. He was of the opinion that it wouldn't look so good on him to have a gay daughter."

"Oh, brother," Devi said, rolling her eyes. "Why does everyone consume themselves with what other people will think of them?"

"It's human nature," Asha said. "No one wants to be judged."

"And yet, Sierra's father judged her," Dee interjected.

"It's a vicious cycle," Sierra replied. "That's why I try to always be open-minded. I believe everyone has the right to be happy."

"I couldn't agree more," Dee said, offering a crooked smile. "My sweet Bill had the same opinion. He once said there was already too much fighting in the name of humanity to wage war against another human being for his or her sexual orientation, ethnicity or social status."

"I remember that speech," Devi laughed. "He went on and on about it over dinner. Then he looked over at Asha, who wasn't really saying anything, and was like 'Do you have anything to add?'"

Asha's lips parted into a glowing smile. "I came out that night."

"That was really sweet," Sierra said, squeezing Asha's hand. "I'm sure that was a huge load off your shoulders."

"Her shoulders?" Devi interjected with feigned exaggeration. "I was the one having to cover for her as she went out each night to go see her girlfriend."

Asha stuck her tongue out at Devi. "At least I didn't get caught."

Devi shook her head in remembrance. "I got so busted that night."

"You sure did," Asha said, laughing. "Of course, it didn't help that you were totally inebriated."

"Don't leave us in the dark, you two," Dee said, winking at Sierra. "Bill never did tell me the whole story. He kept being overwhelmed by fits of laughter every time he tried."

"Do you want to tell it?" Asha asked. "Or do you even remember?"

Devi took a sip of her soda. "I do, but you go ahead."

"You're such a fibber," Asha said, pressing her lips together to keep from laughing. "The thing was I told Grandpa Bill that Devi was going over to a friend's house to practice for their cheerleading squad and would probably stay the night."

"I apparently decided to sneak in around one in the morning, completely blitzed," Devi said, with a shrug.

"Sneaked in?" Asha said, raising an eyebrow. "You walked in through the screen door and started screaming you were covered in spider webs."

"I don't understand," Sierra said, looking back and forth between them.

"She literally walked *through* the screen door," Asha replied. "I'd left the back door ajar just in case she decided to come home. I knew she was going to a friend's birthday party and there was no parental supervision. I told her to crash there if she ended up drinking but she was quite adamant that she didn't even like the taste of beer."

"How was I to know that they would have peach schnapps?" Devi said innocently. "I thought I was drinking liquid candy."

"Anyway," Asha said. "Devi decides the party is getting out of hand after a large vase gets knocked off a table and shatters on the ground."

"And it's a good thing I left," Devi said. "The police were called about an hour later and half the partiers were arrested."

"Bill never told me that!" Dee said. "No wonder he was so evasive."

Devi blushed.

"Go on, Asha," Dee said with keen interest.

"Devi, being the self-proclaimed expert in sneaking in, walks through the screen door in a drunken stupor," Asha continued. "Luckily, it didn't have any glass or wood to impede her entry. She totally freaks out, thinking some mutant spider has invaded our home, and starts flailing around, trying to get the torn pieces of screen off her body. I rush down the stairs to see her stop, drop and roll on the floor."

"You've got to be kidding," Sierra said, laughing along with Dee. "What did you do?"

"I was terrified," Asha replied. "I had no idea what was wrong with her. Bill came out of the garage where he'd been doing some woodworking, with his face twisted in absolute panic. When we finally understood what she was screaming about and noticed the screen door, we both started laughing."

"See how compassionate your girlfriend is?" Devi said, looking at Sierra.

Sierra leaned into Asha. "She's not so bad."

"Thank you," Asha said, kissing Sierra on the cheek. "And I was very compassionate, thank you very much."

"All right," Dee said with an amused grin. "What happened next?"

"We get her calmed down and reassure her that there are no spiders crawling on her," Asha said. "Grandpa Bill and I can smell the alcohol on her breath and just as we're picking her up to take her to bed, she throws up all over him."

Dee hugged her stomach as she busted out in laughter. "No wonder he was doing laundry when I woke up the next day!"

They all laughed.

"And now you know why I wasn't allowed to go out for a month," Devi said.

"Oh my God," Sierra said, tears from laughter streaming down her face. "I'm so sorry, Devi, but that story is hysterical."

"It's okay," Devi said. "It was a sore subject with me for a while. I felt like someone had hit me with a baseball bat the next morning. Then, when I hazily remembered what happened, I wished someone had."

"Live and learn," Asha said. "I think we've all had experiences like that."

"I second that," Sierra said, with a knowing smile.

"Would anyone like some coffee or tea?" Dee said, pushing the afghan off her legs.

"No thanks,' Asha replied. "Sierra and I should probably get going."

"Stay a little while longer," Dee said, pleading with her eyes. "I haven't even had a chance to ask Sierra about her writing."

"You're a writer?" Asha said, glancing over at Sierra.

"Yes," Sierra replied.

"Did I let the cat out of the bag?" Dee said apologetically.

"Not at all," Sierra said, staring into Asha's eyes. "I've been working on something for you for Christmas. I didn't say anything because I didn't want you to wonder why I wasn't showing it to you."

"You're so sweet," Asha said, hugging Sierra. "When do I get it?"

"When it gets finished," Sierra said.

"Do you write articles too?" Devi asked, glancing at the *Outside Magazine* on the end table.

"I used to," Sierra said. "Now, I mainly write novels."

"You're kidding!" Asha said. "Where can I find your work?"

"You already have some of my works on your bookshelf," Sierra said.

"I do?" Asha said, tapping her finger against her temple. "Can you give me a hint?"

Sierra shook her head. "Nope, you'll have to wait."

"That's so not fair," Asha said, pouting her lips.

"Maybe it'll give her surprise away if she tells you," Devi said thoughtfully.

Asha contemplated that statement for a moment. "Okay, I'll wait."

"Good," Dee said. "Since that's settled, would anyone like to take me up on my earlier offer?"

"I'd love some coffee," Sierra said.

"Me, too," Asha said.

"Would you like some help?" Sierra said, getting up.

"That's okay, dear," Dee said. "You enjoy a little peace and quiet with Asha. Devi and I will be back in a few minutes."

Devi looked up in surprise before following Dee into the kitchen. As soon as they were out of earshot, Sierra turned to Asha. "I'm sorry I didn't mention beforehand what I did for a living."

"Don't worry, baby," Asha said, pulling Sierra close. "You have your reasons and I totally respect that. Of course, I'm dying to know what this secret project is."

Sierra pressed her lips to Asha's. "Thank you for being so understanding. It means a lot to me."

"I hope I do, too," Asha said, holding Sierra's gaze.

"You do," Sierra replied. *More than you know.*

CHAPTER THIRTEEN

Sierra unlocked the door to her suite and tossed her laptop bag inside. "I had a great time at Dee's," she said, turning to Asha. "In fact, the last twenty-four hours have been perfect."

"Yes, it has. I'm sorry I have to work tonight," Asha said. "I really wanted to crawl into bed and keep you up all night."

"I would have loved that," Sierra replied, taking Asha's hand and pulling her into the room. "But you were right making Dee stay home. She looked way too tired to go in on such short notice."

"Well, the flu has hit not only our staff hard, but a lot of the other businesses as well," Asha replied. "I'll be surprised if I don't end up working until eight o'clock tomorrow morning."

Sierra sat down on the edge of the bed and slipped off her boots. "If that happens, let's go shopping later on this week instead."

"No way, baby," Asha said, kneeling down in front of her. "I have to see you tomorrow."

"Will you miss me desperately otherwise?" Sierra said, running her fingertip around Asha's mouth.

"What do you think?" Asha replied.

"I think you should kiss me," Sierra said.

Asha brought her lips to Sierra's. Passion flared as though their kisses were the catalyst for the nightly display of fireworks at Disney. Sierra lay back and pulled Asha on top of her. "I'm so horny," she whispered.

"Me, too," Asha replied. "I'll make it up to you tomorrow night if you'd like to stay over after we go shopping."

"You have a deal," Sierra said.

"Good," Asha said. She rolled off the bed and onto her feet. "I should probably get going before all hell breaks loose."

"Okay," Sierra replied, following Asha over to the door. "Try not to work too hard."

"Don't worry," Asha said, kissing Sierra. "I'll have plenty of energy for tomorrow."

"You'd better," Sierra said, slapping Asha on the butt.

"Don't get me all excited like that," Asha said, grabbing Sierra and pulling her close. "I'm having a hard enough time trying to resist ripping off your clothes."

"Ooh," Sierra said, running her finger down between Asha's breasts. "I guess I shouldn't tell you that I'll be sleeping naked, then."

"That's just cruel and unusual punishment," Asha said, reaching for the door.

"No, its truthful," Sierra replied.

Asha opened the door and stepped into the hallway shaking her head. "I'll be by around nine o'clock, so we can grab some breakfast before tackling the last-minute holiday shopping rush."

"Sounds good," Sierra said. "Now get going before I drag you back over to the bed and take advantage of you."

Asha took Sierra's hand and kissed the top of it. "Until tomorrow, then," she said softly.

Sierra watched expectantly as Asha strolled down the hallway. She'd almost given up when Asha turned around and blew her a kiss. Reaching out and grasping the invisible kiss, Sierra returned one of her own. Asha jumped up into the air, pretending to barely catch it. She placed the wind-blown kiss on her lips and wiped her hand across her brow. "That was a close one," she shouted.

"It's a good thing you didn't miss," Sierra said loudly. "It would have been floating out there for any random stranger to grab."

"I think not," Asha replied. "It has my name on it."

"You bet it does," Sierra said. She waved good-bye, closed the door and locked it. She hurried over to the dresser and pulled out a comfortable pair of sweatpants and a white T-shirt. Her fingers itched to write and her mind was swarming with different directions in which to take the next chapter of her novel. *I've got all night*, she thought gleefully. *And I've got Asha all to myself the next night.*

• • •

Sierra paced across the suite, waiting to hear a soft knock at the door. She was starting to worry. It had been over an hour since Asha had called to say she was running a few minutes behind schedule. Gusting winds and blinding snow had wreaked havoc during the early morning hours. Asha had been stuck behind the front desk until five-thirty in the morning when Dee was finally able to make it in. The weather didn't improve with daybreak and neither did the staff. Asha helped out for an additional two hours until Jack got there to relieve her.

Sierra peeked through the curtains and noticed that none of the ski runs appeared to be open. The two- to three-person chairlifts were being battered by the wind rocking them from side to side as though they were boats in a storm battling twenty-foot high swells. Sierra knew a lot of the guests were hard-core winter enthusiasts, so their desertion from the sport, even for one day, was a pretty significant sign that traveling outdoors was ill-advised. She wondered if it would be better for Asha to stay home and get some rest. Reluctantly, she walked over to the phone and dialed Asha's number.

"Hello?"

Sierra tried to speak, but her words were choked off. Her heart felt like it had been ripped from her chest and stomped into the ground mercilessly.

"Hello?"

Tears spilled down Sierra's cheeks. "Is Asha there?"

"She's in the shower, Sierra," Vivian replied. "She needed to...freshen up. I'll see if she wants to take the call."

Sierra dropped the receiver and ran to the bathroom. She fell onto her knees and hung her head over the toilet. Her mouth watered uncontrollably as her body tried to recover from the train of betrayal that had blindsided her. *This can't be happening,* she thought.

Seconds drifted into long, agonizing minutes. Sierra wasn't sure how long she had been in the bathroom when she heard a knock on the door. Dragging herself off the floor, she glanced at her appearance in the mirror. She was hideous. The green in her eyes no longer sparkled as though her inner light had been washed away by the tears. Red splotches covered her face and her hair was drenched in sweat from her unsuccessful attempts to be sick.

Sierra peered through the peephole and choked back sobs as Asha pounded her hand against the door even louder. "Sierra, let me in!"

"Leave me alone," Sierra cried out. "Please just go away!"

"Please, Sierra, talk to me," Asha replied.

"Don't you have someone else that you should be comforting right now?" Sierra hissed.

"Let me explain," Asha pleaded. "It isn't at all what you think."

Sierra ripped open the door. "How in God's name would you know what I'm thinking?" she shrieked.

Asha didn't move. "You think I slept with Vivian, but there's nothing further from the truth."

"It doesn't matter anymore," Sierra said dejectedly. "I just need you to leave me alone."

Asha grabbed Sierra's hand to keep her from closing the door. "Let me go," Sierra warned.

Asha gently pushed Sierra back into the room and closed the door behind them. "I never want to let you go," she whispered. "I swear to you that nothing happened."

Sierra crossed her arms in front of her chest. "How can you possibly explain Vivian answering your phone then?"

"Devi had stopped by to drop off a couple things right before I got into the shower," Asha replied. "I was in the shower when Vivian showed up unannounced."

"I don't understand," Sierra said. "Why did Vivian even think she was welcome to come by your house?"

"That I don't know," Asha replied. "But I do know she told Devi she needed to talk with me for a few minutes in private."

"So nothing happened?" Sierra said, her aggressiveness easing slightly.

"No," Asha said emphatically. "After Devi came in to the bathroom to tell me that Vivian was there, she went back out to the living room. That's when she overheard what Vivian said to you on the phone."

"You expect be to believe that?" Sierra said, collapsing on the bed.

"I do," Asha said, sitting down next to her. "You can call Devi right now and ask her if you want."

Sierra closed her eyes and banished her demons of insecurity. "No, I believe you."

Asha wrapped her arms around Sierra. "I would never do something as foolhardy as cheating on you. I know that Vivian would love for me to, but all I want is you."

Sierra laid her head against Asha's shoulder. "I'm sorry I made such a horrific assumption."

Asha tilted Sierra's chin upward and stared into her eyes. "It's okay," she said softly. "Had the situation been reversed, I might have thought the same thing."

"I highly doubt that," Sierra said. "You're one of the most level-headed people I know."

"Well, I've had a lot of practice," Asha said. "Now, enough about this morning, are you still up for some breakfast and a little shopping?"

"Is anything open?" Sierra said.

"This is Vail, baby," Asha replied. "People own businesses here to make money — a lot of it. It would take a record-breaking snowstorm to shut this place down."

Sierra touched the puffiness beneath her eyes. "But I must look terrible."

"Nonsense," Asha said.

"Aren't my eyes all swollen and red?" Sierra replied.

"Nothing a few drops of Visine and a little love can't fix," Asha said. "Come on, let's get you a cold washcloth."

• • •

If it hadn't been obvious before that Christmas was a little less than a week and a day away, the crowds that descended upon the exquisite boutiques, art galleries and other fashionable shops would have been a dead giveaway. Holiday drivers waited like vultures for parking spaces. They showed their good cheer with colorful words when somebody whipped in front of them and took what they believed was their spot. Last-minute shoppers shuffled from store to store searching for the perfect present to give a loved one at any cost. It didn't matter who they bumped into or almost knocked down as long as they accomplished their mission of making the experience as quick as possible.

Sierra held onto Asha's arm as they hurried across the street to grab a cup of coffee. "I can't believe all these people are out in this. When I looked out this morning, it felt like one of those late-night movies where the protagonist wakes up and discovers everyone has died from a mysterious plague. Now look at it. It's a bustling little town."

Asha held open the door to the coffee shop. "Everything can change given the right motivation," she said.

Sierra hurried into the coffee shop and welcomed the warmth. "It's freezing out there," she said, rubbing her hands vigorously over her upper arms.

"Go grab that table over there," Asha said. "I'll get us some coffee."

"That works," Sierra replied. She hurried over and sat down at the table furthest from the entryway door.

Asha paid for the two cups of coffee and took the seat across from Sierra. "I brought cream and sugar just in case."

Sierra took a careful sip. "I'm so glad you did," she said, rolling her tongue around her mouth and trying to eliminate the taste from it. "It's so strong, I'll be lucky if I don't have chest hair tomorrow."

"We definitely don't want that," Asha said, handing the tiny sealed cups of cream to Sierra. "I happen to like your breasts just the way they are."

"That's good to know," Sierra said, peeling back one of the seals.

Asha leaned back in her chair. "So, are you ever going to tell me which of your books is on my shelf?"

Sierra smiled behind her coffee cup. "Nope."

"Well, can you tell me at least what genre it falls under?" Asha persisted.

Sierra cocked her head to the side. "What genre do you think I write under?"

Asha took a sip of coffee, then another. An ornery smile graced her lips. "Well, if I was a betting girl, I'd guess some sort of lesbian novel."

Sierra set her coffee cup on the table. "Now, what would give you that idea?" she said playfully.

Asha's eyebrow shot up. "I have insider's information, remember?"

"Oh, yeah," Sierra said. "So what type of lesbian books do you think I write?"

Asha leaned forward. "Explicit sex manuals," she whispered.

"You have to be joking!" Sierra said, feeling her cheeks get hot. "I've never been accused of that before."

"I thought that might get a rise out of you," Asha said, a dazzling, white smile spreading across her face.

"You're out of control," Sierra replied. "Do you know that?"

"I thought you liked when I got out of control," Asha said, reaching out and taking Sierra's hand.

Sierra looked away as Asha's bedroom eyes penetrated her soul. "I'll have to get back to you on that."

"That isn't fair," Asha said, whining slightly.

Sierra enjoyed another sip of coffee. "Hmm. Maybe I do like when you're out of control."

"I'm going to show you out of control," Asha said, her warning filled with desire. "I hope you know what you're getting into later tonight."

"I hope it's you," Sierra replied.

A subtle red hue spread across Asha's cheeks.

"Did I embarrass you?" Sierra teased, squeezing Asha's hand.

"I wasn't expecting that," Asha said with a shy grin.

"Not even from the woman you accused of writing explicit sex manuals?" Sierra asked, trying not to smile.

Asha finished her coffee and pushed her chair back. She walked around the table and put her mouth next to Sierra's ear. "I thought maybe the writer of such a book would like help in discovering new and different positions for the next explicit sex manual in the series."

Sierra's mouth went dry. "I think she'd be very interested."

"Then we'd better get back to shopping," Asha replied.

"Come to the bathroom with me first," Sierra said, gulping down the last of her coffee. "I thought you might want to show me one of those standing positions first."

Asha's mouth dropped open. "Are you serious?"

Sierra stood up and looked toward where the single occupancy bathrooms were located. "There's no line," she said, smiling seductively.

"You are serious," Asha said, following after her.

Sierra pushed open the bathroom door and held it ajar with her foot. "Are you coming in or will I have to just pretend you're here?"

Asha walked into the bathroom and locked the door. She grabbed hold of Sierra's belt loops and pulled their hips into one another's. "Now what?"

Sierra reached down and undid the top button of Asha's jeans. She slowly lowered the zipper and slipped her hand beneath

Asha's silk bikini underwear. Her fingers were immediately greeted with a warm, wet welcome. "My God," she said. "You are so sexy."

Asha moaned quietly as Sierra slid her fingers deep inside her. "You feel so good," she gasped quietly. "Please don't stop."

Sierra moved her fingers in powerful, thrusting strokes. She could feel Asha's muscles tensing around her fingers. "Come on, baby," she said. "Let me feel you explode all over my hand."

Asha threw her head back and pumped her hips forward rapidly. "I'm coming," she whispered urgently. Her body shuddered violently and flooded Sierra's hand with sweet nectar.

Sierra removed her fingers and held onto Asha's trembling body. "Was that okay?" she said.

"How do you expect me to walk after that?" Asha said, struggling to stand on her own.

"Are you complaining?" Sierra teased, taking a step back.

"Hell, no," Asha said, zipping up her jeans.

"Good," Sierra replied, brushing her lips against Asha's. "Because my plan for tonight is to rock your world even harder."

"Let's get to shopping, then," Asha said with renewed energy.

"I thought you might see it that way," Sierra said, unlocking the bathroom door.

"I'll see it any way you want me to if that's the end result," Asha replied, following Sierra back into the coffee shop.

"I'll keep that in mind," Sierra said, zipping up her jacket. "Do you want to grab any more coffee before we head out?"

Asha flipped up the collar of her coat. "I'm on fire the way it is."

Sierra headed out the door and stepped onto the sidewalk. "So, where to now?"

Asha wrapped her arms around Sierra's waist. "Let's just take our time and explore as many shops as possible. I'd like to get a feel for the things you like and dislike. Besides, rushing will only make tomorrow morning come too quickly."

And bring me one day closer to having to leave, Sierra thought. She forced the impact of that realization to the back of her mind before her heart had the chance to intercept and channel her pain through an onslaught of tears.

• • •

Sierra accepted the towel that Asha handed her and stepped out of the shower. "My God," she said, drying off her back. "It feels so good to be clean."

Asha nodded her head in agreement as she finished brushing her teeth. "You know what I really love?"

Sierra swallowed hard. *Please be me,* she thought.

"I love climbing into a fresh set of sheets after showering."

"Me, too," Sierra replied, effectively concealing her disappointment by kissing Asha on the shoulder. "Would you like to do that tonight?"

"Do you mean change the sheets?" Asha said, before rinsing her mouth with water.

"Yes," Sierra said, wrapping the towel around her body.

"Sure, I'll go get a set," Asha replied.

Sierra walked over to Asha's bed and peeled off the sheets. A part of her wanted to bag them up and take them home with her. Her feelings for Asha were undeniable and there was no going back. She knew she would miss Asha and what might have been had they lived closer together.

"What do you think?" Asha said, returning to the room and holding up a set of sheets with penguins on them.

"They're so cute," Sierra replied. "I love it!"

Asha tossed Sierra the top corner of the fitted sheet and within seconds the entire bed was remade. Sierra dropped her towel onto the floor, slid between the sheets and wiggled her butt. "It feels so good."

"You are so sexy," Asha said, flipping off the light. She carefully made her way back over to the bed. "I had such a great time today."

"Me, too," Sierra said, pulling the covers back for Asha.

Asha lay down and turned onto her side. "I can't believe the month is almost over."

"Me either," Sierra said. "It's gone by way too quickly."

"Yes, it has," Asha said. She reached out and caressed the side of Sierra's face. "I miss you more every day."

"I miss you more every day, too," Sierra said, her eyes brimming with tears.

"I wish I could stop time," Asha said, scooting a little closer to Sierra.

"If only that was possible," Sierra said. She placed her hand on Asha's side and enjoyed the silky smoothness of her bare skin.

"Tonight," Asha said, her voice trembling slightly, "could I just hold you?"

"Absolutely," Sierra said, curling up in Asha's arms. "Will this work?"

"Yeah," Asha said. "This is perfect."

"I'm glad you think so," Sierra replied.

"I'd like to fall asleep like this every night," Asha whispered, fighting to stay awake.

"I'd like that, too," Sierra said. "Now get some sleep. You have to be exhausted."

"I am," Asha said. "I hope this week is a little less hectic."

"Wouldn't that be nice?" Sierra said.

"It sure would be," Asha replied. "I'll be absolutely miserable if I don't get to see you at least once a day."

"You know my room number, sweetheart," Sierra said, squeezing Asha's waist. "I'll even give you the extra keycard so you can come in and sleep for a few hours if you work through the night again."

"I'm not sure I'll want to sleep," Asha replied.

"Well, I'm not sure I'll let you," Sierra said. "Now close your eyes, baby. We both have a very long week in front of us."

CHAPTER FOURTEEN

Sierra reread her email to Dana before attaching the rough draft of her novel. She hovered the arrow over the send icon, took a deep breath and clicked it. The ring of the telephone interrupted her thoughts about what Dana would think of her first attempt at writing a love story, but not her worry. She hurried over to the nightstand and scooped up the receiver. "Hello?"

"Hi, beautiful," Asha said. "How's my girl?"

"I'm doing wonderful," Sierra said. "How's your day?"

"I'm so happy it's Friday," Asha replied. "I can't wait until six o'clock. We'll actually be able to have a nice, relaxing evening- just the two of us."

"That'll be a welcome change to the past few nights," Sierra said, sitting down on the bed.

"I know," Asha said. "I'm sorry about not being able to see you."

"It's okay," Sierra replied. "Were you able to get Christmas day off with all the overtime you've put in?"

"What do you think?" Asha said, her smile evident her tone.

"I think I'm one lucky girl," Sierra said.

"Sorry, babe," Asha said. "We'll have to keep this short. A guest just blew through the front door looking mad as hell. You're still going shopping with Devi today, right?"

"Yeah," Sierra said. "I'm meeting her in the lobby around eleven."

"Maybe you can make it a few minutes earlier?" Asha replied, a little more professional sounding.

"I love when you talk to me in your work voice," Sierra said. "It's sexy."

"Thank you, ma'am," Asha said.

"Ooh, I could torture you with explicit sex talk right now, couldn't I?" Sierra teased.

"That isn't necessary," Asha said. "We'll be discussing that in greater detail later."

"I like the sound of that," Sierra said. "I'll see you at about ten minutes till eleven. I miss you."

"Likewise," Asha replied.

Sierra hung up the phone and walked back over to the computer. She ejected the flash drive and set it next to her wallet on the dresser. *I definitely can't forget that,* she thought.

• • •

Sierra peeked into the storage room behind the registration desk and saw Asha busily arranging snow boots according to size in ascending order. "Hi, sexy," she said softly.

Asha turned around as an enormous grin spread across her face. "You're early," she exclaimed.

"I couldn't wait to see you," Sierra replied. "I hope you don't mind."

"Of course not," Asha said, stepping over a pile of snow boots. She pulled Sierra into her arms and kissed her passionately. "You're the best sight for these tired eyes."

Sierra used her foot to kick the door closed. "I have another sight for those eyes," she said, taking off her jacket.

Asha arched an eyebrow. "And what would that be?"

"Something I bought this week on a whim," Sierra said, seductively unbuttoning her blouse and letting it slip from her shoulders onto the floor.

Asha stared at the red bra with see-through lace that crossed Sierra's nipples and complemented her ivory skin. "You look stunning."

Sierra wrapped her arms around Asha's neck. "There's more," she said, glancing down. "And it's all see-through."

Asha slipped her fingertips underneath each of the red bra straps and pulled them off Sierra's shoulders. "I'm not sure I can wait until tonight." She peeled the material away from Sierra's breast and pushed her back against the door.

"Then don't wait," Sierra replied. "Take me right now."

Asha unzipped Sierra's jeans and slid them from her hips. "My God," she said, staring at the red pair of see-through thong underwear.

"I guess you like what you see," Sierra said, stepping out of the jeans that were now down around her ankles.

"That's an understatement," Asha said, slipping her hand into the satiny material. "You're so wet."

"I've been thinking about you all day and night for the past seventy-two hours," Sierra replied. "How else would I be?"

Asha slipped her fingers deep into Sierra. "It's been torturous knowing you were only a few floors above me and sleeping naked. All I wanted was to sneak into your room and have you wake with me between your legs."

"I would have loved that," Sierra gasped, her feet starting to lift off the floor from the power of Asha's thrusting hips.

Asha wrapped her lips around one of Sierra's nipples and stroked it with her tongue. Sierra tilted her head back and clenched her teeth. She wrapped one of her legs around Asha's waist. "I need more," she pleaded.

Asha slipped another finger deep inside Sierra. "How does that feel?"

Sierra grabbed Asha by the back of the hair. "I need you to take me harder," she gasped. "I want to know who I belong to."

Asha slammed her hips into Sierra's and drove her fingers even deeper. She bit down on Sierra's nipple and traced its circumference with her tongue. "You belong to me," she said.

Sierra's back thumped against the door. "You feel so good," she whispered.

"How good?" Asha said.

Sierra jerked her hips back and forth passionately. "Incredibly good."

"The best ever?" Asha said, slowing her hips.

"Yes," Sierra said, clawing at Asha's back. "So please don't stop."

Asha picked up her rhythm. "Don't worry, baby. I have no plans on stopping."

Sierra fell forward, digging her nails into Asha's back. "Oh, baby," she cried, trying to keep her voice low. "I'm coming. Don't stop, I'm coming!"

"Asha?" Devi called through the door. "Are you in there?"

"Uh, I'll be out in just a second," Asha said, looking at Sierra in disbelief. "Sierra is helping me with some equipment."

"Can I help?" Devi replied.

"Oh, that's okay," Asha said, removing her fingers slowly from within Sierra. "The door's blocked at the moment."

"Maybe I can squeeze through," Devi said, trying the door handle.

Asha grabbed the handle and held it firmly in place. Sierra frantically grabbed her pants off the floor and hopped around on one foot trying to get them on.

"I think the door is locked," Devi said.

"Hold on, I'll be right there," Asha said. She bent over and picked up Sierra's blouse.

Sierra snatched the blouse and threw it on over her shoulders. She buttoned it quickly, all the while gazing into Asha's eyes. "Okay," she said, panting slightly. "How do I look?"

"Beautiful," Asha replied. "Ready?"

Sierra flipped her hair away from the collar of her shirt. "Ready."

Asha yanked open the door and Devi tumbled into the room. "Are you okay?" she asked, helping Devi back up.

"I'm fine," Devi said, laughing. She smiled at Sierra. "Is my sister being a slave driver?"

"Isn't she always?" Sierra said.

"Hey," Asha said, slipping her hands into her back pockets. "I'm not that bad."

"You're perfect," Sierra replied, her eyes sparkling.

Jack rushed into the room. "Hey, I just heard on the news that the weather is going to get pretty nasty this afternoon."

"We should get going, then," Devi replied, looking over at Sierra. "That is, if you still want to go shopping."

"Absolutely," Sierra said, checking to make sure the flash drive was still in the front pocket of her jeans.

"Don't forget your jacket," Jack said, picking Sierra's coat off the floor.

"Thanks, Jack," Sierra replied.

Jack leaned down next to Sierra's ear. "Make sure you take a moment to rebutton your shirt. It looks like you missed one along the way."

Sierra's cheeks turned a rosy red. "I'll do that," she said, glancing down at her blouse.

"See you tonight," Asha said with an apologetic grin. "Oh, make sure you come back before the weather gets bad."

Sierra walked over to Asha and kissed her on the cheek. "Don't worry," she said. "I'm in good hands."

"Thanks for...helping me with the equipment," Asha said. "It was a pleasant surprise."

Sierra held Asha's gaze. "I'm always here if you need an extra hand with anything."

"I'll keep that in mind," Asha said. "Now hurry so I can stop worrying."

"Yes, ma'am," Sierra replied. "I'll be back before you can miss me."

"I already miss you," Asha said.

"Oh, I'm going to be sick," Devi said. "Come on, Jack, let's wait out here until all the smoochy-smoochy stuff is over."

"Ah, man," Jack said, following Devi out of the room. "I'm a guy. I'm supposed to watch stuff like that."

Asha shook her head. "I'm sorry we were interrupted," she whispered. "I hope it was still okay."

"It was better than okay," Sierra said. "You're an amazing lover."

Asha wrapped her arms around Sierra's waist. "I'm glad you think so."

"Honey," Sierra said, placing the palms of her hands on either side of Asha's face. "There's not a single doubt in my mind or my body."

"What does your heart say?" Asha said.

Sierra fell silent and contemplated her answer. "It says you'd be worth the risk of falling deeply in love with if you didn't live on the opposite side of the world."

"I don't live on the opposite side of the world," Asha said, taking Sierra's hand.

"California might as well be," Sierra said.

"It doesn't have to be," Asha replied.

"What are you saying?" Sierra said, hoping that Asha would just tell her what she needed to hear so badly.

"Sierra?" Devi said, leaning into the room. "Are you coming?"

"Yeah," Sierra said, offering Devi a reassuring smile. "I'll be right there."

Asha pulled Sierra into her arms. "What do you want, Sierra? Just tell me."

Sierra kissed Asha passionately. "You have to figure that out on your own," she said, rubbing the tip of her nose against Asha's.

"What if I don't?" Asha said, genuine concern reflecting in her eyes.

"I have faith that you will," Sierra replied, slipping out of Asha's embrace.

"Now get back to work. I'll see you at six o'clock sharp."

• • •

Sierra and Devi barreled up the steps to the lodge and escaped into the lobby at exactly six o'clock. A gust of wind swept in behind them, slamming the lobby door closed with thunderous force. A group of Vail's top search and rescue team members were gathered around a small card table that had been setup in one corner. They jerked their heads up and stared at Sierra and Devi with their eyes wide in anticipation.

Sierra stomped her snow-covered shoes on the entryway rug and studied their faces. "What's going on?" she said, turning to Devi. "They all look like they've eaten glass."

"I don't know," Devi said. "The last time these guys all got together it was because one of their own hadn't come back from avalanche patrol."

Sierra searched the faces again. "Where's Asha?"

Devi slipped her hand into Sierra's when she saw Jack walk out of the other room with his arm around Dee's shoulder, comforting her. "I think Asha is the one in trouble."

Dee motioned to Sierra and Devi to follow her and Jack back into the recreation room. Devi looked over at Sierra. "This can't be good."

Dee collapsed into an oversized lounge chair. Sierra dropped to her knees beside her. "What's going on?" she said. "Where's Asha?"

"She hasn't come back yet," Jack said, hanging his head.

"Where did she go?" Devi demanded, slapping Jack in the arm.

"It's going to be fine," Dee said, unconvincingly.

"Grandma, you still haven't answered the question," Devi said. "Where's Asha?"

"The storm came in faster than any of us anticipated," Dee replied weakly. "Some of the skiers got caught out in it."

"Asha had tried to warn as many people as she could," Jack said. "When the storm hit, all of our guests were safe and sound, but we got word that a party of five cross-country skiers from another lodge hadn't returned. Asha called, confirmed the report was accurate, and assembled a team."

"That still doesn't answer the question," Devi repeated heatedly.

"They found three of skiers," Dee said. She patted the arm of the chair for Devi. "Come here, dear."

Devi sat down next to Dee. "Asha went after the other two, didn't she?"

"Yes," Dee said, her blue eyes brimming with tears.

"Why didn't anyone go with her?" Sierra said.

"I tried," Jack replied, regret thick in his tone. "I lost sight of her in the blinding snow and we were separated. I tried to backtrack, but it was no use."

"So what's the team doing sitting in there?" Sierra said with disdain. "Hoping Asha will come through the door so they won't have to go out and find her?"

"No one's sure where to even look," Jack replied. "These guys are going over a map of the area now and trying to see if Asha will contact them through her emergency two-way radio."

"Why didn't Asha just come back with everyone else?" Devi said. "I don't get it. The chances of finding the other two skiers alive are one in a million."

"I know why," Sierra said. She wiped at her eyes to keep tears from streaming down her face.

"Why?" Devi said, staring intently at Sierra.

"She remembers how helpless she felt when your parents went missing," Sierra said gently. "She also remembers seeing the rescue team that was meant to bring them home come back every evening to sleep in nice warm beds and fill their bellies with plenty of food."

"Excuse me," a tall, lanky gentleman said, poking his head into the room. "We'd like to talk with Dee privately for a moment."

"Sure," Dee said, pushing herself out of the chair. "I'll be right back."

"What do you think is going on?" Devi said, looking over at Jack.

Jack shook his head. "They're calling off the search until the morning."

"What?!" Sierra said. "They can't just leave her out there."

Dee walked back into the room a short time later with her face twisted in anguish. She opened her mouth to speak but collapsed into Jack's arms, sobbing uncontrollably. The four of them didn't speak for a moment. The only sound was the crackling pop of the fire in the fireplace.

Sierra closed her eyes and thought about Asha's brilliant, white smile and how she might not ever see it again. "This stops now," she blurted out.

"What do you mean?" Dee said, taking Sierra's outstretched hand.

"Devi," Sierra said. "I need you to start calling out to Asha on the two-way radio. I don't care if you get an answer or not. If there's a chance she can hear us, I want her to know we're coming for her."

"Sure," Devi replied. She kissed Dee on the cheek and sprinted into the lobby.

"Jack, I want you to study that map and try to locate where you were when you last saw Asha. That's where we'll start looking."

"What are you talking about?" Jack said. "You've never even been trained in search and rescue."

"Look, I love her," Sierra said, refusing to keep her feelings for Asha hidden any longer. "I'm going to go with or without you."

"You can count us in," Darren said, strutting into the room with Ryan hot on his heels.

Ryan's brilliant blue eyes met Sierra's. "There's no way we're leaving her out there."

Tears streamed down Dee's face. "Thank you all so very much."

Devi hurried back into the room with the two-way radio. "Does anyone know how to tell if this thing is working properly?"

"What's the problem?" Jack said.

"I keep getting this series of beeps," Devi replied.

Sierra's heart pounded in her chest. "Do the beeps come before or after you try Asha?"

"I don't think it's either one," Devi said. "It's like that same series of beeps repeated over and over again."

"Let me see that," Sierra said, taking the radio from Devi. She slowly turned the knob to increase the volume. The series of beeps that Devi had explained only moments before graced Sierra's ears. "It's Morse code!"

Jack sprinted into the lobby and came back with pen and paper. "Last year," he said, scribbling furiously, "Asha and I took an advanced search and rescue course with an option to learn Morse code. I was really reluctant to spend the additional time learning it, especially since cell phones are everywhere, but Asha insisted."

"Do you think it could be Asha?" Devi said, pacing back and forth across the floor.

"Hold on," Jack said, taking the two-way radio from Sierra. He held it up to his ear and began jotting down letters. The room was completely still.

"This is maddening," Ryan said softly.

"I've got it," Jack said, handing the piece of paper over to Sierra.

"What does it say?" Devi asked.

The scribbled piece of paper trembled in Sierra's hand. "Asha's with the two skiers," she said. "One of them needs a stretcher."

"Do we know where they are?" Dee asked, her eyes wide with hope.

"We will," Sierra said, handing the piece of paper back to Jack. "Answer Asha back and find out if there are any landmarks around where they are. Ryan and Darren, come with me. We need to gather some equipment and get ready to go."

• • •

Sierra changed into her snowmobile suit and grabbed her warmest pair of boots. She stopped by the supply room per Jack's instruction and grabbed four hand-held spotlights and a very large first aid bag. Her mind raced back to earlier in the day when she and Asha had been left alone in the very same room. *I'm on my way, baby,* she thought. *Just hang on.*

Jack was waiting for her when she emerged onto the front porch. "Let me take that," he said, taking the first aid kit.

Sierra followed him down the steps to where Ryan and Darren were already waiting. The wind was blowing so hard, she found herself shouting to be heard. "What's the game plan?"

"We have to stay close together," Jack shouted back. "No exceptions."

"Do we know where they're at?" Darren yelled, climbing onto a snowmobile.

"I have a general idea," Jack said, taking one of the spotlights from Sierra and handing it to Darren. "Still, it's going to be very difficult to find them. We have to keep a vigilant look out."

"I don't think that'll be a problem," Ryan said. "We all know what's at risk here."

They all nodded.

"I'm taking the snowmobile with the rescue boggan," Jack continued, taking another spotlight for himself. "Ryan, give Sierra a crash course in operating the other snowmobile while I double-check to make sure we have everything we need. We can't afford to waste any time."

CHAPTER FIFTEEN

Sierra gritted her teeth and hunkered down as low as she could on the snowmobile. She squinted to see Jack through the whirling snow. The blizzard made it appear as though they were traveling through the white static that used to signify that a television station's program had ended. The wind hammered into her body, reminding her of the few times she had gone surfing and been swallowed up and spit out by a large wave. The pounding of her body, the throbbing pain in her head, and the struggle to escape the Grim Reaper's will to give in had uncanny similarities to her present predicament. Instead of the ocean, though, she was in the middle of a forest with unforgiving mountains that would bury her alive if given the opportunity.

Three hours had passed and there was still no sign of Asha or the two skiers anywhere. Jack kept his spotlight sweeping back and forth, reminding Sierra of the warning beacons from lighthouses that still checkered the coastline. When the light suddenly vanished, Sierra imagined a giant crack in the earth's crust devouring the naïve who had ventured out into the present wintry nightmare. She refused to turn back, though, and pushed forward in the direction where she had last seen the light.

Sierra came upon Jack within seconds. He pounded on his spotlight furiously. "The fucking thing stopped working!"

"Take mine," Sierra shouted. "I'll stay as close as I can so we don't get separated."

"What's wrong?" Darren said, gliding up alongside of them with Ryan.

"We need to keep Sierra in our line of sight no matter how tough that might be," Jack instructed. "My spotlight is shot, so I'm using hers."

"You've got it," Darren replied. "Ryan, stay on her right side and I'll stay on her left while Jack keeps the lead."

"That's fine with me," Ryan said. "Which way now?"

"I don't know," Jack said, shining the spotlight in various directions.

"We've been zigzagging around this area for the past hour," Darren said, wiping the snow from his lenses before it had time to freeze. "We're not going to make it much longer under these conditions. We have to find them soon or they'll be sending a rescue party to find us in the morning as well."

"I know," Jack shouted. "Let's keep going this way for another ten minutes or so. I've been trying to search in somewhat of a grid pattern, but I'm not sure if it's going to work."

"It'll work," Sierra said. "It has to."

Jack looked at her and nodded. "If there's still no sign of them, we'll turn and head east. Let's go!"

Twenty minutes passed, then another twenty, when Jack finally gave the signal to turn eastward. Large teardrops seeped from Sierra's eyes and collected at the bottom of her ski mask. *Please, God,* she prayed. *Help us find her.*

Sierra wiped away the snow that had collected on her ski mask again and continued to follow Jack. Though only about ten feet separated her snowmobile from Jack's, the weather made it appear a lot further. For that reason alone, she knew that keeping a constant visual on him was wise, but she couldn't resist searching the wintry darkness that surrounded her in hopes to find three forms huddled together for survival.

A flash of light drew Sierra's eyes forward. Jack traveled the intense beam from the spotlight back and forth between her, Darren and Ryan. He climbed off the snowmobile and waved his arms frantically. "I found them," he shouted.

Sierra barely heard what Jack had said as she careened up next to his snowmobile. He was already on the move with the first aid bag, staggering through the snow toward three dark shapes at the base of a large pine tree. *Asha,* she thought, choking back tears. *Hang on, baby. I'm coming.*

"Where's he going?" Darren shouted, pulling up next to Sierra at the same time Ryan did. "I can't see anything!"

Sierra pointed toward the pine tree. "Over there," she replied. "We need to hurry!"

"We're right behind you," Ryan said.

Sierra struggled forward through the knee-deep snow as the unforgiving wind continued to pound her body. She tried to follow Jack's footprints, but they were vanishing before her eyes. She could hear Darren and Ryan cursing behind her and when she turned around and looked, she understood why. They were also at the mercy of the wind as it collided into the aluminum stretcher, almost ripping it from their hands.

Knowing there was nothing she could do, Sierra pressed forward. She stumbled over next to Jack who was treating one of the skiers and knelt down beside him. The blizzard had caked all of their faces in snow and ice and there was no way of telling who was who. "What can I do?" she said, loud enough for Jack to hear.

"We need to immobilize his leg," he shouted. "He has multiple fractures and Asha has no idea how bad the breaks are. I need the temporary splint from the first aid bag. Can you get it?"

Sierra dug into the bag and found the splint. Darren and Ryan dropped to their knees beside her and placed the stretcher directly next to injured skier. "Anyone else hurt?" Darren said.

"What?" Jack said, cupping a hand to his ear.

"Will we need another stretcher?" Darren bellowed.

Jack looked across the injured skier at Asha and the other skier. "Are you guys able to walk?"

Sierra held her breath, waiting for one of them to speak. Her heart pounded in her chest with anticipation. *Please don't let her be hurt.*

"We're exhausted and cold, but we can make it to the snowmobiles," Asha replied.

Sierra felt every muscle in her body tighten like the strings on a finely tuned guitar. All she wanted to do was spring on top of Asha and cover her in kisses, but she resisted. It was enough to know she was safe, for now.

Jack finished applying the splint as the skier moaned in agony. "All right guys," he said, "Get ready."

Darren and Ryan adjusted their grips on the stretcher.

"Sierra," Jack continued. "Help me roll him onto his side."

"Sierra?" Asha said, her voice trembling.

Sierra nodded in acknowledgment as she continued to help Jack. Darren and Ryan tucked the stretcher beneath the injured skier's body. "We're set," Darren said.

Sierra and Jack gently rolled the skier back onto the stretcher. "Be careful when you lift him," Jack said. "We don't want him flipping over."

"On the count of three," Darren said to Ryan. "One. Two. Three!"

Darren and Ryan lifted the skier off the ground and trudged their way through the snow toward the rescue boggan. "Sierra," Jack said. "Please help the other skier over to Darren's snowmobile. Asha, are you strong enough to hold onto Ryan?"

"I think so," Asha replied, staggering to her feet. "I'm not sure if I have the strength in my legs to make it over there or not."

"That's okay," Jack said, stepping over next to her. He wrapped his arm around Asha's midsection and hoisted her up. He looked back at the other skier. "Are you sure you're okay, ma'am?"

"Just cold," she replied. "And my name's Cynthia."

"Well, Cynthia," Jack said. "I need you to promise me you'll hang on real tight to Darren. We need to get your boyfriend back to the lodge as fast as possible."

"I understand," Cynthia replied. "And thank you for coming after us."

"Don't thank me," Jack said, looking over at Sierra. "She's the one who should be thanked."

"There's no need," Sierra said, stumbling wearily over to Cynthia.

"Well, thank you anyway," Cynthia replied.

Sierra helped Cynthia up onto her feet. The only thing she truly wanted to do was take Asha into her arms and hold her. Still, they were a long way from the lodge and she knew there was a high probability that both skiers and Asha had frostbite. "You're very welcome," she said at last. "Now, let's go."

Within a few minutes, everyone was set and Jack took the lead again. It was an agonizing journey. The wind was even more brutal and it hammered into Sierra without mercy. She couldn't even look over to see how Asha was faring, as she was having a hard enough time keeping track of Jack, who was directly in front of her. The last thing she wanted was to become a victim of stupidity and never have the opportunity to tell Asha how she really felt because her dumb ass got lost.

That would be a tragedy of classic proportions, Sierra thought, sailing over a snowdrift. Her fears were instantly lifted as the bright lights of Vail penetrated the seemingly never-ending blindness that had descended upon them throughout their journey. She could hear Jack shouting into his cell phone, which had finally picked up some reception, for an ambulance. *We're going to make it,* she thought. *We're actually going to make it!*

• • •

Sierra watched the emergency room doors open and close continuously at the Vail Valley Medical Center. From her vantage point, she could see the doctors and nurses scrambling from patient to patient, addressing the most critical first. It seemed that everyone from Eagle to Routt counties had been affected adversely by the storm. There were no rooms left to accommodate the influx of injuries and the staff had to situate patients wherever there was room, including the hallways and the waiting area.

Sierra was one of the latter. She pulled the two blankets wrapped around her even tighter and shivered uncontrollably. Her teeth ached from their continuous chattering. One of the midnight shift nurses hurried over and knelt down next to Sierra. "Miss?" the nurse said softly. "Are you still awake?"

Sierra pulled the blankets away from her face and gazed into bright blue eyes. "Yes," she whispered. "Is everything okay?"

"Yes, ma'am," the nurse replied with a warm smile. She held up a steaming cup of coffee. "I thought this might help to warm you up. The doctor wants to make sure we keep you warm and hydrated."

"Thank you," Sierra replied, taking the cup with trembling hands.

"Would you like me to bring you another blanket," the nurse said.

"That would be wonderful," Sierra said. "Do you mind telling me your name?"

"It's Beth," the nurse replied.

"Mine's Sierra."

"It's a pleasure," Beth said. She looked down at the bucket of water Sierra's feet were soaking in. "How's that feeling?"

"It's starting to feel a little cool," Sierra said.

"I'll send Rachel over to change out the water," Beth replied. "Try to rest."

Sierra reached out and touched Beth's arms. "Can I ask you something real quick?"

"Sure," Beth said.

"There's a patient who was brought in a few minutes before I arrived," Sierra said. "Her name's Asha. Do you know if she's okay?"

"I'll find out for you," Beth said. "I'll be back in a few minutes with one blanket and an update on your friend."

"Thank you," Sierra replied. She pulled the blankets back over her head and tried to keep her eyes from closing.

A few minutes had passed when another nurse came by, presumably Rachel, and refilled the bucket with warm water. Beth returned a short while later and placed another blanket around Sierra's shoulders. "Your friend is fine," she said softly, respectful of the other patients and their families who had drifted off to sleep. "She's exhausted, but she'll make a full recovery."

"Will she be able to go home soon?" Sierra asked.

"Well, she had a moderate case of hypothermia when she arrived," Beth said. "The doctors are working on warming up her core and supplying her with the hydration and fuel supplements that she needs."

Sierra looked at her quizzically.

"She should be able to go home tomorrow," Beth said, chuckling. "You, on the other hand, can leave whenever you feel up to it. The color in your face has returned and your teeth are no longer chattering. Do you have someone you can call?"

"That won't be necessary," Devi said, walking up to them. "Asha gave me strict instructions that you're supposed to let me take you back to her place."

"I don't have any clothes there," Sierra said.

"Well, that's my cue," Beth said, getting to her feet. "Take care of yourself, Sierra, and have a Merry Christmas."

"You do the same," Sierra replied.

Devi sat down next to Sierra. "Asha said you can wear anything in her closet. She just really wants you to be home when she gets there."

The word "home" resonated in Sierra's ears and traveled to her soul. "Okay," she squeaked, tears welling up in her eyes.

Devi wrapped her arms around Sierra and hugged her. "Asha loves you," she said. "She's terrified to tell you that, but I know she does."

Sierra wiped at her eyes. "How do you know that?"

"I know my sister better than anyone," Devi replied. "She started asking for you the moment she arrived at the hospital. When the doctor said that wasn't possible, you would have thought someone had stabbed her. It tore her up not being able to see you."

"I wish she would tell me," Sierra said. She smiled up at Rachel, who brought her a towel to dry her feet and removed the tub of water.

"Give her time," Devi said. "Besides, anyone who looks at the two of you together can tell that you're madly in love with each other."

"You can see that?" Sierra said, slipping her feet into a pair of slippers the hospital had given her.

"Everyone can see that," Devi replied. She rose and helped Sierra to her feet. "I already have your snowmobile suit and boots in the Jeep. We should probably get going since it's going to take a while considering the weather."

"Who's going to stay with Asha?" Sierra asked, walking with Devi toward the nurses' station with the three blankets.

"Dee is going to stay over, so don't worry," Devi replied. "She'll be dropping Asha off in the morning. She was wondering if you'd look after her for the next few days."

Sierra handed the blankets to a red-headed nurse who offered a tired grin. "Happy Holidays," she whispered.

"The same to you," the nurse replied.

Devi led Sierra toward the exit doors. "So can you stay with Asha?"

"Of course," Sierra replied. "I'll need to stop by the lodge, though. Will that be a problem?"

"Not at all," Devi said. "Wait here while I bring the Jeep around."

"You don't have to do that," Sierra said.

"Oh, yes, I do," Devi replied. "You didn't see your face when you climbed off the snowmobile and passed out from exhaustion."

"True," Sierra said. "What if I wait right here?"

Devi laughed. "I'll be right back."

CHAPTER SIXTEEN

Sierra paced back and forth across Asha's living room. She'd been up since eight o'clock, and four painstaking hours had passed without word from anyone on Asha's condition. *This is driving me insane,* she thought. *Somebody pick up the fucking phone and call me!* She collapsed onto the couch and tried to calm her nerves with long, deep breaths. Her body was still suffering from exhaustion and needed to rest, but her mind was relentless.

A car door slammed and Sierra sat straight up. She tried to listen over the ferocious beating of her heart. Footsteps plodded across the porch toward Asha's front door, and the metallic sound of a key engaging broke the silence in the room. Sierra got to her feet and looked through the window to see Devi's Jeep backing out of the drive. She hurried toward the front door as it swung open slowly.

"Asha?" Sierra said, praying it wasn't Dee.

"Hi, beautiful," Asha said, stepping from behind the door and closing it behind her. "How's my girl?"

Tears streamed down Sierra's face. "I'm good," she said, touching Asha's cheek. "I've been so worried about you."

Asha pulled Sierra into her arms. "I need to kiss you."

"Then kiss me," Sierra said, closing her eyes.

Asha leaned forward and brushed her lips against Sierra's. "I want more than to kiss you."

Sierra opened her eyes. "And you'll be able to have more once you're feeling better."

"But," Asha said.

"No buts," Sierra said, gently kissing Asha's chapped lips. "I want you to rest today."

Asha took Sierra by the hand and led her back toward the bedroom. "You're not going to leave, are you?"

"I'll stay as long as you need me," Sierra said.

"I might need you to stay with me for the rest of your vacation," Asha said, crawling into bed fully dressed.

Sierra pulled off Asha's boots and pulled the covers up around Asha's shoulders. "I'll be here," she said, walking over and switching off the light. "Now try to sleep."

"Will you lie with me?" Asha asked, turning onto her side.

I'd lie with you forever if you'd only ask, Sierra thought. She walked around the bed and slipped beneath the covers.

"Sierra?" Asha whispered.

"Yeah," Sierra said, moving her body closer to Asha's.

"Thanks for coming after me," Asha whispered. "It was the most selfless thing anyone has ever done for me."

"Well, I've been meaning to tell you something," Sierra said, fearing the words that warmed her soul. "I love you."

Asha was silent.

Sierra felt the mighty claws of disappointment rip into her heart. "Aren't you going to say anything?"

Asha didn't move. The only sound that escaped her lips was that of her rhythmic breath. "Asha?" Sierra said. "Are you still awake?" There was still no reply.

Sierra leaned over and looked down at Asha. Her eyes were closed and her face was a picture of tranquility. Sierra almost laughed out loud with joy, but instead kissed Asha's cheek. "Sleep well, my love," she whispered.

Rolling onto her back, Sierra stared up at the ceiling and listened to Asha breathe. Soon she found herself drifting off and thinking about falling asleep beside Asha every night. *If only real life played out like one of my signature endings*, she thought. *I would have the one thing I've always wanted— my soul mate.* She moved her hand so that it barely touched Asha's back, and fell asleep.

• • •

Sierra awoke to the sound of running water. The room was pitch black, but she didn't have to reach for Asha to know she was no longer lying beside her. The chill that had settled where Asha's body had warmed the bed was enough. "Asha?" she said softly.

Climbing out of bed, Sierra shuffled across the floor and peeked into the hallway. She tiptoed toward the bathroom and knocked on the door.

"Just a sec," Asha said.

Sierra heard the water shut off. "Are you okay?" she said.

"I'm fine," Asha replied, opening the door.

Sierra stared breathlessly at Asha, standing in nothing but a towel wrapped around her waist. "Wow," she said, biting her bottom lip and glancing away.

Droplets of water from Asha's hair trickled down her shoulders and onto her breasts. She walked over to Sierra and took her by the hand. "I missed you."

"I missed you, too," Sierra said.

Asha ran her fingertip around Sierra's mouth. "Do you want to...?" she asked, nodding her head toward the bedroom.

"Yes," Sierra said, her eyes darting to Asha's breasts. "But are you up for that?"

"Try me," Asha said, dropping the towel to the floor.

Sierra's mouth went dry and she licked her lips as her eyes traveled down Asha's body. "I plan on it."

• • •

"Lie down," Sierra said softly, switching on the light.

Asha pulled the covers back and crawled on top of the sheets. "Is this want you want?"

"Yes," Sierra said, watching Asha spread her legs further apart.

"Now what?" Asha said, running her hands over her breasts. "Do you want to just watch?"

Sierra shook her head and carefully lowered herself down on top of Asha. "Not this time," she said, taking Asha's breast into her mouth.

Asha arched her head back and her hips thrust upward. Sierra slipped her fingers deep inside Asha and gingerly moved her hand back and forth. "Don't stop," Asha pleaded.

"Don't close your eyes," Sierra said, staring into the dark chocolate pools. "I want to be looking into them when you climax."

Asha nodded and rocked her hips harder against Sierra's hand. "Oh, baby," she said, gazing into Sierra's eyes. "I'm..."

Sierra felt Asha's muscles tighten around her fingers before they were flooded with sweet nectar. She lowered her lips to Asha's and kissed her. When their lips parted, she couldn't help but wonder if she would ever get the chance to stare into Asha's brown eyes again while making love.

"What's the matter?" Asha said. She reached up and touched the side of Sierra's face. "You look sad."

Sierra gently removed her fingers from Asha. "It's nothing."

"Don't lie," Asha said. "You're terrible at it."

Sierra glanced away. "I need to tell you something."

"What is it?" Asha said, smiling up at Sierra. "Whatever it is, it can't be that bad."

Tears streamed from Sierra's eyes. She knew that everything she believed love to be was right in front of her. "Asha," she said, taking a deep breath. "We haven't known each other for that long, but you've made me feel happy to be alive again."

"I know that feeling," Asha replied. "It's exactly how you make me feel."

The doorbell sounded and Sierra fell back onto the pillow. "This is ridiculous!"

"I'm not answering it," Asha said. "Finish telling me what you were going to say."

Sierra placed the palm of her hand against Asha's chest. "It might be Dee."

Asha shook her head. "What is it with people's timing?" She climbed out of bed and quickly got dressed. "I'll be right back."

Sierra waited for Asha to leave the room before grabbing her pillow. She buried her face in the softness that smelled of Asha's shampoo. *What am I going to do if she doesn't love me,* she thought. *How will I be able to continue to see her until I leave?*

Asha's angry voice interrupted Sierra's thoughts. "I'm not going to ask you again," she shouted. "Please leave!"

Sierra scrambled out of bed and crept down the hallway. She pressed her back against the wall next to the foyer. She knew of only one person who could elicit such a reaction from Asha. *Vivian.*

"Please," Asha said. "Please leave me alone."

"But you know you want me," Vivian replied. "That little bitch you're running around with can't please you the way I can and you know it."

"Sierra is not a bitch," Asha hissed. "And for your information, she risked her life to save mine."

"Do you love her?" Vivian asked, stepping closer to Asha.

Sierra held her breath. The moment of truth had rocketed to the forefront.

"That's none of your business," Asha replied.

"You told me you loved me," Vivian said viciously. "Did you tell her you loved her just so you could get her into bed, too?"

"That isn't fair and you know it," Asha said, lowering her voice. "You were the one who lied."

"I never lied to you," Vivian said. "I did love you while we were in bed."

"Get out," Asha said, her voice trembling. "If there was one thing I learned by almost freezing to death, it was that I'm completely over you."

Sierra held her breath.

"Now, Vivian," Asha said softly. "I'm tired and hungry, so please leave me alone."

"Good-bye, Asha," Vivian replied. "You'll live to regret this."

"I wouldn't give yourself that much credit," Asha said.

Sierra tiptoed back to the bedroom and sat down on the edge of the bed. She shook her head when she heard the telephone ringing in the other room. Asha walked into the room a few minutes later and handed her the portable phone. "It's for you, honey."

Sierra placed her hand over the mouthpiece. "Who is it?"

"I think she said her name's Dana," Asha replied. "She said she's a colleague of yours."

Sierra took Asha's hand. "Is everything all right?"

"It was Vivian at the door," Asha said. "I'll tell you more after you get off the phone. Are you hungry?"

"Starving," Sierra said.

"I'll get something started for dinner," Asha said, kissing Sierra on the forehead. "Take your time and come join me when you're finished with your call."

"I will, honey," Sierra replied. She waited for Asha to leave the room before raising the phone up to her ear. "Hello?"

"Sierra?"

"Dana?" Sierra replied. "How did you get this number?"

"That's not a very good way to greet your number-one fan," Dana teased.

"I'm sorry," Sierra said. "The last couple days have been a little insane."

"So I've heard," Dana replied.

"And what have you heard?" Sierra said, walking over and closing the bedroom door.

"Well, the owner of the lodge informed me that she owes you a great deal of gratitude for saving her granddaughter," Dana replied.

"I'm guessing that's how you got this number," Sierra said.

"I wouldn't have had to," Dana said. "But someone didn't bring her cell phone on vacation."

"That's why it's called a vacation," Sierra said.

"Good point," Dana admitted.

"So what'd you think?" Sierra said, leaning against the dresser.

"About what?" Dana said.

Sierra drummed her fingers. "Dana, you know what I'm talking about."

"It's your best yet," Dana replied.

"Better than my mysteries?" Sierra said.

"A lot better," Dana said. "So now I have one question let to ask."

"What is it?" Sierra said.

"Are you coming back?" Dana said. "Or are you going to stay with the woman this book is about?"

Sierra slid onto the floor. "I don't know."

"How can you not know?" Dana said, her voice rising an octave. "It's obvious you love her."

"I'm just not so sure she's in love with me," Sierra replied.

"Why don't you just ask her?" Dana said matter-of-factly.

"I'm terrified that she'll say she's not," Sierra said softly.

"But what if she does?" Dana replied.

"It's a big what-if," Sierra said.

"According to your novel," Dana said. "It's not such a big what-if."

"I have to go," Sierra said.

"You know where I'll be if you need me," Dana replied.

"Thanks," Sierra said.

"Good night," Dana said.

Sierra clicked off the phone and thumped the back of her head lightly against the wall. *It's now or never,* she thought. She pushed herself up off the floor and opened the bedroom door. *I can do this. I just need to have faith.*

• • •

"So, who's Dana?" Asha asked, dropping a spoonful of fried rice onto Sierra's plate.

"She's my literary agent," Sierra replied.

"Is everything okay?" Asha said, setting the bowl of rice down in the center of the table.

"Yeah, she loves my latest project," Sierra said.

"Oh," Asha teased. "Is it that top-secret project you won't tell me anything about?"

Sierra smiled. "Christmas is a little more than thirty-six hours away. I think you can wait until then for me to tell you."

Asha's brow was furrowed. "What's on your mind? You seem a little distant."

"Nothing," Sierra replied.

"I thought you had something you wanted to tell me," Asha said, putting down her fork.

"It can wait," Sierra said, reaching across the table and holding Asha's hand.

Asha pushed her chair away from the table. "I know just the thing to make my girl smile."

Sierra twisted around in her chair and watched Asha remove a present from beneath the Christmas tree in the far corner of the room. "I want you to go ahead and open this one," Asha said, handing the brightly colored package to Sierra.

"Are you sure?" Sierra said, taking the package.

"Absolutely," Asha replied.

Sierra tore through the wrapping paper and ran her hand across the velvet covering on the top of a long, rectangular box. "It looks expensive."

"Well, open it," Asha said excitedly.

Sierra opened the box. "Oh my," she said, staring at the gold rope necklace from its pillow of satin. "How did you know I wanted this?"

"I noticed you looking at it when we went shopping," Asha replied. "I had to get it for you."

"Thank you," Sierra said, pulling it out of the box. "I love it."

"Would you like me to help you put it on?" Asha said, stepping behind Sierra.

"Sure," Sierra said, lifting up her hair.

Asha took the necklace and placed it around Sierra's neck. "There you go," she said, clasping it together.

Sierra leaned her head back and looked up at Asha. "Thank you again so very much."

"You're very welcome," Asha said.

Sierra took Asha's hands in hers. "I need to ask you something."

"Sure," Asha said, kneeling down so they were at eye level. "What is it?"

Sierra took a deep breath and gazed into Asha's eyes. "Wow, this is harder than I thought it would be."

"I know what you're going to ask," Asha said.

"You do?" Sierra replied, bracing herself for the inevitable.

Asha kissed Sierra on the lips. "You want to know what the conversation I had with Vivian was about."

Sierra ran her fingers through Asha's silky black hair. "No, baby, I don't care about that."

"Then what is it?" Asha replied, touching the side of Sierra's face.

"How do you feel about me?" Sierra said, unable to keep her body from trembling.

"You know how I feel about you," Asha replied, glancing away from Sierra's intense gaze.

"No, I don't," Sierra said.

"You're the most amazing woman I've every met," Asha replied, leaning forward to kiss Sierra.

Sierra pulled away. "Do you love me?"

"You know I do," Asha replied.

"Then tell me," Sierra said, her eyes pleading. "Tell me you love me."

"Why?" Asha said angrily. "So you can leave in a week?"

Sierra looked up in surprise. "This isn't about me leaving in a week."

"Then what's it about?" Asha said.

"You and me," Sierra replied, tears filling her eyes.

"If that's true," Asha said, "then how do you feel about me? Do you love me?"

"Why should I give you the pleasure?" Sierra snapped. "Besides, you already have your answer."

"Really?" Asha said sarcastically. "Did I somehow miss that memo?"

Sierra's tears spilled onto her cheeks. "I made love with you," she whispered. She pushed herself out of the chair and walked toward the bedroom.

"Sierra, wait," Asha said, rushing after her.

"Just forget it," Sierra said, unable to look at her. "I'm the one who made the mistake."

Asha grabbed Sierra by the arm. "It's very difficult for me to say those words when I know you're leaving."

"You knew Vivian was leaving," Sierra replied, trying to keep from sobbing. "And yet, you still told her you loved her."

"I know," Asha said. "I wish I could explain the difference in my feelings toward you, but I can't."

"If you ever figure it out," Sierra replied. "I hope you let me know."

"Everything I'm saying is coming out wrong," Asha said, following Sierra down the hallway.

"Can we just not talk about this anymore?" Sierra said, sitting down on the edge of Asha's bed.

"I'm afraid if I agree with that, we'll never talk about it again," Asha replied, reaching for Sierra's hand.

Sierra closed her eyes. "Will you just hold me tonight and maybe we can talk more about it the morning? Will that work?"

"Okay," Asha said reluctantly. "Let me just make sure everything is turned off in the kitchen."

"Sure," Sierra said, crawling into bed. "I'll be right here when you get back."

"I'll hurry," Asha said, rushing out of the room.

Sierra pressed her hands against her chest. *I just won't be here when you wake, my love,* she thought. *But you'll always have my heart.*

CHAPTER SEVENTEEN

Asha was awakened by the relentless ringing of the telephone. She covered her head with the pillow to drown out the noise and rolled onto her side. Instantly, she sat up and pulled the covers back to confirm what she already knew. Sierra was gone.

Tossing the covers to the side, Asha grabbed her robe from the closet and headed out of the bedroom. She searched every room as the phone continued to ring. Finally, she picked it up. "What!"

"What the hell is wrong with you?" Devi said angrily.

"What are you talking about?" Asha countered.

"Grandma just called and said Sierra checked out of the lodge this morning," Devi replied incredulously. "What happened?"

Asha collapsed onto one of the dining room chairs. "I couldn't tell her I love her."

"Why not?" Devi asked, softening her tone.

"Because how I feel about her is beyond love," Asha admitted, running her fingers through her hair. "I love her so much more than love. Does that make any sense?"

"It does," Devi said. "But I'm not the one you should be telling this to."

Asha shook her head. "It's too late."

"You know what?" Devi said. "You're right. I mean, why chase after the only woman who's ever really loved you and vice-versa. That would be ludicrous."

"Did Sierra tell you she loved me?" Asha said.

"You're an idiot," Devi hissed. "That's what I'm telling you. I'll see you tonight at dinner. Merry Christmas Eve."

The line went dead. Asha hurled the phone across the room and it smashed into the far wall. She got up and headed down the hallway. Once in the bedroom, she paced back and forth, unable to take her eyes off the pillow where Sierra had laid her head.

Tears poured from Asha's eyes and her mind swarmed with memories. "Why couldn't I just say it?" she said, falling to her knees. She covered her face with her hands. "What am I so afraid of?"

Crawling up onto the bed, Asha wrapped her arms tightly around Sierra's pillow and wept. "I love you," she cried. "I love you more than love. That's what you needed to hear. That's what I needed to say. I was just so afraid, Sierra. I was just so afraid. If only I had another chance."

Asha looked over at the clock. "Maybe there's still time." She sprinted over to the closet and yanked open the door. Grabbing a pair of jeans and a sweater, she dressed in record time and raced into the living room. She grabbed her spare set of truck keys off the kitchen table and headed out the door. She stopped dead in her tracks when she realized her truck wasn't out front. "Shit!" she shouted.

The sound of an approaching vehicle froze Asha in her tracks. "Please, let it be her."

Devi turned into the drive and honked her horn. "You coming or what?" she shouted out the driver side window.

Asha trudged through the snow and climbed into the passenger seat. "How did you know I would go after her?"

Devi shoved the Jeep into reverse. "I didn't," she said.

"Then why are you here?" Asha said, strapping the seatbelt across her chest.

Devi reached into the backseat of the Jeep and handed Asha a shirt box wrapped in holiday paper with glittering snowflakes on it. "Sierra asked Dee to give this to you tomorrow for Christmas," she said, shifting into drive. "We both thought waiting until tomorrow might be a horrific mistake, so here I am."

Asha looked down at the present. Her bottom lip began to quiver as she read the note taped to the top: "Never forget that I love you."

"Sierra," Asha whispered, running her fingers over the words.

Carefully removing the red ribbon wrapped around the box, Asha peeled the tape off one end and pulled the box free without ripping the Christmas paper. She removed the lid and set it on the floorboard. With trembling hands, she folded the tissue paper back over the edges of the box and pulled out the three-ring binder.

"What is it?" Devi asked, turning the Jeep onto the main road out of town.

Asha took a deep breath and opened the binder to the very first page. Tears flooded her eyes as she ran her fingers over the inscription written simply in permanent black ink on the inside cover.

Devi glanced over. "What does it say?"

Asha wiped at her eyes, but was unable to stop the tears that were flowing down her cheeks. "It's her new book."

"I figured that," Devi replied. "What does the inscription say?"

"It's dedicated to me," Asha said, sobbing. "It reads: 'My dearest Asha. I came here looking to escape my past and in return, found the woman I wanted to spend forever with. I have fallen madly in love with you and I'm sorry I couldn't just tell you that. I was afraid for so many reasons. I know that though our time together was short, you touched my soul like no other. I hope this novel will only be a reminder of the good times we shared and not of our fight. I love you. Always, Sierra.'"

Devi looked over at Asha with tears in her eyes. "If you don't win her back," she said, wiping away a tear, "I'll never forgive you."

"I'll never forgive myself," Asha replied. "Can't we go any faster?"

"I'm trying not to kill us," Devi said. "Don't worry, we'll make it."

"We have to," Asha said, staring out the window.

"You never told me the title," Devi said.

Asha hugged the binder against her chest. "It's called A *Season of Change* by S.A. Webb."

"S.A. Webb?" Devi replied. "Is that like her pen name?"

"Yeah," Asha replied.

"Didn't she say you have a few of her books on your shelf?" Devi asked, turning the heater on a little higher.

Asha thought back to the night she had lain in Sierra's lap and read *Screaming Silence* aloud to her. "I have every book she ever wrote."

• • •

Sierra handed the suitcases over to the airline associate and leaned against the counter for support. Her legs felt wobbly and she clenched her teeth, determined not to break down. She had cried continuously throughout the cab ride; the driver had obviously taken pity on her because he had charged her only $120 for the entire trip, which had started at Asha's front door, included a stop at the lodge, and ended at the airport.

"Ma'am?" the airline associate repeated for the third time.

Sierra's eyes were on the verge of tears. "I'm sorry," she said, accepting the plane ticket that the woman handed her.

"Your flight is currently boarding at this time," the associate said, keeping her tone from sounding too scripted. "I'll call ahead and let them know you're on your way."

"That's very kind of you," Sierra said, adjusting her grip on the laptop bag.

"It's the least I can do," the associate said, securing an identification tag around each suitcase handle.

Sierra got in line with the other travelers waiting to be checked through security. She showed her I.D. and boarding pass to the security guard and proceeded through the rest of the screening. As she put her shoes back on, an overwhelming sense of sadness sneaked up on her again. Her cheeks were instantly saturated with tears. She grabbed the laptop bag and headed toward her gate. *I love you, Asha,* she thought. *Forgive me for not saying good-bye.*

• • •

Devi stomped on the brakes and slid to a stop next to the curb outside the airport terminal. "What are you going to do?"

"I'm going to see if I can find her," Asha replied, taking the three-ring binder with her as she climbed out of the Jeep.

"What if you're too late?" Devi asked.

"Then expect a call from me on your cell phone asking you to find out what Sierra's home address is," Asha said.

Devi shook her head. "You're not going to chase her all the way to Florida, are you?"

"If that's what it takes," Asha said. "Wish me luck." She closed the door and sprinted into the airport.

Looking around frantically, Asha hurried over to the Delta Airlines counter. Dee had called on Devi's cell phone just before they had reached the airport to report that she had managed to get hold of Dana and learned that Sierra had flown in on Delta. The chances of her taking the same airline out were in Asha's favor.

"Can I help you?" the airline associate greeted her.

"I need to know if you can help me locate someone," Asha said. "Her name's Sierra Stanton and I believe she's catching this morning's flight to Miami. Is there any way you can check that for me?"

"I'm sorry, ma'am," the airline associate replied. "That information is restricted."

Asha closed her eyes, trying to hide her tears. "Are there any other flights heading to Miami today?"

"Yes, ma'am," the associate said. "There's one departing in two hours."

"How much for a seat?" Asha said, pulling out her wallet.

The Delta Airlines associate typed furiously into the computer. "Do you want a one-way or round-trip ticket?"

"One way," Asha replied. "I don't know when I'll be coming back."

"The cost for a one-way ticket is $497.00," the associate said.

Asha handed her credit card over to the woman. "Whatever."

The associate took the card and swiped it. "Do you have any luggage to check in?"

"No," Asha said, losing her battle to hide her tears.

"You should know," the associate said, lowering her voice significantly. "This flight will arrive within ten minutes of the other one that's leaving here in a few minutes, due to its hour layover in Atlanta. If your friend had luggage, you might be able to catch her at the luggage claim in Miami."

Asha looked up in complete disbelief. "Thank you," she said, shaking the woman's hand. "You have no idea how much that means to me."

"You're very welcome," the associate replied. "Now stop wasting time. You still might be able to catch your friend at the gate."

Asha grabbed her credit card and boarding pass and hurried over to the

security line with the binder. She tucked
her credit card back into her wallet and
removed her driver's license. *Please don't
let her get on that plane,* she thought,
picturing Sierra's face. *I'll never be able
to forgive myself.*

• • •

Sierra looked down at her plane ticket, then
back over at the few remaining passengers
left to board the plane for Miami. *Pick up
your bag and get on the plane,* she thought,
closing her eyes. *It's over. She doesn't
love you.*

"You can't leave."

Sierra recognized the voice instantly
and opened her eyes. Her heart pounded in
her chest as she stared into Asha's tear-
streaked face. "What are you doing here?"

Asha held up her plane ticket. "I
needed to tell you something and it just
wasn't something I wanted to say over the
phone."

"I have to go," Sierra said, looking
over at the airline personnel motioning at
her to hurry up. "They're not going to hold
the flight for me."

"Sierra," Asha said, grabbing her by
the arm. "Please, I'm begging you. I only
need a few minutes."

"I think we've said all there is to
say," Sierra replied.

"You have, but I haven't," Asha said.
"All this time, I've been trying to figure
out the right words to express how I feel.
Last night, everything I said came out wrong
and I need you to know something before you
walk out of my life."

Sierra's eyes filled with tears. "I'm
listening."

"You asked me if I loved you last night and I didn't know what to say," Asha said.

Sierra picked up her laptop bag. "I know you don't feel the same way about me," she said, turning away from Asha and heading toward the gate as tears dampened her face. "You don't have to explain. I can take a hint."

"What I feel for you is more than love!" Asha cried. "I want to spend my life with you!"

Sierra heard the truth in Asha's words and it penetrated deep into her soul. It erased every hurt that had been thrust upon her heart. She turned around and stared at Asha. "What do you want me to say?"

"Say there's still a chance that I can win your heart back," Asha replied.

Sierra shook her head. "You don't understand."

Asha's face fell. "What is it that I don't understand?"

"You'd have had to have lost it, to be able to win it back," Sierra replied, taking a step toward Asha.

"Does that mean I still have it?" Asha said, her eyes brimming with tears.

"Yes," Sierra said, dropping the laptop bag and running into Asha's arms. "Yes, you still have it."

"Oh, baby," Asha said, kissing Sierra passionately. "I'm sorry for being so stupid last night."

"You're forgiven," Sierra replied, hugging Asha tightly. "Just don't let it happen again."

"I promise," Asha said. "Now, would it be alright if we went home? We have some making up to do."

"I'd love to," Sierra said.

Asha held up the binder. "By the way, Devi went ahead and gave this to me this morning."

"Oh," Sierra said.

Asha took Sierra by the hand. "I read a lot of it on the way here."

"What do you think so far?" Sierra said.

"I love it," Asha replied. "I have one question, though."

"Okay," Sierra said. "Let's have it."

Asha caressed Sierra's face. "How does the story end for the two main characters?"

Sierra was momentarily lost in the love reflected in Asha's eyes. "Their story is only beginning," she replied. "But I know they'll have a fairy-tale ending."

"So they will live happily ever after?" Asha said.

"There's not a single doubt in my mind," Sierra replied.

Asha kissed Sierra tenderly. "I love you with all my heart."

"I love you with all my soul," Sierra replied.

"Forever?" Asha said.

Sierra's eyes were unflinching. "And ever."

∞